A Novel by

John V. Madormo

Cover art by
Lauren Patterson

To my parents, James and Marie Madormo, for their unending support and guidance, and for their unconditional love.

Also by John Madormo

Charlie Collier, Snoop for Hire
The Homemade Stuffing Caper

Charlie Collier, Snoop for Hire
The Camp Phoenix Caper

TABLE OF CONTENTS

Chapter 1

The Well-Disposed Of Caper

Scarlett appeared impatient. "I've got better things to do with my time than wait around here for clients who may never show up."

"I've told you before," Henry said. "We have to maintain certain office hours for walk-ins. It's the way we've always done things."

"Well, then I'd like to propose a new policy," she said. "From now on, we don't see anyone without an appointment. Then we won't have to sit around here and waste our time."

Henry made a face. "You can't make up a new policy just like that. We have to vote on it—and I vote *no*. Charlie, what do you say?"

You would think that after weeks of working together, Henry and Scarlett would have at least learned how to tolerate one another. It was almost as if they enjoyed confrontation. Most people go out of their way to avoid fighting, but not these two. They seemed to embrace it.

"So what's your vote?" Henry said. "Vote *no* if you want to continue to offer a necessary service to your fellow man...or *yes* if you're self-centered, self-absorbed, or self-indulgent." He smiled. He was proud of his command of the language. It didn't hurt that our list of vocab words at school today all began with the word, *self.*

I folded my hands and set them down on the card table. "Why don't we just call it quits for today," I said. "We don't need to vote on any new policies. And besides, my mom's due back any time now."

"Fine with me," Scarlett said.

I removed my fedora and flipped it across the room in the direction of the hook that I always seemed to miss. I wasn't even close this time. I unbuttoned my trusty trench coat and hung it up as Henry folded the card table and slid it behind a ladder on the wall.

"Bye, guys," Scarlett said. "See you tomorrow." She swung open the garage door and stopped in her tracks.

Standing in the doorway, completely out of breath, was Danny Reardon, one of the basketball jocks from school. He squeezed by Scarlett.

"I'm glad I found you, Charlie," he said. "You're still open for business, I hope."

"We were just closing up shop for the day," Scarlett said.

Danny was having a hard time catching his breath. "Listen, guys, this is an emergency. I need help…right now."

Henry reached for the cash jar on one of the shelves, and shook it for Danny's benefit.

"There's an additional fee for a rush job," he said.

Danny threw up his hands. "Whatever, I'll pay it. We just gotta hurry."

"Okay," I said. "Let's get to work." While Henry and Scarlett opened up lawn chairs, I retrieved the card table and set it up. As I slid on my trench coat and fedora, I felt my heart racing. This is what I lived for—a chance to tackle a real caper—and one with urgency, to boot. Danny had come to the right place. We wouldn't rest until the client was completely satisfied. It was the only way *The Charlie Collier, Snoop for Hire Agency* did business.

"Okay, Danny," I said, "what's seems to be the problem?"

Danny stood and began pacing. "It's Rita. She's going crazy. I don't know what to do."

"Who's Rita?" Henry asked.

"She's my dog," Danny said. "We just got her from a shelter."

Scarlett folded her arms. "This is about some crazy dog? I'm afraid you've come to the wrong place. Shouldn't you be taking her to a vet?"

Danny shook his head. "No, you don't get it. A vet can't help with this problem." He sat down and tried to compose himself. "Rita loves this one tennis ball. And it fell down this hole in our yard…and we can't get it out. You just gotta figure out a way to get it for me."

I leaned forward. "How deep is the hole exactly?"

"Ten or fifteen feet."

"Why don't you just go buy her another tennis ball?" Scarlett said. "If you can afford to pay us, you can afford a new ball."

Danny plopped down into a lawn chair and squeezed the handles. "I've tried that already. It won't work. She only likes this one tennis ball."

"This doesn't sound like a real emergency," Henry said.

"Oh, no?" Danny said. He was getting upset. "Just how exactly would you define an emergency then? Try this—Rita stayed outside all night. She refused to come in the house. She just stands over the hole and stares down into it. She hasn't eaten anything in twenty-four hours. Is that good enough for you?"

Before Henry could respond, I held up my hand. "Tell me, Danny, how wide is this hole exactly? And can you slide a ladder down into it?"

"No way. It's only about five inches in diameter," he said.

Henry got up and leaned against the wall. "What kind of hole is this anyway?"

"There was this old water pipe in there. Some workmen from the city came by yesterday and removed it."

"And they didn't fill it back up?" I said.

"They're gonna do that tomorrow," Danny said. "So we gotta get Rita's ball outa there before they come back."

I reached for a small pad of paper on a shelf behind me and began sketching images of the hole. I tried to think of what might be long enough to fit down there, as well as something that could grab the ball. The more I drew I more frustrated I became.

"Have you tried using a long pole with some double-faced tape on the end?" Scarlett said.

"It won't work," Danny said. "The hole goes straight down for about six or seven feet but then it turns to the right…maybe thirty degrees or so. There's no way to get something down there. I don't know what I'm gonna do."

"Why don't you just trade this dog in for a less crazy one?" Henry said with a grin.

Danny didn't seem to appreciate Henry's attempt at humor.

I sat back in my chair. There just had to be a way—an easy way—to get that ball. I tried to recall any Sam Solomon episodes that might help us find a solution, but I kept coming up dry. Then just when I was about to surrender, I had it. Of course, Episode #41—*The Well-Disposed Of Caper*. In this particular story, Sam was hot on the trail of a country doctor who had improperly prescribed a drug that had left his patient clinging to life. To avoid getting caught, the doctor decided to discard the empty pill bottle at the bottom of a dried up old well. The bottle might have remained there forever had not a torrential downpour occurred that raised not only suspicion, but the evidence as well.

I slid my chair up to the table. "Danny, you said this hole is in your backyard, right?"

He nodded.

"Do you by any chance have a hose long enough to reach it?"

"Yeah, I think so."

I rolled up the sleeves on my trench coat. "Here's what I want you to do. I want you to fill the hole with water—all the way to the top."

"What good would that do?" he said. "Then it'd be even harder to get the ball."

Scarlett grinned. She knew exactly what I had in mind.

"It's brilliant, Charlie," she said. "Don't you see, Danny. A tennis ball is hollow. If you fill the hole with water, it'll float to the top."

A smile began to form on Danny's face. "It might work. You *are* brilliant, Charlie."

"As long as Rita doesn't mind a ball that's soaking wet," Henry said.

Danny jumped out his chair, dug into his pocket for a pair of dollar bills, and stuffed them into the change jar.

"Trust me, that won't be a problem," he said. "It's always covered in her slobber anyway. She won't mind a bit." He waved as he exited. "Thanks, guys."

And so the trio of Henry Cunningham, Scarlett Alexander, and yours truly, Charlie Collier had managed to crack yet another unsolvable case. You know, there was a time, not so long ago, when I had gotten tired of the ho-hum cases presented by fellow sixth graders. I wanted nothing to do with them. Instead, I dreamed of tackling the types of capers found on the pages of a Sam Solomon novel. But after the Rupert Olsen and Colonel Culpepper capers, I've since learned that if you are patient enough, one of those lightweight cases could actually turn into the big score. The lost tennis ball was obviously not going to lead us to our next adventure, but I always made it a point to look at every client who walked into our garage as someone who might just present us with a challenge that could turn out to be life-altering.

Scarlett had only been with the agency for a few weeks now, but I was pleased with her progress. She wasn't as dedicated as Henry, and she didn't possess his Rottweiler mentality for collecting cash, but she had an above-average intellect, and frequently offered solutions to problems nearly as quickly as I did. It was also nice to have an extra set of eyes when surveillance missions presented themselves. And it was still hard to believe that I actually had the chance of spending time with her not only in class, but after school at the agency as well. Scarlett and I would never be an item. I had come to accept that. We traveled in different circles. But I figured that as long as I had a stage to demonstrate my amazing powers of deduction, then anything was possible.

We were deciding whether to close up for the day or prepare for another unexpected walk-in when the side door of the garage swung open. A cloud of smoke filled the doorway. In the haze I recognized a familiar face…in unfamiliar attire. My grandmother, Constance Collier, a free spirit who sported a new identity on an almost daily basis, unveiled her latest personality. She had a towel wrapped around her head like a turban, a short purple vest over a tight yellow tee shirt, red satin slippers with the tips pointing up, and sheer turquoise pants.

This was almost too much to bear on an empty stomach. All my fantasies about genies went right out the window at that moment. Gram placed her hands together with her fingertips pointed straight up and bowed repeatedly as she entered.

"Thought you'd might like to know that your mom is on her way," she said.

"Oooh, thanks, Gram," I said. I turned to the others. "We'd better break this stuff down…and fast."

"Thanks for the warning, Mrs. Collier," Henry said.

Henry had seen my grandmother assume any number of identities over the years. It was nothing new for him, and he actually seemed to enjoy them. But this was all relatively new for Scarlett. I was hoping she wouldn't hold it against me that I had a rather eccentric grandmother.

Gram continued bowing as she backed out of the garage. "Gotta run. Time to squeeze back into my lamp. See you later, kids."

Henry was holding back laughter. He waited for the door to close. "I love her, man."

"She is so cute," Scarlett said.

Phew, was I glad to hear that. If Scarlett somehow found Grandma's unusual behavior *cute* rather than *odd*, then I'd have nothing to worry about the next time she reappeared in one of her unpredictable ensembles.

As we flicked off the overhead light and slipped out, we could hear the grinding of the garage door opener. My mom was home and we had escaped in the nick of time. Had she found us conducting business again, there would have been serious consequences. I still was on probation following the Camp Phoenix Caper. They were proud that I helped expose Colonel Culpepper and successfully tracked down Sherman's brother, Josh, but they were still upset about how I had deceived them into thinking I was on a camping trip. It wasn't that my parents weren't impressed with my amazing deductive reasoning skills, it's just that they would have preferred if I had exercised them at school rather than using them to solve problems for fellow classmates. My grandmother had lectured my parents at length about how they shouldn't suppress my talents, and that they should embrace them. That would never be the case. My folks just wanted a normal kid who did normal kid things and didn't engage in life-and-death adventures every few weeks. My dad threatened to ground me if he caught me taking on clients again. And not just ground me—he went out of his way to use the term *house arrest*.

Henry and Scarlett were on their way home and I was safely in the house by the time my mom arrived. I had carefully positioned myself at the kitchen table and was downing a glass of chocolate milk when she came in. I sprinkled cracker crumbs on the table in front of me to suggest that I had been there for a while.

"The traffic was just horrendous downtown," she said as she plopped down bags of groceries on the counter.

"I wonder why," I said.

"I'll tell you why," she said. "The police had Belmont Avenue blocked again. They were back at that carpeting store. They're still trying to figure out who stole all those Persian rugs. It's been almost a week now."

"Really?" I said.

"Yeah, and they have no clues, no suspects, no nothing."

Gram appeared in the doorway—still in her genie outfit. "Sounds like a job for the Charlie Collier, Snoop for Hire Agency if you ask me."

"I would love that, Gram."

My mom made a face. "Please, that's the last thing we want." She pulled out a chair and sat down across from me. "Promise me, Charlie, that you won't interfere this time."

"But, Mom, it sounds like the police could use my help. They're obviously stumped. I might be able to turn up something they may have overlooked."

"Just let the professionals handle it," she said.

"Charlie's *almost* a professional," Gram said.

"Please, Mom," my mother said. "Don't encourage him."

"The boy's got a gift," Gram said. "It'd be a shame if his talents went to waste."

My mom got up and began putting away groceries. "If he wants to go into law enforcement when he grows up, I won't stand in his way. But for now, I just want him to be a normal kid. Is that asking too much?"

"But how will he ever know what he wants to be if you don't let him explore a little?"

My mom slammed the refrigerator door shut. "Do you call nearly getting himself killed *exploring a little*? Mom, you have to let us raise our own son."

Gram sneered at my mom and motioned for me to follow her into the living room. Once we were out of harm's way, Gram put her arm around me.

"Ahh, don't worry about her," my grandmother said. "She and your dad'll come around one of these days."

"And if they don't?"

She smiled. "That's why I'm here," she said, pointing at her outfit. "You get one wish." Maybe she really was a genie.

I thought to myself for a moment. "I got it. I'd like to be able to keep the agency open, without any interference from my parents, and to become a real private detective someday."

"You *are* a real private detective, Charlie. And as far as keeping the agency open...your wish is my command. Consider it done."

"But what about...?" I nodded in the direction of the kitchen.

"You just keep doing what you're doing," Gram said. "And let me worry about Mr. and Mrs. Killjoy." She leaned in and kissed me on the cheek. "Now where the heck is that lamp of mine?" She winked. "Can't keep Aladdin waiting." She leaned over and whispered. "He's a nice kid, mind you, but very demanding. It's *all* about him."

Chapter 2

The Mummy and Daddy Caper

The next day at school began like all the rest—lectures, discussions, in-class projects, quizzes, homework assignments, and so on. As we waited for science class to begin, Henry and I talked about Danny Reardon's dog, Rita, and her obsession with the tennis ball. That was one crazy canine. We expected to see Danny back in the office sometime soon with another dilemma. But at least he was a legitimate client, and one who never squabbled about paying. We couldn't say the same about some of our other clients whose unpaid tabs kept growing.

"We ought to just cut 'em off," Henry said. "That'd show 'em."

"I have a hard time turning people away," I said.

"No kidding. It's no way to run a business."

Mrs. Jansen cleared her throat. "Okay, let's get started," she said.

We had successfully made it to the final period of the day, and our favorite class. It wasn't that we especially enjoyed biology or chemistry or anything like that, it was all about the teacher. Mrs. Jansen had the ability to take the driest, most boring material and turn it into something fascinating. And having to wait until the end of the day for her class was torturous. It was kind of like a delicious dessert after a meal of broccoli, cauliflower, and Brussels sprouts.

"Okay, gang, let's start off with a brain teaser," she said.

Jackpot! This was the best part of the class. I could feel a smile beginning to grow on my face. It was hard to hide it. I noticed a handful of classmates glancing in my direction. I was used to it. Whenever Mrs. Jansen unveiled one of her patented brain busters, most of the kids expected me to solve it. It's not that they wanted me to, it was just how things tended to work out. I had this gift—these amazing reasoning skills—that seemed to come alive whenever a brain teaser or puzzle or riddle was served up.

I often wondered why I was fortunate enough to possess these talents. I guess I inherited them from my grandmother. That would make sense, right? Then again, why hadn't my dad been so lucky? He couldn't care less about brain teasers, and he had no real aptitude for solving them. I guess these gifts just skipped a generation.

"Okay, imagine this," Mrs. Jansen said. She stood in front of her desk and held out her hands. "You're holding a bowling ball."

Henry raised his hand.

"Yes, Henry."

"How heavy is it?" he asked.

"It doesn't really matter," she said. "Oh, let's just say it's twelve pounds."

Stephanie Martin, an annoying girl who sat two rows over began nodding. She did that a lot. Actually all the time. She threw her hand into the air.

"Yes, Stephanie,"

"Is it a man's bowling ball or a woman's?"

Mrs. Jansen smiled. "It doesn't really matter."

"Well, technically..." Stephanie began.

Mrs. Jansen sighed. "Okay, let's say it's a man's. And how about if we do this—let me give you the entire problem, and *then* you can ask questions, okay?"

A few kids glared at Stephanie. She responded by nodding. What else were you expecting?

"Okay," Mrs. Jansen said, "You're holding a *twelve-pound, man's* bowling ball. On the floor in front of you are a pair of two thirty-gallon garbage cans—one red and one blue. Each can is filled with water."

I wasn't sure where this was going but I listened carefully to each clue. Solving a brain teaser in class was great practice for any budding private detective. I knew that it was all about the details.

"The temperature of the water in the red garbage can is forty degrees. The temperature of the water in the blue can is twenty degrees. If I drop the bowling ball into each can, will it hit the bottom faster in the can with forty-degree water or twenty-degree water?"

I sat back and closed my eyes. I wanted to picture the scenario that Mrs. Jansen had described. I tried to remember anything that I might have learned in science class about water temperature and its effect on falling objects. I knew that the color of the cans was meaningless, as was the weight of the bowling ball. This was all about water temperature. I was sure of it.

And then, all at once, it hit me. I started to chuckle under my breath. I was surprised that it had taken me as long as it had to figure out. This one was a no-brainer. I looked around the classroom. Some kids had sketched pictures of the bowling ball and the cans of water. Others sat back, their arms folded, with pained expressions on their faces. I couldn't believe no one else had figured it out by now.

"So, what do you think, gang?" Mrs. Jansen said.

Sherman Doyle, by far the largest kid in class, raised his hand. A couple of months back, I was deathly afraid of Sherman. He'd grunt a lot and always had this menacing look on his face. But since the last two adventures with Rupert Olsen and Colonel Culpepper, we had gotten to know him better. Peel away the oversize body and what you have left is a pretty normal kid, and a nice one at that.

"I think it'll take the same time to hit bottom in both cans. I just don't think the temperature of the water has anything to do with it," he said.

"Oh, but it does," Mrs. Jansen answered. She looked around and saw Henry's hand in the air. "Okay, Henry."

"It'll take longer for the ball to go through the twenty degree water. I don't know why but I think it will."

Mrs. Jansen smiled. "You are absolutely correct."

Henry jumped up and threw his arms into the air. "Yesss!"

"But I'm afraid the answer is incomplete," she said. "It's important to know why."

Henry dropped back into his seat and curled up. He didn't handle rejection well.

I looked around to see if any more hands were raised. I noticed a lot of confused faces but no one was volunteering an answer.

"That's it?" Mrs. Jansen said. "No more takers?" She waited a few moments to see if anyone else wanted to venture an answer. "I have to say I'm a little surprised. I didn't think this one was that difficult."

It wasn't. At least for someone like me, it wasn't. I decided to wait until the last second to respond. There was a time in the not so distant past when I would have fought the urge to raise my hand. I used to be worried about how people would feel if I showed them up. It used to really bother me. But in the last few months, I had learned a lot about myself. I now realized that even though there may be a handful of jealous classmates out there who would like nothing better than to see me fail, the sensation that I would experience when I was able to tackle a brain buster, to deduce the answer, and to share my findings in class was like no other. So, a few occasional sneers or catcalls no longer discouraged me. The ultimate payoff was just too good to pass up.

"Last call," Mrs. Jansen said.

I knew it was my time to shine. I raised my hand slowly.

She smiled. "I was wondering when you'd decide to speak up, Charlie. Enlighten us."

A few kids rolled their eyes.

I wasn't going to let it bother me. "Well, this one is so easy, it can seem hard if you try to overthink it," I said. "Henry was right. A bowling ball will drop faster in water with a temperature of forty degrees than in twenty-degree water. And the reason is pretty simple. Twenty-degree water is frozen. The freezing temperature for water is thirty-two degrees Fahrenheit."

Groans filled the room. Some of the brighter kids were angry with themselves. They knew they shouldn't have missed that one.

"Well done," Mrs. Jansen said. "Okay, now get out your books and open them up to page 147."

As we dug out our science texts and flipped through the pages, there was a soft knock on the door. Mrs. Jansen seemed surprised. She walked over and opened it just slightly. A smile began to form on her face as she conversed with someone in the hallway. And within a few seconds, she returned and sat down on the edge of her desk.

"Boys and girls, we have a special guest this afternoon," she said. "So why don't you put away your textbooks for the time being." She motioned for the mystery guest to join her in the classroom.

In what could only be described as theatrical, Thaddeus Miles, Roosevelt Middle School's longtime drama teacher, entered the room. He bowed at the waist and waved his hand in a formal manner. Mr. Miles was no stranger at Roosevelt—he was a legend. The longtime actor, well past retirement age, had directed nearly every school production in the past thirty years. Before joining the faculty, he had acted in dozens of Broadway plays and an untold number of old-time radio dramas. In his day, Mr. Miles was known as *the man of a thousand voices,* and he frequently demonstrated them to anyone who would listen. He stood off to the side and waited for a formal introduction.

"For those of you who are unfamiliar with this esteemed gentleman," Mrs. Jansen said, "I'd like to introduce the head of our theater department, Mr. Thaddeus Miles. He's stopping by the sixth grade classrooms to share some pretty exciting news." She turned to her guest. "Mr. Miles, the floor is yours."

The silver-haired drama instructor proudly strutted to the front of the room, oozing confidence. And why not? He had performed before countless audiences in his career, both local and national. He smiled as he scanned the room. It was almost as if he was performing a formal inspection. He brushed a speck of lint off his fire-engine red blazer and repositioned the white ascot around his neck.

"Good afternoon, theater lovers," he said, throwing his arms into the air. Mr. Miles was a master of body language. He moved and swayed in a manner that suggested that his appearance today had been carefully choreographed. He could really work a room. "As many of you have undoubtedly heard, we are about to hold open auditions for our annual sixth grade spring play. Have any of you ever considered a career in the acting profession?"

A couple of hands went up in the back of the room. The response was underwhelming.

"Well, it looks like I have my work cut out for me," he continued. "Let me tell you about this year's production."

Mrs. Jansen, standing off to the side, waved her hand. "Just wait until you hear this, kids."

"In the past we have staged traditional works, but this year will be different," Mr. Miles said. "This year you have a chance to make history. We will be performing an original production, penned by…" Mr. Miles smiled and waved his hand, "yours truly." He paused. It almost seemed like he was waiting for applause. When it became clear that we had missed our cue, he frowned and continued. "It's the story of Rebecca Ramsey, a spoiled young heiress who is facing criminal charges following the disappearance of her wealthy parents. All of the facts point to her as the guilty party. The accused then hires a private detective to help uncover evidence that will prove her innocence."

Mrs. Jansen took the lead this time by waving her arms so we would applaud. It worked.

"That sounds just fascinating, Mr. Miles," she said. "So, is there more?"

"Yes," he said. "Rebecca has a deep, dark secret that she keeps hidden from almost everyone. She has a bit of a gambling problem. She likes to play the ponies. But instead of showing up at the track and risk being recognized, she places her bets through a bookie. And it just so happens that this bookie is her alibi, but he's disappeared." He smiled. "I'm giving too much away."

"So, what's next?" Mrs. Jansen asked.

"All that's left now is the casting. I'm hoping to discover some talent right here in this room."

I looked around. To be honest, I couldn't imagine anyone in class actually sticking their necks out to audition for a part. There weren't any actors in this room. Why would any of us want to risk public humiliation?

"Mrs. Jansen," Mr. Miles said, "I came to your classroom first for a reason."

"Oh, really?" she said.

"I wanted to ask one of your students to consider trying out for a particular part in the play."

"And who might that be?" she asked.

Mr. Miles put his finger to his lips and looked around. It was as if he was searching for someone.

"Is there a Charles Collier in the room?" he said.

Every head turned at the same time. All eyes were now on me. It was the same feeling I would get when I answered a brain teaser in class. But this sort of attention I could do without. I felt Henry nudge me from behind. For some reason, I resisted the urge to raise my hand and be identified.

"Well, we call him *Charlie*," Mrs. Jansen said. "And he's sitting right over there." She was pointing in my direction. "Please stand up, Charlie."

I slowly rose to my feet.

"Mr. Collier, your reputation precedes you," Mr. Miles said. "I've been following your exploits in the news the last couple of months. I'm very impressed."

"Thank you, sir," I said.

"One of the principal characters in my play is a tough, old-school, no-nonsense private eye by the name of Nick Dakota. Rebecca hires Nick to locate the bookie. Without him, she faces life in prison. Mr. Collier, with your background, I think you'd be the perfect choice for this part."

I couldn't believe what I was hearing. Did this guy really think that I had any acting abilities? There was no way I would embarrass myself on stage. I considered myself a real private detective, not an actor playing a private detective. I knew my own limitations. I could solve brain busters, help classmates with their problems, but I was no actor.

"What do you say?" Mr. Miles said.

I shuffled my feet and swallowed hard. "Sir, I appreciate the invitation but—" I didn't want to seem ungrateful. "I've just never…I mean…I just really…" I exhaled. "Mr. Miles, I'm not an actor."

Mr. Miles folded his arms and smiled. It was one of those knowing smiles. "I beg to differ." He strolled across the front of the room and stopped at the window. He gazed out momentarily, and then suddenly spun around. "Have you ever assumed a new identity during an investigation?"

"Well, sure," I said. "Plenty of times."

"So you pretended to be someone you weren't?"

I nodded.

"And when you were doing that," he said, "what exactly *were* you doing?"

I didn't know how to answer the question. "I don't understand."

Mr. Miles threw his hands into the air. "Charlie, you were acting? You might not have thought so at the time but you were. Let me ask you another question. In order to solve a case, did you ever have to fib to your parents?"

Henry immediately started laughing. Then the entire room joined in.

I smiled sheepishly. "I'd rather not answer that question."

Mr. Miles chuckled. "I already know the answer." He began to walk down the aisle toward me. "When you stretched the truth, you were acting." He was now standing a foot away from me. "Don't underestimate yourself. You have hidden talents. It would be a shame to see them go to waste." Mr. Miles extended his hand. "What do you say? Will you audition for the part?"

I knew that I should just shake his hand and tell him what he wanted to hear but I couldn't. I guess it was fear of failure that held me back. I lowered my eyes.

Mr. Miles withdrew his hand. "Will you at least consider it?" he said.

That I could do. "I will, sir. I'll consider it."

"Wonderful," he said. And for the next fifteen minutes, Mr. Miles described in detail each scene, each act, each character description, etc.

I found myself wondering what to do. I knew what I wanted to do. I wanted this whole thing to just go away. I didn't want to disappoint Mr. Miles, but I also didn't want to embarrass myself. Going undercover and assuming a new identity during an investigation may have been acting, but it sure didn't give me the courage to step onto that stage if front of a live audience. And then there was the agency to consider. It would be impossible to attend play rehearsals *and* run a business. I couldn't walk away from my clients just like that. And what about this unsolved crime in town— this Persian rug burglary? That could very well be my next caper. Gram certainly thought so. And if that turns out to be the case, I'd want to be ready to drop everything and jump in. I didn't know which way to turn. Maybe this had nothing to do with the agency. Maybe it had everything to do with the fear of embarrassing myself.

As was the case whenever I found myself in a fix, my mind drifted to Sam Solomon. What would Sam do in a situation like this? Would he attempt something he knew he wasn't qualified to do? There had to be an episode where something like that may have happened. I closed my eyes and concentrated. Think, think. And then it hit me. Of course, Episode #38—*The Mummy and Daddy Caper*.

In this particular story, Sam had been hired by a movie producer who was shooting his latest horror film. Apparently, a number of mishaps had been taking place on the set, and several of the actors had been injured. To conceal his identity, Sam was hired as a film extra. He had a walk-on part and a handful of lines. Because of his inexperience, he was concerned that veteran actors would be able to detect a fraud in their midst which would blow his cover. So he worked with an acting coach to help him prepare for his theatrical debut. Not only was the veteran P.I. able to fool the cast and crew, but he was able to expose the perpetrator—a disgruntled actor who had been denied a part in the film and who would sneak onto the set each night and booby-trap various props.

So if Sam was able to leave his comfort zone and attempt to do something completely foreign to him, then maybe I should at least consider it. I had promised Mr. Miles that I would. And if I managed to build up the courage to actually audition for the play, then I would do so knowing that my literary hero had faced a similar dilemma and had conquered it with dignity and grace. If Sam could do it, so could I.

Chapter 3

The Hymn and Her Caper

The next day after school Henry and I decided to poke our heads into the auditorium just to see how many brave souls actually showed up to the open auditions for Mr. Miles' play. We entered from the rear so that we could sneak out quickly if necessary. We crouched down behind the last row of seats. That would provide the perfect cover. When we peeked at the goings on in the front, we noticed about a dozen kids standing around the stage. Most of them had their backs to us so we couldn't really tell who was who, and we weren't able to hear their conversations but it didn't matter. We just wanted to get a sense of what was going on.

"You couldn't pay me to audition for this play," Henry said. "Why anyone would want to risk embarrassing themselves is beyond me? And in public no less."

"Then again, if you've got talent, you might want to flaunt it," I said.

Henry wasn't buying it. "How many sixth graders in this school do you really think could pull that off? Gimme a break."

"We won't really know until we see them in action."

Henry shrugged. "Whatever. At least I'm glad you came to your senses and decided not to try out."

"Actually I haven't really made up my mind yet."

"Oh, really?" he said "If you're still considering it, then why are you back here while everyone else is up there?"

I didn't have an answer. "I haven't ruled it out, but I'm leaning *against* doing it."

Henry pointed to the kids standing near the stage. "Wait a minute. Somebody's turning around. It's…it's…oh, brother…it's the *nodder*.

"Stephanie?"

"Uh huh.

"Hey, and who's the kid standing off to the side all by himself? I can barely make out his profile."

Henry chuckled. "Standing all by himself? Who do you think?"

It was Brian Hart, better known as the *hisser*. Brian was, for a lack of a better word, a germophobe. He had a mortal fear of coming into contact with other human beings for fear that he might pick up germs from them. If you ventured within six feet of him, he would begin to hiss at you. The closer you got, the louder the hissing. It was unnerving and it didn't take long to get the message.

Henry elbowed me. "You're not gonna believe it. Look."

Making a rare appearance at school was Patrick Walsh, known affectionately as the *slacker*. This kid was the master of deception. He'd get a part for sure…but would he show up for rehearsals? That was the question. No one, and I mean no one, missed more school than Patrick. To the teachers, and even to his parents, he was frail and sickly. But we all knew better. His faked illnesses were legendary. There was no one better. He even knew exactly how many school days he could miss before he'd need to attend summer school or be held back a grade.

"How do you like that?" Henry said. "The nodder, the hisser, and the slacker. Pretty elite company. Now aren't you glad you're not up there? It's a geeks' convention."

"Henry, take a look at some of the kids we hang around with. We aren't too far removed from that bunch, you know."

"Speak for yourself," he said. "We're a lot closer to the *in crowd* than the *clod squad*. I'm not her biggest fan, mind you, but the fact that Scarlett is a member of *our* agency says something about our ever-increasing popularity."

I wasn't so sure that we were any closer to the clique of popular kids because of the Scarlett connection but I was okay with that. And that was another reason not to audition. Why waste away my afternoons here when I could be spending them with Scarlett at the agency? I'd hate to miss out on the chance of working on a real caper, with Scarlett by my side, because I had to attend play practice. There—that settled it.

And another thing—what if Gram was right? What if we did get involved in this Persian rug burglary? I wouldn't want to miss an opportunity to get my teeth into that one. I couldn't get it out of my head lately. If I were lucky enough to get the chance to assist the police on this caper, I know the first thing I'd do. I'd find out why someone would want to steal rugs anyway. I mean—if you wanted them so badly, why not just steal some money and then go buy the rugs? It would certainly be a lot easier to jimmy open a cash register and slip a wad of cash into your pocket, than trying to lug a bunch of rugs down the street. It just didn't make any sense to me. This criminal must have really wanted them for some reason. I decided to wait a few days, and if the police still had nothing, I just might throw my hat into the ring.

Henry slid the backpack off his shoulder, plopped in on the floor and sat on it. "Since it seems we're going to be here for a while, are you ready for a challenge?"

That could only mean one of Henry's illustrious brain teasers.

"Let 'er rip," I said.

"Okay, now listen carefully. Which one is correct? The yolk of an egg *is* white, or the yolk of an egg *are* white?"

I repeated the question—the yolk of an egg *is* white, or the yolk of an egg *are* white? It didn't take an expert in English grammar to know that yolk is singular and therefore would take the verb, *is*. Not only that, the other way just sounded wrong. But because it was so obvious, I knew that there had to be a catch. This wasn't a grammar question. It was a trick question. I repeated it in my head a couple more times. And then it hit me. How could I have been so dense?

"I'll tell you the answer if you're stuck," he said.

"I hate to disappoint you but I'm not stuck. The answer is…neither statement is correct. Because the yolk of an egg is *yellow*."

Henry rolled his eyes. As was always the case, he had failed to trip up the master.

"You're so smug sometimes," he said. "I'm gonna get you one of these days, Collier. And you can take that to the bank."

Before the war of words could escalate, our attention was drawn to the front of the auditorium. We noticed the kids beginning to quiet down. Something was happening. A moment later, Mr. Miles appeared on stage. He had a stack of scripts under his arm.

"Everyone, please take a seat," he said. "I'm delighted with this turnout. Frankly, I wasn't expecting to see so many of you…which is actually good *and* bad, I'm afraid. You see, we have a limited number of speaking parts. So I don't want you to be disappointed if you aren't cast in one of the lead roles. But we *are* going to need an understudy for each of the three main actors."

I tapped Henry on the shoulder. "What's an understudy?"

He shrugged. "You got me."

"And then, of course," Mr. Miles continued, "we'll have plenty of opportunities for extras in many of the scenes. Suffice it to say that I'll do my best to fit everyone in the show somehow."

Henry squinted. "Can you see any more faces yet?"

I shook my head. We were dying to know who the others were. And it was at that very moment that I began to feel uncomfortable about spying on my classmates. Something about it just didn't seem right. A private eye was certainly no stranger to undercover surveillance. Heck, a well-executed stakeout could bust a case wide open. But this seemed different. It seemed…nosey. Had I reached a new low? I wasn't quite sure.

Then I thought of Sam Solomon. Would Sam have spied on his own classmates? And then I remembered something? Not only would he have done so, Sam once snooped in, get this, a church. In Episode #42, *The Hymn and Her Caper*, Sam had been hired by a local minister who noticed that the collections at his church were decreasing dramatically each week. Sam was convinced that a member of the congregation was responsible for the theft, so he hid in a small compartment in the massive church organ and watched through a tiny vent as the collection basket made its way up and down each pew. It didn't take him long to identify the culprit—a woman who had recently joined the congregation. She had apparently applied stickum to her hands, and instead of giving alms like all the others, she was actually making a withdrawal.

Spying on others was a nasty business, but at times it was absolutely necessary, and although we weren't working on an actual case, I convinced myself that this little exercise would enable me to brush up on my surveillance skills.

Mr. Miles, meanwhile, was addressing the troops. "Okay, now, who among you is trying out for the role of the private eye?"

Two boys raised their hands.

"The police detective?"

A couple more hands went up.

"The bookie?"

The hisser waved his hand. "Mr. Miles, I'm interested in the role and all…but…what exactly is a bookie?"

What is a bookie? I couldn't believe this kid didn't know that. If he had read as many Sam Solomon novels as I had, he wouldn't be embarrassing himself with such a dumb question.

"Bookie is short for bookmaker," Mr. Miles said. "And a bookmaker is someone who takes bets and pays off winners for horse races, but he doesn't actually work for the racetrack, making it illegal. It's a dying art. Off-track betting parlors have pretty much put the bookies out of business. But our play is a period piece, so for our purposes, bookies are alive and well. Does that help?"

"Yes, sir."

"Okay," Mr. Miles said. "Who's interested in the role of Rebecca, our heroine?"

Three girls raised their hands.

Mr. Miles spent the next minute reading off the names of all the characters in order to determine who was interested in what parts.

"Okay, everyone up on stage, please," he said. "I have a script for each one of you."

The dozen or so hopefuls paraded onto the stage and encircled Mr. Miles.

"What I'd like you to do is spread out across the front of the stage in groups," he said. Mr. Miles pointed to his right. "Private eyes over here, police detectives here, those vying for the role of Rebecca right here," and on and on until everyone was a member of a group.

Henry and I were now able to determine the identities of some of the other brave souls. Most were kids we knew casually— none that we really hung around with. Henry was right. Most were of the nodder/hisser/slacker variety. And then, all at once, he hit me in the shoulder, nearly knocking me over.

"Did you see who's up there?" he said.

It was Scarlett.

"What does she think she's doing?" he said. "If she thinks she has time to rehearse for a play and remain an active member of the agency, she's in for a big surprise." Henry was beside himself. "She's got to make a choice. If she gets the role, then she's out. Agreed?"

Henry was right about one thing. If Scarlett won the role of Rebecca, then she'd be spending the majority of her after-school hours right here. She'd never have time to help out at the agency. But who was I to deny her a chance at stardom? If this was something she really wanted to do, I wouldn't stand in her way. This just might turn out to be her passion in life, and if that was the case, then she should do it. She shouldn't have to choose. There had to be a better way to handle this.

"If she gets the part," I said, "then she can just take a leave of absence from the agency. We can't just kick her out."

"There you go again, Charlie, thinking with your heart instead of your head."

"Henry, you and Scarlett are never going to be best buds. We both know that. But let's be gracious here. If she makes it, we should congratulate her, and then welcome her back when the play's over. Can you do that?"

Henry sighed. "It's your name on the door, pal. Whatever you say." He had surrendered but he wasn't happy about it.

We decided to stay a little while longer and listen to some of the kids read lines from the script. Most were pretty green. Mr. Miles asked each student to find a page where his or her character spoke, and then to read some of the dialogue. It was clear after only a few minutes that none of the kids in the group were in need of a theatrical agent to manage their acting careers. Of course, I based that having heard from everyone but Scarlett. She was the last to go.

"Let's get out of here," Henry said.

"No, I want to see how she does."

"It's a waste of time. She's gonna be brutal like all the rest."

"Maybe," I said. "But let's listen anyway. It's not as if we have a pending case that needs our immediate attention. Let's enjoy this little break between capers. Okay?"

With an expression that could only be described as a combination of disgust and disinterest, Henry leaned up against the seat and closed his eyes.

"Wake me when it's over."

I was unprepared for what came next. I listened as Scarlett read from a passage in the script's third act. The look on Mr. Miles' face said it all. Her delivery was so expressive, so passionate, so flawless, that I couldn't believe what I was hearing. I glanced at Henry. His eyes were wide open. He was now staring at Scarlett, as were all of the others on stage. A star had been born before our very eyes. If Scarlett hadn't found her calling in life before today, it was clear to everyone within earshot of her performance that this girl belonged on a stage, or on screen, or wherever else amazingly talented folks showcase themselves.

"Scarlett," Mr. Miles said. "I'm…I'm speechless. That was brilliant." He looked to the others. "I think it's safe to say that we've found our Rebecca."

I nudged Henry. "Can you believe that?"

He was speechless—which was completely out of character for him. He had never had a hard time coming up with a dig for Scarlett in the past.

"Splendid, just splendid," Mr. Miles said. "And now we need to find her co-star. The role of Nick Dakota, our private eye, is very important. He's in nearly as many scenes as Rebecca." The aging drama teacher glanced at the two sad sacks who were auditioning for the role. He frowned. Having heard their readings moments before, he knew he was in trouble.

I felt bad for him, especially since he went out of his way to personally invite me to audition for the role. Part of me wanted to jump up, run to the stage, and save the production. But, to tell you the truth, I wasn't sure if I was any better than the competition. Heck, I might even be worse. The one thing I had going for me, though, was insight—the knowledge that only a real private detective could possess. I knew how they thought…how they performed under stress…how they would deduce a solution to every problem. And if I hadn't experienced that situation personally, then I certainly knew what was going in the mind of Sam Solomon.

"Can we go *now*?" Henry said.

I didn't want to leave but I knew that I didn't have the courage to audition for the part. I was only delaying the inevitable.

"I guess so," I said.

From a crouched position, we began our escape. We didn't want anyone to see us sneaking out. I glanced back at Mr. Miles who seemed troubled.

"I was hoping to cast all of the parts today," he said to the group. "But I'm just not sure. You see, the role of Nick Dakota is critical. He has to be shrewd and cunning, and at the same time, mindful and compassionate. And he must also be *romantic*."

I grabbed the back of Henry's shirt. "Wait a minute."

"What?" Henry said.

I wanted to hear more about Nick Dakota.

"Nick is the only one who believes in Rebecca," Mr. Miles said. "He's the only one who can save her from life in prison. And as you might guess, the two eventually fall in love. And in the final scene, they embrace."

Embrace? I had no idea. What was I doing running away? This was my big chance. If I couldn't get Scarlett to like me in real life, then this was the next best thing.

"Are we leaving or not?" Henry asked.

"You can, but I'm not."

"What's going on?"

"Didn't you hear what he said? Rebecca falls in love with Nick Dakota. That could be Scarlett and me."

Henry shook his head. "Big deal. It's make-believe."

"It's good enough for me." I took a deep breath and stood up. If Sam Solomon could learn to act, then so could I. "Excuse me, Mr. Miles," I yelled out.

"Who is that? Where's that voice coming from?" he said.

"It's me, sir, Charlie Collier."

He walked to the edge of the stage. "What are you doing back there?"

"I came to audition for the part of the private eye. I'm sorry I'm late." I wasn't sure how Mr. Miles would react. Then I saw a smile begin to form on his face.

"Well, get up here!" he said. "Let's get to work."

I ran up the aisle as fast as my stocky legs could carry me. I hopped up onto the stage. I couldn't help but glance at Scarlett. I wondered what she was thinking right at the moment. I don't suppose that I was the kind of leading man she had me in mind. But that was okay. I'd just need to win her over, that's all.

"Here's a script, Charlie," Mr. Miles said. "Can you read the highlighted passage for me?" He paused, as if in thought. "Better yet, since this is a jail scene with Rebecca, perhaps Scarlett can read along with you." He motioned her over.

The expression on Scarlett's face was confusing. It wasn't welcoming, I knew that. It was more skeptical than anything else. Maybe she wasn't upset. Maybe she doubted my abilities to pull this off. Well, I'd just have to convince her that I was more than capable of handling this challenge.

Mr. Miles pointed to where he wanted me to read.

I let out a long breath and jumped in. "You're not making this job easy for me, Miss Ramsey. All the evidence points to you as the murderer. The cops have suspended their search. They're not even lookin' for anybody else. I need something…anything."

Scarlett stood opposite me. "I told you. You have to find that bookie. He's my alibi. I was with him when my parents disappeared. He'll swear to it."

"He'll swear to it? Gimme a break. Do you really think he's gonna tell the cops that he was taking bets—and risk going to jail—just to save your neck?"

"He has to," she said. "He just has to."

"Don't count on it. And even if we do find him, once he's on the witness stand, the prosecution will eat him alive." I sighed for effect. "He's not what you'd call a credible witness."

"He's my only chance. If you can't find him, my life is over. The cops don't believe he exists. They want to pin it on me. It makes their job easier. Especially that detective."

I was beginning to think that I could actually do this. "What detective?"

She paused momentarily as if thinking to herself. "Reynolds. Lieutenant Reynolds. He has it in for me."

"Now why would you say that?" I asked. "The man's probably just doing his job."

Scarlett waved her arms dramatically. She was good—really good. "Don't you understand? He despises women like me— wealthy socialites. He's a civil servant who obviously hates his job…along with his tiny salary. And so, he takes it out on people with money." She sighed. "I may have my faults but I'm no murderer."

"Listen, I have a few friends in the department. Let me rattle some cages and see if I can get a gander at the evidence."

"And if not?"

"Then I reel in some of my favorite snitches," I said. "I won't rest until I find your bookie friend or something that'll get you outa here, lady. It's the least I can do for a paying client—a well-paying client at that."

Mr. Miles started chuckling. Oh, no, did he think my performance was laughable? Did I blow my big chance?

"Wonderful, just wonderful," he said. "Scarlett, beautifully done. And Charlie, let me say this. You definitely have some natural talent. I can see that. You're like a piece of clay. But I think I can spin you around on my pottery wheel and mold you into an exquisite vase." Except he pronounced *vase* the funny way—like how it sounds when it rhymes with Oz.

I wouldn't call it a ringing endorsement but at least I appeared to be in the running. I noticed Henry now seated in the front row of seats. What was he doing up here? I was sure he had left. Then all at once, he started waving his arms. It appeared he wanted to get Mr. Miles' attention.

"Mr. Miles. Oh, Mr. Miles," he yelled out.

"Yes, can I help you, young man?"

"Is it too late to audition for the play?" he asked.

What was going on here anyway? Was this the same kid who wanted nothing to do with this production? Why had he suddenly done an about face? Henry was up to something.

"What's your name, son?"

"Henry Cunningham."

"And what part were you interested in?"

"The police detective—Lieutenant Reynolds."

Mr. Miles glanced at his watch. "I suppose we have a few minutes left. Why don't you come on up here."

Henry sprinted to the front and hopped up onto the stage.

"Oh, by the way," Mr. Miles said, "let me remind all of you that if everything falls into place, I will be deciding which of you will be receiving speaking roles this evening. When you arrive for school tomorrow morning, look for a cast list on my office door."

Henry was now standing opposite Mr. Miles.

"Okay, now, Mr. Cunningham, let me find an appropriate passage for you," he said as he began flipping through pages. "Ah, yes, right here." He handed the script to Henry.

"I have a question," Henry said. "What's my motivation?"

Scarlett rolled her eyes. She was just starting to figure out what Henry was up to.

"Well, that's a very good question," Mr. Miles said. "Every actor should know his motivation." He pressed his finger to his lips and paused. "Let's see now. You're a hard-nosed, veteran cop. Been with the force for as long as you can remember. You're respected, but feared by your subordinates. Your job is to locate supporting evidence that will convict Rebecca Ramsey. You don't particularly like her. You don't like her kind—a wealthy heiress who's never worked a day in her life. A guilty verdict would be a feather in your cap—and would bring some personal satisfaction as well." He smiled. "How's that?"

"Perfect," Henry said. "Couldn't be better, sir. I was made for this part." He sneered at Scarlett.

And believe it or not, Henry went on to give a pretty respectable interpretation of the character. At one point, it was almost if he wasn't even acting. I had to hand it to him. Henry was living his greatest fantasy—a chance to be mean to Scarlett and get away with it.

Chapter 4

The Loan Arranger Caper

Henry and I made it a point to get to school early the next morning. We were anxious to see who had been selected for Mr. Miles' production. As we got closer to his office door, we noticed a crowd of kids camped out in the hallway. The cast list still had not been posted.

"What do you think our chances are?" Henry said.

"Based on the competition, I think we have as good a chance as anybody."

"And Scarlett?"

"Scarlett's a shoo-in," I said. "That's a no-brainer."

We sat on the floor to wait for the announcement. We didn't have much time. Classes were scheduled to start in fifteen minutes. We were all hoping to know our fate before then. I could feel my heart racing. It was the same sensation I would get when I was immersed in a case. As each minute passed, I could feel myself getting more anxious. I wiped my hands on the front of my pants. They were clammy. I hated the waiting. I wished I could handle it better—like Sam Solomon.

Sam was the master of patience. Just consider Episode #44—*The Loan Arranger Caper*. In this case Sam had been hired by the family of a man whose business had failed. The distraught businessman, whose credit made it impossible to get a bank loan, made the fateful decision to seek out the services of a Mafia loan shark. When the man was unable to repay the loan and suddenly disappeared, Sam decided to penetrate the seedy underworld of loan sharking. He posed as a down-on-his-luck gambler in need of a temporary cash fix. But his timing couldn't have been worse. A police raid interrupted the transaction, and Sam was arrested for interfering with an ongoing police investigation. His private investigator's license was suspended, and he spent the next week waiting to hear if the suspension would be permanent.

So if Sam could wait out a potentially life-altering decision, then I was happy to give Mr. Miles all the time he needed to announce his cast.

"Maybe we should just go and stop back at lunch," I said.

But before Henry could respond, the door to Mr. Miles' office began to open, and a moment later he appeared. He seemed surprised by the turnout.

"I didn't realize you all were out here," he said. He pulled a rolled-up piece of paper from his sport coat pocket and smiled. "This is it." He grabbed a push pin from the bulletin board on his door and was just about to attach the list when he stopped and turned toward us. "Now mind you, this was a very difficult decision. If you didn't receive a speaking role, don't be discouraged. I promise that everyone will be on stage." He turned back and posted the list. "Okay, kids, have at it."

Mr. Miles was unprepared for the response from the assembled throng. He was nearly swallowed up by the crowd, but did manage to squeeze through and escape to his office.

Henry immediately began to muscle his way to the front of the line. I, on the other hand, waited several feet back. No need to tackle the mob. Nothing was that important. A minute later, Henry had returned. He was sporting an ear-to-ear grin.

"Well?" I said.

"There was never a doubt. You're in. I'm in. And what's-her-name is in."

"Really?" I said. "Henry, do you realize what this means? It's my chance to win over Scarlett. When she sees me in action on that stage, anything's possible."

"Don't get your hopes up, partner. You might think this is real life but I guarantee that she sees it as two people reading lines that someone else wrote. And nothing more."

I knew he was right. Every so often I'd get my hopes up that Scarlett might see me, not as some weight-challenged classmate who solves capers for fellow sixth-graders, but rather as a suave and debonair mystery man. I knew it was a long shot—and by long shot, I meant *beyond the realm of possibility*—but I had to keep my hopes up.

"Excuse me, Charlie, do you have a minute?" It was Mr. Miles.

"Sure," I said.

"Will you excuse us, Henry, I'd like to have a word with our new leading man."

"Not a problem, sir," he said. "See you in class, Charlie."

I waved good-bye to Henry and followed Mr. Miles into his office. He pointed to a chair opposite his desk.

"Well, first let me tell you how happy I am that you decided to take me up on my invitation to audition. A person with your credentials is a perfect fit for Nick Dakota."

"Thank you. I appreciate your confidence, but I know I have a lot to learn."

"And that's what I'm here for," Mr. Miles said. "But first, I wanted to share something with you—something I think you'll find really interesting."

I wasn't sure what was coming. I assumed it was good news. Although whenever a teacher asked you to step into his office, it usually meant that you might soon need the services of a good attorney.

"Charlie, would you believe that we have something in common?"

"What's that?"

"Actually, we have mutual friends—two of them."

I smiled. I didn't know who he was referring to.

"Would you believe that Eugene Patterson and I are old fraternity brothers?"

I sat up in my chair. This was getting interesting. "Really? I didn't know that."

"And what if I told you that I could have been your grandfather?"

Now, wait just one minute. This was starting to get weird. "What do you mean exactly?"

Mr. Miles sat back in his chair and laughed. "Well, not really, I guess. But your grandmother and I did date years ago. Actually it was only one date. She met your Grandpa Jim about a month later and the rest is history."

It was hard to imagine Gram with anyone else. Grandpa Jim was my mentor. He taught me so much. He was the one who introduced me to Sam Solomon. And that in itself changed my life. Without Grandpa Jim's influence, I wouldn't be the person I am today. I think about him a lot—whenever I think about Sam Solomon.

"That's pretty interesting," I said.

"And your grandmother is just as pretty today as she was back then. You might not know this but she was a real looker in her younger days."

I was starting to get creeped out. It wasn't as if Mr. Miles had said anything wrong. It was just hard to think about my grandmother as a *looker*...even though I had seen pictures of her when she was a teenager, and she did look pretty good. But I'd rather not think about those things. It was like seeing your parents kiss. I mean it was nice that they still got along and all, but I wasn't a fan of their public displays of affection. Spare me.

"So, please say hello to your grandma and Eugene the next time you seem them. Will you do that?"

"I will."

"Just tell them that Thad says hi."

"I'll do that," I said as I slid out of my chair and headed for the door.

"Remember. We start play practice next Monday after school. See you then."

I waved and slipped out. Whoa, now that was weird. I was hoping we wouldn't be having any more conversations like that any time soon. I tried to picture Mr. Miles as my grandfather. Then I spent the rest of the day trying to get that painful image out of my head.

*   *   *   *   *

When I got home from school that day, I looked for my grandmother. I wanted to tell her about my conversation with Mr. Miles. I found my mom in the kitchen cutting up vegetables for dinner.

"Mom, do you know where Gram is?"

"Shhh," she said. "Just a minute." She leaned in and turned up the volume on the radio. The local news was on.

"Police continue to investigate the burglary last night at Vito's Italian Bakery on the east side," the newscaster began. "When owner, Vito Dalesandro, opened up the shop this morning, he discovered that a cash register drawer had been jimmied. More than twenty-five hundred dollars was taken. But more interesting than that—the thief also made off with at least a dozen loaves of bread. Anyone with information is asked to contact the Oak Grove Police Department. In other news—"

My mom reached over and turned off the radio. She shook her head. "To think that something like that could happen right here in our little town is…is very disturbing." She sighed. "I'm sorry, Charlie, what did you ask me before?"

"I was wondering where Gram was."

"She's in her room, I think."

"Thanks." As I made my way to Gram's room, I thought about this new crime wave. First, several Persian rugs were stolen, and then exactly one week later, to the day, a bakery is burglarized. It didn't seem to me that there was a connection between these two crimes since they were so different. I was convinced they had to be random acts. I decided not to mention the bakery theft to my grandmother. Whenever a crime went unsolved around here for a few days, she had it in her head that our little agency should assist the authorities. Who knows? She might end up being right but now was not the time to mount a new investigation. I needed to concentrate my efforts on the play.

And if I even suggested to Henry that we take an active role in solving either crime, I knew exactly what he'd say. He'd lecture me about the evils of taking on cases without a paying client. But that never mattered to me. It was never about making money. For that matter, if it were up to me, I doubt if I'd even charge people for what we do. I'd always get such a rush whenever we'd successfully solve a really tough caper that no amount of money could ever match that.

I tapped lightly on my grandmother's door. I wasn't sure what she was up to so I didn't want to startle her.

"Who goes there?" a voice said from behind the closed door.

"It's me, Gram, Charlie. Can I come in?"

The door flew open and standing there was my grandmother decked out in a meter maid uniform.

"Do you have a minute?" I said.

She put her arm around me. "Come with me. I gotta make my rounds. We can talk on the way."

I followed her down the hallway, into the kitchen, and past my mother, who did a double take when she saw what Gram was wearing. We then proceeded out the back door, through the yard, and into the garage. Gram flipped on the overhead light and immediately leaned down to look at the driver's side front tire on the minivan. There was a chalk mark on it.

"Just as I thought," she said. She pulled out a small pad of paper from her back pocket, flipped over a few pages, and began scribbling. "Why people ignore these signs is beyond me. It's as if they can't read." She pointed to a rake hanging on the back wall. "It says right there—*four-hour parking*. What's wrong with these people?" She ripped off a page and inserted it under one of the front windshield wipers. "So, what was it that you needed?"

"I wanted to tell you that I bumped into a friend of yours today."

"A friend of *mine*? Who was it?"

"He told me to tell you that Thad says hi."

Gram leaned back against the car and smiled. "Thad? Thad Miles?"

"Uh huh."

"Good old Thad. I haven't seen him in the longest time." She slipped the pad of paper back into her pocket. "Don't tell me he's still teaching?"

"Yep."

"And directing plays?"

I nodded. "Actually he's directing a new one—one that he wrote himself."

"You don't say."

"And you'll never guess who the leading man is." I said. Gram shrugged.

"Moi."

She clapped her hands. "You? I didn't know you could act."

"Well, the jury's still out on that one," I said. "To tell you the truth, I wouldn't even have considered it but Mr. Miles personally invited me to audition for the part since one of the main characters is a private detective. And I won the role."

Gram hugged me. "Oh, Charlie, that's so exciting. And a private detective—how perfect. Have you told your folks?"

"Not yet."

"Well, you tell them when you're ready. I won't spoil it." She thought to herself momentarily. "You know who you have to tell all of this to?"

I shook my head.

"Eugene. He'll get a real kick out of you playing a private eye. He can probably give you some pointers. Eugene was in a few plays in college. That's how he and Thad met."

"I didn't know that." And then I remembered what I wanted to tell her. "Gram, Mr. Miles said that you and he once dated."

She smiled. "I wouldn't really call it a date. He was more interested in me than I was in him. You know how that is."

Oh, brother, did I. That had been the case with Scarlett and me for as long as I could remember.

"I liked Thad. He was a nice enough guy, but a little too dramatic for me. He was on stage even when he wasn't on stage. You know the type." She flipped off the light in the garage. "Hey, you want to have a little fun with your mom?"

"Sure, I guess." But I knew that whatever Gram had in mind, my mother would not be referring to it as *fun*.

I followed her back into the kitchen. She approached my mom who was still preparing dinner at the counter. Gram pulled out her pad, ripped off a page and presented it to my mom.

"What's this?" she said.

"It's a parking ticket. What does it look like?" Gram said.

"A parking ticket? For what?"

"I'm afraid you exceeded the four-hour parking restriction."

My mom smiled. "The car's parked in our garage."

"*Your* garage?" Gram said. "Prove it."

I could see my mom about to say something she would probably later regret. But fortunately, cooler heads prevailed. She paused long enough to compose herself.

"Tell you what—I'll go down to city hall first thing in the morning and be sure to take care of it. How's that?"

"Just like you took care of your other outstanding tickets? Seventy-six of them to be exact," Gram snapped.

My mom continued to play along. "I'll pay all of them tomorrow. I promise."

"Well, it's a little too late for that, sister. You're under arrest." And with that, Gram made her move. Before my mom knew what hit her, she found herself handcuffed—one end to her wrist and the other to a handle on one of the counter drawers."

My mom began tugging at the handcuffs and tried to open them. When she realized that it wasn't a toy, she scowled.

"Okay, Mom, you've had your fun," she said to my grandma.

"Fun? You're a scofflaw. You think that's fun?"

"So what do you want me to do now?" my mom asked calmly.

"If I were you," Gram said, "I'd get yourself a good lawyer. See you in court." She turned and walked into the hallway.

My mom motioned me over. "See if you can find the key for these," she said.

I turned and followed my grandma to her room. I didn't want to spoil Gram's fun but I could see that my mom was close to reaching her boiling point and she appeared anxious for this little performance to reach its conclusion. This was slightly out of character for Gram. She usually pulled pranks on my dad but on occasion she would share the wealth. I didn't want to see things escalate, so I decided to try to defuse things on my own.

"That was pretty funny, Gram. So, would you like me to release the prisoner?"

"Release? Before she's had her day in court? I don't think so."

Gram walked into her closet, and about a minute later, reappeared wearing a full-length, black judge's gown.

"Want to stick around?" she said. "I could use a good bailiff."

I politely declined. Right at that moment, I wanted to get as far away as physically possible. And that was precisely what I did.

Chapter 5

The Faulty Breaks Caper

I left via the front door, walked along the side of the house to the backyard and into the garage. I hopped on my bike and fled the scene. I didn't want my mom to think that I had abandoned her but what was I supposed to do? I wasn't proud of myself but the last thing I wanted was a family scene where I had to take sides. It was never pretty. I would usually side with Gram, but because it was my parents who doled out justice, I would more often than not find myself reluctantly agreeing with them, at least publicly. Gram never seemed to hold it against me though. She realized that these family crises placed me in a precarious situation and that for reasons of self-preservation, I needed to align myself with my parents. I was glad she understood.

As I biked my way to Eugene's office, I tried to imagine the scene taking place in our kitchen. I didn't want to think about it. I knew one thing for sure—my dad was in for an earful as soon as he walked in the door. My mom would usually escort him into their bedroom, close the door, share the sordid details, and then ask him what he planned to do about it. This had happened more times than I cared to remember. I knew the routine fairly well since I had eavesdropped on a few of their conversations in the past. If things played out true to form, my mom would ask him to consider placing my grandmother in a home with other senior citizens. She would argue that Gram would actually be happier there since she'd be around more people her own age. My dad would always resist. He either realized that Gram had full use of her faculties and was perfectly fine living with us, or he was just too afraid of what she'd do if he even suggested it. Whatever the reason, I was just glad that things would always remain the same. And after a few days, it would all blow over and things would be back to normal—although normal at our house would probably be considered *abnormal* anywhere else. No big deal. I was used to it.

I wished sometimes that I could share with my mom certain details about my grandmother's past. She'd have a completely different opinion of her mother-in-law if I were able to do that. But Gram had sworn me to secrecy. My mom was aware that Gram was an overseas telephone operator during World War II, but what she didn't know was that Eugene, a commander with U.S. Naval Intelligence, had recruited her to intercept and decode enemy messages that were communicated over phone lines. Gram had a real gift when it came to deciphering secret codes. I think they call it *cryptography*. And since she handled international calls, the government figured that she'd be in a perfect position to recognize sensitive messages, especially conversations, from enemy countries. Gram served her country well but had always kept it a secret—from everyone but me, that is.

And if that weren't awesome enough, Gram joined Eugene after the war when he set up his own private detective agency. She accompanied him on countless cases. Eugene had a nickname for her that I just recently learned—the Chameleon. Since Gram was asked to do a lot of undercover work, she frequently needed to blend into a crowd without being noticed. She became a master of disguise that allowed her to collect evidence and help solve a bunch of cases. And I guess that Gram never got tired of those disguises. It would explain her fondness for taking on new personalities on an almost daily basis. When you come from a background filled with adventure and intrigue, it must be hard to give that up. To me, it was pure entertainment. To my parents, however, it was anything but.

By the time I made it across town to Eugene's, my legs ached. I never complained though. I always considered it a great way of working off a few calories—a few calories that I'd never miss. I parked my bike in the back of the building and climbed the stairs to Eugene's office. As I did so, I thought about how lucky I was to have someone like Eugene in my life. He was more than just a friend—he was a mentor, and at times, a lifesaver. He had come to our rescue in the nick of time in each of our last two adventures— with Rupert Olsen and Colonel Culpepper. I can honestly say that I'm not sure I'd be standing here today without the help of one very cool senior citizen.

When I reached the top of the stairs, I immediately noticed the sign on the door. It was new. It read *Eugene Patterson, Private Investigator*. Someday, I thought, I'd like to have a real office somewhere, and I could picture the sign: *Charlie Collier, Snoop for Hire. Charlie Collier, Proprietor.* I knocked twice, scratched my fingernails over the surface of the door, and then knocked three more times. It was a special password informing Eugene that a friend was on the other side of the door.

"Come in," a voice said.

Since the door was always getting stuck, I put my shoulder into it. It easily gave way. Eugene, seated behind his desk reading the newspaper, greeted me with a broad smile.

"Charlie, what a surprise." He set the paper down.

"I didn't mean to interrupt anything, Eugene."

"Don't worry about it," he said. "I was just reading about those burglaries. You know, the rug store and the bakery. The boys in blue are stumped." He winked. "Maybe you and I ought to lend a hand. What do you think?"

"That's what Gram suggested. But maybe we should wait for a formal invitation."

"Couldn't agree with you more," he said as he sat back in his chair and folded his arms. "So, what brings you here? Need help with another case?"

"No, not really. Although I reserve the right to return if I do," I said with a grin.

"My door's always open," he said. "If it's not stuck, that is."

I walked in and pulled up a chair opposite his desk.

"So, what's on your mind?" Eugene said.

"Actually, it's a social call."

Eugene got up, walked around to the front of his desk, and sat on the edge. "Even better."

"I had a nice conversation today with an old friend of yours," I said.

"And who would that be?"

"An old fraternity brother by the name of Thad."

Eugene smiled. "That would have to be Thaddeus Miles. Am I right?"

I nodded.

"Is he still teaching at Roosevelt?"

"Uh huh. And he's directing a play too."

"You don't say. Well, Thad certainly loved the theater. Maybe a little too much."

I leaned forward in my chair. "And I have some really big news."

Eugene raised his eyebrows.

"I got one of the leading parts in the production. And get this—I play a private detective."

Eugene clapped his hands and laughed. "I love it. When do you start?"

"Play practice begins next Monday after school," I said. "I'm afraid it's going to occupy a lot of my time. So I guess we won't be taking on any new clients for a while. I might not even have time to read any Sam Solomon novels."

Eugene snapped his fingers as if he had just remembered something. "Sam Solomon. Thanks for reminding me." He slid off the front of his desk, walked around and sat down behind it. He picked up a pencil and began scribbling something on a piece of paper. "Gotta remember to listen to Sam's new episode next week. If I don't write it down, I'm sure to forget."

"What new episode? What are you talking about?"

"Didn't you know?" he said.

"Know what?"

"About *The Sam Solomon Mystery Theater*. The radio station in town is rerunning highlights from the series."

Sam Solomon Mystery Theater? What was Eugene talking about? I knew all about the Sam Solomon novels. Heck, I had read each one of them multiple times. But this sounded like something completely different.

"Eugene, I'm confused. You mean to tell me that Sam Solomon was on radio?"

"Your grandpa never told you about it?"

I shook my head.

Eugene sat back in his chair and crossed his arms. "And you call yourself a Sam Solomon fan?"

Not just a fan, I considered myself an expert on the world's greatest master detective. How could I have missed this?

"Let me tell you about it, Charlie. *The Sam Solomon Mystery Theater* was a popular old-time radio program back in the late 1930s and early 1940's. And this year just happens to be the 75th anniversary of its premiere. So, the local radio station in town is rerunning one episode each week from the collection. That's the good news. The bad news is that they're airing them at eleven o'clock on Monday nights—well past your bedtime I would guess."

"I'd gladly lose some sleep for a chance to hear them," I said.

"Just don't let your parents catch you, okay?"

I nodded. "I can be very discreet when I need to be." This was such great news. I had a hard time believing it. A whole new world of Sam Solomon was about to open up to me. "Are the stories just like the ones in the books?"

"Yeah, just shorter," Eugene said. "Sam needs to conduct his entire investigation and find the bad guy in just thirty minutes. A little bit tougher, but he can do it. After all, he's Sam Solomon."

This was amazing. I wasn't sure if I could emotionally handle everything that had happened in the last few hours. First, I'm a leading man. And now, my hero on the radio. It just didn't get any better than this.

"So, do you know what the next episode is about?" I asked.

Eugene placed finger to his lips. "Let me see if I can remember. After last night's program, I seem to recall hearing something about *coming attractions*." He closed his eyes, gritted his teeth, and made a face. I had seen it before. Eugene was in full concentration mode. He opened one eye. "I'm getting it. Something's coming." When his other eye popped open, I knew he had it. "A crooked promoter bets on prizefights that he illegally fixed."

"Sounds interesting," I said. "So, that's this Monday night at 11:00, right?"

Eugene picked up a pad of paper. "Want me to write it down for you?"

I smiled. "No, I'm sure I'll remember." I didn't need any reminders. There was no way that I would forget about *The Sam Solomon Mystery Theater*. I was certain that it would soon become my favorite program.

Eugene got up, walked over to the window and opened it a crack. "Getting a little stuffy in here." It got a little stuffy in Eugene's office on a regular basis. This unique space was an exact replica of Sam Solomon's 1938 Chicago office—including climate control—which meant a radiator that worked whenever it wanted to, and absolutely no sign of air conditioning. He returned to his desk. "So, tell me about this big production you're starring in?"

"Well, it's about this young, spoiled socialite who's a suspect in the disappearance of her wealthy parents. The police are convinced that she's the guilty party, although no bodies have been recovered. No one seems to believe her, so she hires this private eye named Nick Dakota," I pointed to myself, "to dig up evidence that will hopefully convince the authorities she's innocent."

"Sounds like Thad's got himself a winner," Eugene said. "And if you need any help, just yell. I was in a few productions in college. Glad to give you some pointers."

"I may take you up on that," I said. "This is all new territory for me."

"By the way, are any of your other friends in the play?" he asked.

I smiled. "Believe it or not, both Henry and Scarlett are in it. Henry plays the police detective intent on convicting Rebecca Ramsey—that's the heroine's name. And Scarlett plays Rebecca."

"With all you kids in the play, it looks like your little agency may become a ghost town for the next few weeks."

A ghost town? I didn't like the way that sounded. And the more I thought about it, the more it bothered me. I was determined to win over Scarlett with my acting prowess, but was I really willing to abandon the agency? At the time, it seemed like the right thing to do, but now I found myself rethinking my options. Had I acted hastily when I agreed to play the role of Nick Dakota? Did I even for a minute think about potential clients who'd be denied our services? What will they do when they stop by the garage and find it empty? I was beginning to feel guilty…and selfish. I needed to rethink all of this.

"Eugene, I better get going."

"Need a ride?" he asked. We can toss your bike in the back of the car if you want."

I glanced at the clock on the far wall. "No, that's okay. I have just enough time to make it home for dinner. Thanks anyway though."

"Well, break a leg," he said.

"Huh?"

"Theater talk," he said. "It means *good luck*."

"Oh, thanks. Well, see you later." I hightailed it to the door and raced down the stairs. I jumped on my bike and was off. All I could think about was how I'd feel a day, a week, or a month from now if I hadn't solved a case for someone. I was guessing that I'd feel pretty empty inside. As badly as I wanted to be Scarlett's leading man, I wasn't really sure I wanted to devote all of my time to the play and miss out on the chance for a big caper. Suddenly I didn't know what to do.

I made it home in record time. When I pulled up in back of the house, and entered the garage with my bike, I noticed, hanging on the walls, all of the paraphernalia I had accumulated for my role as a super sleuth. My fedora and trench coat hung from hooks. The card table—the official agency desk—was stuck behind a ladder. Lawn chairs, for me and potential clients, were folded up and stacked in the corner. A set of binoculars and a magnifying glass were tucked away high on a shelf behind some paint cans. And the clipboard that held our appointment calendar was stuffed behind boxes of Christmas ornaments. Best to keep that one hidden. If it fell into enemy hands—namely my parents—the agency might be forced to close its doors permanently.

As I stared at all of our tools of the trade, I continued to question my decision to audition for the play. Did I really want to give up all of this for a few weeks? Could I even make myself walk away from it? To have been selected for one of the leading parts in Mr. Miles' production was unimaginable. It was an amazing accomplishment for someone with no formal training as an actor. But somehow I had managed to pull it off. After having done that, was I really willing to just walk away from this new opportunity? Not to mention all of the quality time with Scarlett that I'd be losing. I had to make a decision, and fast. I had to choose—my love of the P.I. business vs. the glittering lights of Broadway.

My mind drifted to Sam Solomon. I tried to remember a time when Sam might have made a decision to close the office for a few weeks, voluntarily or not. And if so, how had he coped with it? I thought hard for several minutes and then I had the answer. Why had it taken me so long to remember? The answer was so obvious—Episode #45—*The Faulty Breaks Caper*.

In this particular episode, Sam had been hired by the business partner of a man who was suspected of embezzling funds from the company. When Sam contacted the accused and asked for a meeting, he was invited to the man' mountain retreat. Why in such a remote location, he wondered? Could it be a trap? Would he come back alive? Against his better judgment, Sam agreed to the meeting—which turned out to be pretty uneventful. As he drove back down the mountain, however, he realized his greatest fear. During the meeting, someone had poured acid over his car's brake lining. As he approached a treacherous turn, and without the ability to stop, the car veered off the road and down an embankment. Sam suffered multiple contusions and half a dozen broken bones. He was forced to close the agency for three months. And it was during that hiatus that Sam learned that he *could* live without the adventure, the intrigue, and the danger. He actually found himself enjoying the break, but was anxious to resume business when he was fully healed.

So if Sam could survive for three months, then I could certainly survive for six weeks. It was decided. I would hang the *Gone Fishing* sign on the door first thing Monday morning and immerse myself in the play. I was determined to be the best private eye in town—even if I was mouthing someone else's lines.

Chapter 6

The Miss Information Caper

I met up with Henry and Scarlett on the playground before school the next day.

"I'm glad I caught you guys," I said. "I have a plan. Since play practice begins on Monday, why don't we at least keep the office open for the rest of the week? That way we might get a last minute walk-in before we close up shop for the next month and a half."

"I can't today," Henry said. "My little sister has a dance recital after school and my mom's making me go."

"And I can't tomorrow," Scarlett said. "I have an appointment at the orthodontist."

"Then that just leaves Friday," I said. "Does that work for you guys?"

Henry nodded. "I can do it."

Scarlett frowned. "Can't you guys ever give me a little more warning?"

Unlike Henry, I liked the idea of having a third brain at the agency. And I really liked being able to spend more time with Scarlett. But sometimes she made it so difficult. She wasn't committed yet, and I wasn't sure if she would ever be.

"That's forty-eight hours from now. That's plenty of notice," I said. "It may be the last chance for us to help out our fellow man for who knows how long. We owe it to the client."

Scarlett sighed. "I'm just not a big fan of this walk-in business. We're just sitting around doing nothing until someone decides to show up. It seems like a big waste of time. Do we absolutely have to?"

"Well, you don't," Henry snapped. "But me and Charlie'll be there. And if a client with a killer case happens to stroll in, we'll be sure to call you…if we remember, that is."

The first bell went off. We now had five minutes to get to our first class.

"So that's how it's going to be, huh? Blackmail," she said. "If I don't come, you're going to freeze me out of the next caper."

Henry shrugged. "What can I say? It's just business. It's like the story of the Little Red Hen. You wanna piece of nice, warm, oven-baked bread, you gotta help roll out the dough."

Scarlett rolled her eyes. "I'll be there," she said as she squeezed past a group of kids standing near the front door.

Henry grinned and wiped his hands. "If you need any more help handling the princess, you know who to call."

It was funny the way things seemed to work out. Henry, who could barely tolerate Scarlett, knew all of the right buttons to push to get her to do exactly what he wanted. Then there was me, a kid who'd do anything for her attention, and who was totally clueless when it came to girls. At times I thought about adopting Henry's strategy—complete rudeness—but I knew it'd never work for me. As soon as I'd utter a negative comment, I would immediately feel the need to apologize. I needed a new approach, but I had nothing in mind. I could only hope that my theatrical debut would ultimately win her over.

*   *   *   *   *

The next couple of days were a blur. All I could think about was Friday afternoon when we'd meet up in the garage for one last session at the agency. Since it would be weeks before we'd get a chance to take on new clients, I was hoping that someone with a quick and manageable problem would stroll in. And as strange it may sound, I was actually hoping that no one would walk in with a killer, Sam Solomon-type case. Our schedule simply wouldn't allow it.

When I got home from school on Friday afternoon, I changed clothes and ran downstairs to meet up with Henry and Scarlett. Timing couldn't have been more perfect. My mom was at her monthly book club meeting. We would be safe for a good two hours. On my way out to the garage, I passed through the kitchen and immediately spotted a plate of brownies on the counter. For a kid who was supposed to be monitoring his calorie intake, brownies presented the ultimate temptation. There weren't really any foods that were absolutely forbidden as far as my parents were concerned, but if there had been, I was fairly certain that brownies would have been in the top ten. My mom, who had struggled with her own weight for as long as I could remember, had always preached *moderation*. Nothing was off the table, but you were expected to exercise prudence when choosing portions. I knew that a small sliver of a single brownie would be acceptable, so I cut off a corner and promptly inhaled it.

While savoring the moment, I spotted a headline in the newspaper lying on the kitchen table. It read: *Mystery Cards May Link Crimes*. I sliced off another corner of the same brownie and sat down to read the article. It recounted the story of the theft of Persian rugs from the carpeting store a little more than a week ago. Then it mentioned the burglary of the bakery shop this past Tuesday. I remembered both stories and I also recalled thinking to myself that they seemed unrelated. But now there appeared to be a connection.

On the floor of the rug shop, police recovered a business card with the letters *SS* on it. There was a red circle around the letters and a red slanted line over the *SS* lettering. I had seen the red symbol before. It usually meant that something wasn't allowed somewhere. Then, according to the story, exactly one week later on the floor of the bakery, the same card was found. The article said that the discovery of the cards may indicate a connection between the two crimes. Or it may just be a complete coincidence. At press time, police had been unable to explain the significance of the *SS* markings on the card.

I glanced down at the plate of brownies. No less than six of them were now missing all four corners. This is not what my mom would refer to as *moderation*. I knew that I would have to answer for this crime. I could only hope that my punishment would be swift and relatively painless. As I walked out the back door and into the garage, I found myself thinking about the *SS* lettering on the business cards found at the crime scenes. Had the perpetrator inadvertently dropped them at each location? Or had he done so intentionally?

That immediately made me think of Sam Solomon. In Episode #43—*The Miss Information Caper*, he was on the trail of a notorious female assassin. After each hit, she would leave a flower called a Black Spider—an Asiatic black lily—at the foot of each victim. When police struggled to identify a suspect, Sam was hired by the family of one her potential targets who hoped to stop the killer before she struck again. Within days, Sam had managed to track her down. It was later learned that the woman was playing a game of cat and mouse with police, and had deliberately left clues for them, with the hopes of being caught.

I doubted if we were dealing with the same sort of psychopath in tiny Oak Grove but it sure was interesting. And then there was the question about the markings on each card. What did the *SS* mean anyway? The only times I recalled seeing that abbreviation was in a history class when we were studying World War II. I seemed to remember that the *SS* was an elite corps of the Nazi Party that guarded Adolf Hitler. I could see where someone might not be particularly fond of that group. Or it could stand for Secret Service or Selective Service or even Social Security. Maybe the guy was an anti-government type. Whatever it turned out to be, this story had piqued my interest, and I was determined to follow it to its conclusion.

When I entered the garage, Henry was already waiting for me. He had set up the card table and lawn chairs. He had even laid out my trench coat and fedora. He was ready for business.

"She's late as usual," he announced.

"She'll be here," I said. "Don't worry."

And before Henry had a chance for a clever retort, Scarlett strolled in.

"Sorry," she said. "It took me a while to get past that long line of walk-ins out there."

"Very funny," Henry said.

It appeared that I needed to intervene—as usual. "Why don't we all just take a seat and relax. When someone does eventually walk in, we need to have our game faces on."

Each of us dropped down into our respective lawn chairs. I smiled weakly at the others, hoping to preserve the peace. Scarlett crossed her legs, folded her arms, and did her best to avoid eye contact with either of us. Henry stretched out his legs, leaned back in his chair, closed his eyes, and pretended to be napping. After a couple of minutes, Scarlett jumped out of her chair.

"I just can't sit here like this," she said. "It's making me crazy."

Henry opened one eye and smiled. He apparently was going to let me get myself out of this.

"Well, we could have a conversation," I said. "We could talk about the play. We do have that in common. Scarlett, you go first."

She made a face and sat back down. "I think I'd rather just sit here."

I shook my head. Now I was completely confused. Wasn't she the one, about twenty seconds ago, who couldn't stand just sitting around. Oh, well. I would never understand girls. For the next few minutes, an uncomfortable silence followed. Scarlett would shift in her chair every so often. Henry would let out an occasional snore just to irritate her. And from the expression on her face, it was working. I kept glancing at the door. I so prayed that someone would walk in just to end the standoff. When it was clear that a prospective client was nowhere to be seen, I decided to ease the tension myself.

"So, has anyone heard any good brainteasers lately?" I said. I doubted if Scarlett would react to my question, but I was almost certain that Henry would be unable to pass up a chance to stump us.

He sat up in his chair. "Since you asked," he said, "I just happen to have a little something for you."

"Great, let 'er rip," I said. This would hopefully pacify Scarlett. If she was forced to do a little critical thinking, she might feel that the afternoon hadn't been a total waste of time.

"Here goes," Henry began. "A man, convicted of murder in Canada, is sentenced to life behind bars. He vows to escape. He's sent to a prison on an island off the coast of Nova Scotia. One day he does manage to escape without anyone's help. There is no bridge connected to the mainland, yet he is able to walk away." Henry sat back in his chair. "How'd he do it?"

Scarlett uncrossed her legs. It had worked. We now had her attention.

"Maybe the water was shallow and he was able to wade to the shore," she said.

"Nope," Henry said. "It was twenty feet deep, and he couldn't swim."

This was getting interesting. The fact that this happened in Canada is either an important clue, or it's meaningless and just intended to throw us off. Even if the inmate managed to escape from the prison himself, I was having a hard time imagining how he could just walk away. I began to concentrate on the facts: the prison, the island, the water, and maybe Canada. The combination had to lead to a solution.

"He had a boat stashed somewhere," Scarlett said.

Henry shook his head. "No boat. And he walked. He didn't paddle."

I stared straight ahead and tried to imagine the scenario that Henry had described. There had to be a logical way to get the prisoner off the island, across the body of water, and onto the mainland. What was I missing? I decided to toss Canada into the mix to see if that would help. What was unique about Canada, I thought? And then suddenly, I had it. In this particular brain buster, the location *was* important.

"So, do you give up?" Henry said.

"Yeah, whatever," Scarlett said. "What is it?"

"Not so fast," I replied. "I've got it."

Henry and Scarlett both turned in my direction.

"Here's how he did it," I said. "Since the prison is so far north, the prisoner just waited until the dead of winter, when everything was frozen, including the body of water between the island and the mainland. And then he just walked away."

Henry, foiled again, sat back in his chair. "Wake me when a client walks in." And that was it. No congratulations. No 'nice going, partner.' No nothing. Henry was too competitive for his own good. But that spirit did come in awfully handy when we found ourselves embroiled in an unusually challenging case.

"Are we done here?" Scarlett asked.

"No," Henry said. His eyes never opened.

She began tapping her fingers on the card table. "How long are we expected—" She stopped in mid-sentence.

There had been a knock at the door. Henry sat up and smiled.

"What did I tell you?" he said. He raced over and threw open the door.

And almost as if he had planned it, a walk-in client stepped into the garage. It was a familiar face—Derrick Hirsch. Derrick was a fellow sixth-grade classmate at Roosevelt. The most interesting thing about him was his mouth—it was full of metal. This kid was a dentist's dream. He had been in braces for as long as I could remember. Derrick would regularly pop out his retainer, along with other dental paraphernalia, and set them on his desk. If that wasn't bad enough, they were always dripping in drool. Not an appetizing picture during lunch, let me tell you.

"Collier, you open for business?" he asked.

"You bet," I said. "Pull up a chair."

Henry reached for the change jar and shook it just for Derrick's benefit.

Derrick reached into his pocket and pulled out a handful of change. "There's at least a buck here. Don't worry."

"Just checking," Henry said.

With that ugly business out of the way, it was time to get to work. "Okay," I said, "what can we do for you?"

Derrick leaned in, folded his hands and set them on the table. "Here's the deal, Collier. My grandpa is a big coin collector. Been saving coins all his life. He's got this awesome collection. And he's always telling me that someday he's going to give me it to me. So yesterday, he says: 'Derrick, it's time for you to become steward of my collection.' So naturally I'm pretty excited. Then he says: 'But before I hand it over, you'll have to earn it.'"

I couldn't stop staring at Derrick's braces. I could see these little rubber bands in his mouth moving up and down as he spoke. I knew I should have been concentrating on what he was saying but it was tough.

"So my grandpa pulls out this jar," he continued. "It's about this high." Derrick held one hand about eight inches above the other. "Then he drops a coin in there. It's an 1875-CC twenty-cent piece."

"Twenty-cent piece?" Scarlett said. "I've never heard of that before."

"Yeah, they made them from 1875 to 1878," Derrick said. "But let's not get hung up on details."

"What's it worth?" Henry asked.

"About five hundred bucks," he replied.

Henry, Scarlett and I looked at one another. It was obvious we weren't charging this guy enough.

"Then he sticks a cork into the top of the bottle. He looks at me, smiles, and says: 'If you want my collection, you have to remove the coin from this bottle, but you can't take the cork out, and you can't break the bottle.'" Derrick sat back in his chair. "How the heck am I supposed to do that? Collier, you gotta help me."

I turned to my colleagues. "Any thoughts?"

Scarlett shook her head.

"How wide is the opening at the top of the bottle?" Henry asked.

"About an inch," he said. "Just large enough for the coin to fit in."

I tried to imagine a bottle with a cork in it and a coin sitting at the bottom. I grabbed a pad of paper from the shelf and began to sketch. I sat there and stared at it for a good minute. Nothing was coming. I glanced at Henry and shrugged. He shook his head. As did Scarlett.

"You mean you don't know?" Derrick said. "What am I gonna do, guys?"

"Maybe if we think about it overnight, we might come up with something," I said.

"I'm not getting my money's worth here," Derrick said disgustedly.

Normally, I would immediately have tried to put an end to the bickering but I was too deep in thought. I repeated the directions to myself: *you have to remove the coin, but you can't take the cork out, and you can't break the bottle.* I began to stress each phrase, and then each word. *You can't take the cork out...you can't take it out...out,* that's it. I sat up in my chair and grinned.

"I got it," I said to Derrick. "Here's what you do. Your grandpa said that you couldn't take the cork *out*, but he didn't say anything about *in*."

"Huh?" Derrick said.

"All you have to do is push the cork *into* the bottle. Then turn it over and shake the coin out."

A wide grin began to form on Derrick's face. "That's it. It's mine, all mine." He got up and headed to the door.

"Got a problem with walk-ins now?" Henry said.

Scarlett sneered, stood up, and headed for the door. "See you in a month and a half, gentlemen."

And with that, the Charlie Collier, Snoop for Hire Agency was officially on hiatus.

Chapter 7

The Hammond Eggs Caper

I spent the better part of the weekend studying my lines. I had never been great at memorization so this play business was going to be a real challenge. I thought it might help if I were able to get into character so I pretended to be the real Nick Dakota. Then I imagined what he might say. If it had been Sam Solomon, it would have been simple. Not only did I know how Sam thought, but I could recite virtually every line of dialogue from the entire mystery series. There was one advantage—the two characters were somewhat similar. Like Sam, Nick Dakota appeared to be the same sort of hard-boiled, no-nonsense private eye. But Nick was a contemporary private detective, not a 1930s sleuth. He never referred to a woman as a *dame*. He was more politically correct.

At dinner on Sunday, I told my parents that their little boy had won the part of leading man at the upcoming sixth grade play. My mom could barely contain herself. She demanded to know all the details—the entire story line, scene by scene; what other kids were in it; and most importantly, the date of the performance. She apparently planned to invite a bunch of relatives. Now that I could have done without. But I decided not to say anything. It wasn't often that she got a chance to brag about her only child. I did put my foot down, however, when she volunteered to help make costumes. That was the last thing I needed. I couldn't afford having her snooping around at school. It would cramp my style big time.

My dad reacted in typical "dad" fashion. "Just don't screw it up," he said.

But that was okay. I decided to use it as motivation, and to surprise him with a stellar performance. Maybe that way he'd go easy on me the next time I got caught taking on new clients.

When Monday morning finally arrived, I was pumped. This promised to be a red letter day. Not only would I have an opportunity to showcase my talents on stage for Scarlett, but I was also counting the hours until eleven o'clock tonight, when I'd be curled up under the covers—with headphones, of course—listening to *The Sam Solomon Mystery Theater*. I remembered Eugene mentioning that tonight's episode was about a crooked fight promoter. I could hardly wait. I knew that I'd be tired tomorrow morning, but that didn't matter. It was nothing compared to the dozens of sleepless nights that Sam Solomon experienced. Take, for instance, Episode #50—*The Hammond Eggs Caper*. Sam sat in the corner booth of a northwest Indiana all-night diner for seventy-two hours straight just waiting for a chance to get a glimpse of a suspicious character suspected of smuggling thousands of laying hens across the Illinois/Indiana border. So I had nothing to complain about if I missed an hour or two of sleep.

As was usually the case when I was excited about an upcoming event, the school day seemed to drag. I found myself glancing at the clock the entire time. The minute hand seemed frozen in place most of the day. At recess, I pulled out the script and practiced some of my lines. Henry, on the other hand, appeared unusually calm, just hours before his theatrical debut.

"Relax, Charlie, we don't have to know all of our lines today," he said. "Some of the other kids told me that Mr. Miles lets you read from the script for the first few rehearsals. So don't kill yourself."

"Well, that's good to hear," I said. "Because you know me and memorizing. I'm no good at it."

"Who is?"

"I am," a voice said proudly. It was Stephanie—Stephanie the nodder. She wasn't part of the conversation but she decided to weasel her way into it anyway. "Typical boys. You never want to make the necessary effort to succeed. All you do is the absolute minimum. Serves you right if you can't remember your lines." She smiled in a smart-alecky way.

"Who asked you?" Henry said.

"I'm just trying to explain to you that everyone has the aptitude to succeed *if* he's willing to work hard enough," she said.

"We don't need you to tell us that," Henry snapped. "Maybe you haven't been reading the papers lately. Charlie and I single-handedly thwarted a black market taxidermy operation, not to mention capturing a notorious criminal responsible for a string of burglaries in the area. So don't lecture us about hard work."

Stephanie snarled. "I must have missed that," she said. And having made her point, she huffed and was on her way.

The remainder of the afternoon was a snore. Even the final period, Mrs. Jansen's science class, was intolerable. Since her daughter recently had a baby, Mrs. Jansen took a couple days off to help her out. Our sub was a strange bird named Theodore Montague. He was bald on top with shoulder-length hair. It wasn't a good look. Every time he had subbed in the past, he wore the same clothes—a rust-colored corduroy suit—even when it was hot out. He had a glass eye—at least that's what the eighth graders told us. You could never tell if he was looking at you or not. That really messed up some of the less-than-honest kids who were never sure if he was watching them borrow answers from fellow classmates. Mr. Montague spent the entire period reading to us from the textbook. I always hated it when teachers did that. I could have done that myself.

The minute that class had mercifully come to an end, Henry and I made our way to the auditorium to meet up with Mr. Miles and the rest of the cast. Everyone sat in the first couple of rows anxiously awaiting our director, who eventually arrived fashionably late.

"All right, let's get to work, everyone," he said. "I want all of you up on stage, but you can leave your scripts on your seats. We won't need them today."

I nudged Henry. "You said he'd let us use our scripts today. This isn't gonna be pretty."

We all hopped up on stage and prepared for the worst.

Stephanie began nodding, and raised her hand.

"Yes, Miss Martin," Mr. Miles said.

"This doesn't affect me, mind you," she said, "but what if we haven't memorized all of our lines. Will you be handing out detentions?"

Mr. Miles' eyes narrowed. He seemed unaware of the fact that Stephanie was the official whistle-blower in the sixth grade.

"There won't be any detentions. In fact, none of you will be asked to recite any of your lines today."

A collective sigh followed.

"Today you'll we doing a series of exercises to strengthen your instrument."

"What instrument?" Henry asked.

"Your voice, Mr. Cunningham. What else?"

Henry shrugged.

"Okay," Mr. Miles said, "everyone in a straight line across the front of the stage facing me with your backs to the audience."

And for the next hour, we performed various voice techniques. We started by rolling our heads forward, back, right and left. This was supposed to relax our neck and shoulders. Then we massaged our faces, from our hairlines to our jaws. I felt pretty silly doing this, but since everyone had to do it, it was kind of fun. After that Mr. Miles passed out pencils to each of us. He told us to hold the pencils in our mouths crosswise, and then try to recite the Pledge of Allegiance. At first, everything sounded really garbled, but after a few minutes, I could see what he was trying to accomplish. Since the pencil made it difficult to speak, we were forced to over-enunciate each word in order for it to be heard correctly. After we had performed a few more physical exercises, Mr. Miles instructed us to turn around and face the audience.

"Now it's time to hear you project," he said. "With our budget, we don't have the luxury of placing a wireless mic on everyone. Wired microphones will be hanging from the rafters. The only way they can pick you up is if you speak clearly and loudly." He grabbed his chest. "From the diaphragm. Always remember— from the diaphragm." He walked over to the side of the stage and opened his briefcase. He emerged with a handful of papers, which he distributed. "Each of you should be holding a tongue twister. I want you to read it over, and then when I cue you, I want you to belt it out, as if it were opening night."

We each read over the material on the papers. Some of the kids made faces. Others appeared confused. This was going to be interesting.

"Okay, let's begin." Mr. Miles danced down the stairs leading to the main floor, walked to the middle of the auditorium, and sat down in one of the seats. "From left to right," he called out. "Here we go. Miss Martin, begin."

Stephanie nodded and yelled out "When one black blood bled black blood, the other black blood bled blug." She made a face. The rest of us were enjoying this. "Let me try it again," she pleaded. But she never got a chance to say *when one black bug bled black blood, the other black bug bled blue.*

"No mulligans," Mr. Miles said. "Next...Mr. Hart?"

The hisser took a deep breath and let 'er rip. "Mommy made me mush my muffy mummins."

Mr. Miles sighed. He was hoping to have heard *mommy made me mash my mini-muffins.* "Mr. Walsh?"

The slacker just stood there. He must have been daydreaming. He was probably thinking up a new illness to get him how of tomorrow's practice.

Mr. Walsh?"

"Oh, sorry," he said. And then proceeded to rattle off "a proper cup of coffee in a coppa cuppa coffee." Instead of *a proper cup of coffee in a copper coffee cup.* "I messed that up. I can do better."

Henry, Scarlett, and I stood at the other end of the line listening in as fellow actors were humbled by relatively simple tongue twisters. Mr. Miles was making his point in a most effective way. Until we learned to speak clearly and crisply, there was no sense reciting lines from the script. When Mr. Miles pointed at Henry, it was do or die.

"Mr. Cunningham?"

Henry stepped forward and let fly. It wasn't pretty. "The sixth ship's sick sheep is six." He groaned and stepped back into line. He was trying to say *the sixth sheik's sixth sheep is sick.*

"Mr. Collier? This one is perfect for you."

It was time to wow Mr. Miles and Scarlett. I could do this. I was certain I could. It was time for my close-up, Mr. DeMille.

"Charlie chooses to choose choice chilled cherries." I had done it. Only one flub. I should have read *Charlie chooses to chew choice chilled cherries.*

"And Miss Alexander?"

Scarlett was cool as a cucumber. She smiled and delivered a flawless performance. "Moses supposes his toses are roses, but Moses supposes erroneously."

Mr. Miles sat back in his seat and folded his arms. "Very nice, Scarlett. I wish I could say the same for the rest of you." He stood and approached the stage. "We're going to continue this exercise until each one of you is able to deliver your line five times in a row—mistake-free. It could happen later today, or two weeks from today. It's up to you. And we won't read from our scripts until then."

And for the next half hour, we repeated our tongue twisters over and over. When we reached the end of our first rehearsal, we still had failed to master our task.

"We'll continue this same exercise tomorrow," Mr. Miles said painfully, "until we get it right. Any questions?"

Even if there had been questions, most of us were too drained to string together more than a couple of words. I was upset that I was unable to nail a relatively simple tongue twister. I was better than that. I vowed that tomorrow would be different. If not, there would be no way to win the hand of the fair Rebecca Ramsey—not by a long shot.

*   *   *   *   *

That night following dinner, I went up to my room to finish my homework. I had a hard time concentrating. And who wouldn't? When your hero, your idol, your mentor—Sam Solomon—was about to be featured in his own old-time radio program, how could you think of anything else? I found a portable radio and headphones and slid them under my pillow. I even set the alarm on my clock radio for eleven o'clock just in case I fell asleep waiting for the program to start. Since my parents might still be awake at eleven, I had to make certain that they weren't able to detect what I was up to. I wanted everything to appear normal so as soon as I finished up an English composition, I went downstairs for a few minutes to watch a little television. That would make it seem like a typical evening.

When I entered the living room, I found my parents seated on the couch. My mom was watching TV while working on a crossword puzzle. My dad was reading the newspaper. Gram—at least I think it was Gram—was sitting in an easy chair in a Darth Vader costume. A lightsaber rested in her lap. She nodded to me when I came in, then turned and pointed her weapon at my dad. Another painful family melodrama was about to unfold. I didn't need this tonight so I decided to defuse it. I stepped into Gram's line of fire and just stood there. I knew she'd never use me for target practice. A moment later, she shrugged, then turned and lowered her weapon. My dad will never know how close he came to being vaporized.

He dropped the newspaper on the coffee table. "Did you see this story?"

"What story?" my mom asked.

"This one about the people who got poisoned."

"No," she said as she set down her crossword puzzle.

My dad picked the paper back up and began reading. "Thirty people attending a campaign fundraiser for State Treasurer, Miranda Pickens, were rushed to the hospital last night complaining of stomach distress. Blood tests revealed that they had ingested some type of poison that has yet to be identified."

"Food poisoning, maybe?" my mom said.

"Now get this," my dad said. "After the health department inspected all the food and beverages at the affair, they found traces of poison in the punch."

"The punch?" my mom said. "How could that be?" She paused. "Unless someone put it in there. How awful."

I found myself listening carefully to each detail. It reminded me of being in Mrs. Jansen's class when she would unveil one of her patented brain busters.

"Following the toxicology report," my dad continued, "the police began questioning each guest who had attended the party. They started with the caterer who supplied the punch. Before the affair had begun, witnesses indicated that they had watched the caterer prepare the punch. He had mixed the ingredients, added ice, and then tasted it himself. But there were no signs of poison in his system."

"Then one of the guests must have put it in there," my mom said.

"I don't think so," my dad replied. "A closed-circuit camera captured everything that took place at the beverage table the entire evening. And no one was seen putting anything into the punchbowl." My dad set the paper down. "What do you make of that?"

As would always happen when an unsolvable problem presented itself, my brain went into overdrive. I tried to think of how someone could have placed the poison in the punch without being seen. And how did the caterer drink it and not get sick? I could feel the wheels turning. And within a minute, I had it solved.

"I'll tell you who did it," I said. "It *was* the caterer."

"But, Charlie," my mom said, "people saw him drink from the bowl, and he's fine. No, it has to be someone else."

I sat down on the couch next to my mom. "Don't you see. He mixed all of the ingredients in front of everyone to throw off suspicion, but one of the ingredients actually contained the poison."

"Then how come he didn't get sick?" my dad said.

I smiled. "Because the poison was in the ice cubes. And since he took a sip right away, the ice hadn't melted, and the poison hadn't been released yet."

My parents stared at one another. They were speechless. I had seen this look before.

Gram ripped off her Darth Vader helmet. "He just did it again," she said. "When are you people going to recognize that this boy has a natural gift, and let him use it in whatever way he wants…including his little agency."

"Mom, let's not have this conversation again, please," my dad said.

Gram turned to me. "Have you been following the news? The police are now dealing with *two* unsolved burglaries. Your community needs you, Charlie. Think about it."

The exchange that followed was predictably heated. Gram listed all of my investigative accomplishments over the years, while my parents countered with concerns about some of the slightly unethical tactics I had used to solve some of my more memorable cases. They could have argued all night. It really didn't matter. I appreciated Gram coming to my defense but I knew I'd never win this one. As I headed upstairs to escape the drama, I could still hear the bickering even when I closed the door to my room.

Chapter 8

The Fright to the Finish Caper

Bzzzz... The alarm on the radio next to my bed woke me up from a sound sleep. I glanced at the clock. Instead of seeing the usual 7:00 am, it read 11:00 pm. What was going on? I pulled up the curtains next to my bed and looked out the window into darkness. Had my mom been messing around with my clock radio? Why would she do that? And then all at once, it hit me. *I* had set the alarm in case I fell asleep...which I had. It was time for *The Sam Solomon Mystery Theater.* I fumbled for the portable radio under my pillow, put on headphones, and waited to be transported into yesteryear.

A booming voice told me that I was at the right place. "Welcome, mystery fans. Welcome. It's time once again for The Sam Solomon Mystery Theater starring Peter Wentworth as Sam Solomon. And brought to you by Ipana Toothpaste."

The audio was a bit muffled and there was some occasional static, but I didn't mind. The broadcast actually sounded pretty good considering that it was seventy-five years old. I had to sit through a commercial before the announcer returned.

"Episode number 60 – The Fright to the Finish Caper," the announcer said.

The next words I heard were spellbinding.

SAM SOLOMON (NARRATOR):
Good evening, folks. Sam
Solomon here. Why don't you sit
back, relax...if you can...and join
me for the next thirty minutes.

I couldn't believe my ears. It was really Sam. Oh, I knew it was just an actor, but he sounded so real. And, you know, the voice was pretty close to what I had always imagined Sam might sound like. This was going to be outstanding.

SAM SOLOMON (NARRATOR):
It was Friday night, about ten
thirty. I had just finished up a
plate of Egg Foo Young and was
about to wash it down with a
nightcap when there was a knock
at my door.

SAM SOLOMON:
Go away. We're closed.

SAM SOLOMON (NARRATOR):
The knocking continued. The visitor was
relentless.

SAM SOLOMON:
Did you hear what I said? Take a hike.

SAM SOLOMON (NARRATOR):
Then a muffled voice from the hallway called out.

WOMAN:
Please, Mr. Solomon, I need your help.

SAM SOLOMON (NARRATOR):
It was a dame's voice. Now what
did she want at this hour of night
anyway? I got up, dragged myself
to the door and reluctantly opened
it. Before my eyes stood a
goddess—a red-haired goddess.
She was in a white dress, and her
tanned complexion made for a
striking contrast.

WOMAN
May I come in?

SAM SOLOMON (NARRATOR):
My first inclination was to tell her
to come back during business
hours but I was afraid she'd never
return, and I couldn't take that
chance. I escorted her to a chair
opposite my desk.

SAM SOLOMON:
So, what can I do for you?

WOMAN:
I need your help. My boyfriend's in trouble.

SAM SOLOMON (NARRATOR):
Now why did dames like this
always have to have boyfriends? I
couldn't get a break. She
proceeded to tell me about her
boyfriend, Butch—Butch
Kaminski—an up-and-coming
prizefighter. The name sounded
familiar.

SAM SOLOMON:
Killer Kaminski?

WOMAN:
So you've heard of him?

SAM SOLOMON:
I follow the boxing circuit when I
get a chance. And, yes, I've heard
of him. Supposed to have a
promising career.

WOMAN:
Well, not anymore.

SAM SOLOMON:
I don't understand.

SAM SOLOMON (NARRATOR):
She began to tear up. I had struck
a cord and I wasn't sure why.

WOMAN:
Last Friday night, Butch fought an
east coast boxer named Peter "The
Prince of" Paine. Butch was an
easy two-to-one favorite. He
should have had no problem
defeating his opponent. But
shortly after he answered the bell
in the eighth round, he got light-
headed and dizzy in the ring. He
couldn't defend himself. An
uppercut from Paine sent him to
the canvas...and the hospital. He's
still in a coma.

SAM SOLOMON:
I'm sorry, but how can I help you?
I don't understand.

WOMAN:
He was drugged. I know it.
Somebody wanted him to lose that
fight, and they made sure he did. I
want you to find out who did
this...and I want them to pay.

SAM SOLOMON (NARRATOR):
The attractive redhead opened her
purse, pulled out two crisp one-
hundred dollar bills, and slid them
across the desk.

WOMAN:
How soon can you start?

     This was incredible stuff. I couldn't believe that I had never heard of *The Sam Solomon Mystery Theater* before. For the next thirty minutes, I was transported back to 1938 Chicago. I had a ringside seat for a heavyweight bout between the world's greatest literary detective and every hood, conman, and mobster in the Windy City. I could feel my heart beating from beneath the covers. My hands were clammy. It was as if I was standing right next to Sam. I almost felt as though I could reach out and touch him. He seemed that real. To think that I would be able to experience this rush every Monday night for the next few weeks was dizzying.

     The program itself was mesmerizing. Sam reluctantly agreed to take on the case. He knew in his heart that there were hidden dangers. He knew that every time a beautiful woman, especially a redhead, walked into his office, his life would soon be in peril. The mystery woman identified herself as Roxanne Wainwright. She and Butch were just about to announce their engagement when he was hospitalized. Their impending nuptials would have to wait. In order to solve this case, Sam had to immerse himself in the seedy underbelly of professional boxing. His investigation ultimately led him to the fight promoter, Anton Sawyer, an ex-con who had been banished from the sport ten years earlier but who had assumed a new identity to infiltrate the ranks.

     Sam discovered that Sawyer had rigged dozens of fights in the months leading up to Butch's match. When the promoter decided to bet against Butch, he had to guarantee his stable of bettors a victory for The Prince of Paine. In order to do so, he spiked Butch's water bottle, the one that his manager would squirt into his mouth between rounds. And although the boxer would just swish around the water and spit it out, there was still enough of a chemical present to have an effect. When Butch returned to the ring, he experienced dizziness and lightheadedness, and was easy prey for his opponent.

Once Sam had collected enough evidence against Sawyer, he presented his findings to both the boxing commission and the police. The crooked promoter was soon KO'd by authorities—permanently. And I'm happy to report that within a few days, Butch emerged from his coma. His boxing days were over but he began a new chapter with Roxanne. The program ended with the happy couple exchanging vows in a wedding chapel with Sam in attendance. Then the announcer made reference to next week's show—something about baseball and blackmail.

I placed my hands behind my head, leaned back against the pillow, and savored the moment. It didn't get any better than this. I thought that my devotion to the world's greatest detective couldn't get any stronger, but the bond now was unbreakable. We were brothers for life. In order to get my Sam Solomon fix each day, I would usually read a chapter or two from one of his many novels— novels that I had read countless times before. But a radio show? This was incredible. And although it *was* radio, the images in my head were crystal clear. It was all good.

From the hallway, I heard a sound. I slid the headphones off and jammed them, along with the radio, under my pillow. No one could know I was still awake. Someone was definitely out there. I heard footsteps getting closer. I pulled the covers over my head. If it wasn't a family member, I didn't want to know who it was. I kept perfectly still and hoped that whoever it might be would assume I was fast asleep, and just go away. A second later, I heard someone flip on the light switch.

"I know you're awake," the voice said.

I sat up and decided to confront my accuser. I was unprepared for what stood before me. It was Gram in a robe. But not just any robe. It was the satiny kind of robe that prizefighters wear when they get into a ring. She had on black, hightop leather shoes, headgear, and boxing gloves. There was also a white towel hanging around her neck. She was in appropriate garb. It was almost as if she had also been listening to the Sam Solomon program.

"I could use a good cutman right about now," she said, pointing to a bandage over her right eye.

Relieved that she hadn't commented on why I was still awake, I was happy just to play along.

"Sure, Gram, what can I do?" I said as I threw off the covers and slipped out of bed.

"*Gram?*" she said. "Please refer to me as *Bonecrusher.*"

I smiled. "Sure, Bonecrusher, why don't you let me see if I can close up that cut for you?"

Gram plopped down on the bed and started laughing. "You're so much fun to play with, Charlie. Unlike your dad."

I shrugged. I didn't want to take sides. It had proven dangerous in the past.

"So, tell me," she said. "Why are you still awake anyway?"

"Awake? I...um...woke up when I heard you come in."

She grinned. "You can't fool a senior sleuth, you know. You were listening to the Sam Solomon radio show, weren't you? Eugene told me all about it."

"Don't tell Mom and Dad, okay?"

"As long as you don't tell them what I'm up to most of the time. Agreed?" She held out her hand, or rather, glove.

We shook on it. "It's a deal," I said.

She jumped up and began shadow boxing. "How'd you like the show?"

"Gram, it was sensational. I couldn't believe I was actually listening to Sam's voice. It was just as I had imagined it."

"Well, I'm glad to hear that," she said. "By the way, have you given any thought to those crimes the police are still investigating—the stolen Persian rugs and the burglary at the bakery? They haven't been solved yet, you know. You might be able to help."

I pulled out my desk chair and sat down. "To tell you the truth, I've been too busy."

"Why? Did you take on a new case or something?"

"No. We decided to close up the agency for a few weeks. We have play practice every day after school."

"Oh, that's right. You're a star now."

I shook my head. "It's nothing like that. But you ought to see Scarlett on stage. Now she's a star."

Gram continued punching the air. "Maybe when the play's over, if the police are still stumped, then you can help 'em out."

"Works for me," I said. But wait a minute. Did I actually mean that? Would it actually work for me? The play was going to tie us up for at least a month and a half. By that time, the police will have easily wrapped up this case. And I will have missed out on the chance of a lifetime. I hated the thought of it. But what could I do? I made a commitment and I had to see it through, no matter how painful. Right?

"Oh well, gotta go," Gram said. "I got a fifteen rounder with Lucy "Left Hook" Lacy."

"Good night, Gram…I mean Bonecrusher. Good luck."

She winked and waved goodbye with one glove. "Sweet dreams, Charlie."

And as I lowered my head onto the pillow and thought about Sam Solomon, I had some pretty sweet dreams that night.

Chapter 9

The His and Hearse Caper

Talk about rude awakenings. All I can remember is someone hovering over me...shaking me...yelling at me. I was in such a sound sleep that I wasn't sure what was going on. Was I still in my own bed? Was I a captive in a Sam Solomon mystery? What the heck was happening? Then through the haze, I was able to make out a face, and then a voice.

"Charlie! Wake up! You must have slept through your alarm. Your bus leaves in ten minutes. You'll never make it. Let me see if I can catch your dad. He'll have to drive you." My mom was standing over me with her hands on her hips. She didn't look pleased. "This isn't like you. Hurry up and get dressed." She scurried out of the room and pulled the door shut—loudly.

I sat up in bed and stared at my clock radio. What happened, I wondered? Was I in such a sound sleep that I never heard the alarm? I don't recall ever doing that before. And then it hit me. After listening to the Sam Solomon program, and following the conversation with my grandmother last night, I had forgotten to reset the alarm. It was still set to 11 pm. This one was on me. I had screwed it up. Although I'd rather have my parents think that it wasn't carelessness on my part but rather a young man who should be forgiven since he was tired and overworked. Somehow I didn't see that happening.

I jumped out of bed and threw on the same clothes I had worn yesterday. My mother would cringe when she saw that. I ran into the bathroom and washed and brushed. I grabbed my backpack and hustled downstairs. When I reached the last step, my executioner was waiting for me. My dad, his arms folded, was tapping his foot.

"So that *you* can be on time for school, young man, *I'm* going to be late. Does that seem fair?"

"Dad, this is like the first time this has ever happened. I'm sorry." Then, of course, there was the response I was thinking but dared not speak: "Lighten up, geez. Can't you just chill out for once?" Every so often I worried that I would say something out loud that I was thinking, but never intended to actually say. I had a dream once about that—where I was saying all these awful things to people, and I couldn't stop myself. I was so relieved when I woke up.

"Your mom's making you something for breakfast," he said. "I'll be waiting in the car. You can eat on the way." He turned and walked out the front door.

I stared at the floor as I entered the kitchen. I tried to look remorseful. It wasn't as if I didn't feel bad about my dad being late for work, it was just that he had made it seem like a capital crime. What was the big deal anyway?

"Here," my mom said, as she handed me a paper towel with two pieces of toast lightly buttered. She slid a banana into my coat pocket. "You'd better get out there. Your dad's late as it is."

I needed to make sure that my mom and I were still on friendly terms. I couldn't afford to lose both of them at the same time. It always paid off to have at least one ally during a dispute.

"I'm really sorry about this, Mom. It won't happen again."

"These things happen. Don't worry about it." She leaned over and kissed me on the forehead. "You'd better get out there now."

Okay, that was a good sign. I knew I could count on my mom's vote in a jam. Of course, no one made a better co-conspirator than my grandmother. She was always on my side.

I scooted down the hallway, through the living room and out the front door. My dad was sitting in the car with the engine running. I threw open the back passenger side door, tossed in my backpack, and hopped in the front seat. My dad didn't say a word for the better part of the trip. Then at one point he flipped on the radio. It was on a news station. The anchor was reading the top stories from the previous night.

"Police are investigating a break-in early this morning at Pet World on West Lake Street. According to witnesses, shortly after three a.m., an alarm sounded and a car was seen speeding away from the scene. When police arrived, they discovered a broken window in a backroom. The suspect is believed to have made off with two-to-three thousand dollars, along with several purebred dogs. This is the third major crime of this nature in the Oak Grove area in a little over two weeks. And each one has occurred, interestingly enough, on a Tuesday morning. And like the others, police found a business card on the floor of the pet shop with the familiar SS insignia."

My dad reached over and flipped off the radio. "What's going on here? It's not safe to live in this town anymore. Let me tell you—these things weren't happening around here when I was your age."

I knew my dad was ranting about something but I didn't hear a word of it. I kept thinking about the fact that each of these crimes, three of them in total, had been committed early on a Tuesday morning. There was something about the timing that got me to thinking. The crimes had been perpetrated just hours after a Sam Solomon radio drama had aired on Monday night. It was almost as if there was a connection—like the suspect waited to hear the program before striking. Was he somehow influenced by the subject matter of each drama? I only knew the storyline from last night's program—the crooked fight promoter. But what did that possibly have to do with a burglary at a pet shop? And then there was the mysterious business card with the SS crossed out on it that had been found at each crime scene. How did that factor into all of this? Was there any connection between the business cards and the radio dramas? And then it hit me. It was so obvious. I found myself thinking out loud which proved to be a huge mistake.

"SS—that's for Sam Solomon. Of course. They *are* connected. They must be."

"What are you talking about?" my dad said.

Oh, no. Did I just rat myself out? Did I just say something about the Sam Solomon program to my dad? What was I thinking? I was getting careless. He couldn't find out I was up late last night listening to it.

"No, I didn't mean it that way," I said. "What I meant to say was…well, um…what I meant was that…oh yeah…I was reading a Sam Solomon novel last night…and I just figured who the bad guy is…I made the *connection*…that was all."

"You're still reading that stuff? I would have that you'd have outgrown it by now."

Did I hear him correctly? Why that's blasphemy. No one, and I mean no one, bad-mouths Sam Solomon and gets away with it. Not even my dad. I didn't want to overreact or anything, but I placed my hands over my ears. I couldn't listen to any more of it.

My dad nudged me. "What's wrong with you anyway?"

"Dad, do you know who you're talking to? You're talking to a Sam Solomon fanatic. He is undoubtedly the greatest literary detective of the last century. Of course, I still read those books. And I can't imagine a time when I wouldn't be."

My dad shook his head. "Instead of re-reading those books all the time, why don't you try picking up something new? Maybe if you read something other than Sam Solomon, you might forget about this silly little agency of yours. I blame him for all of this."

I sighed. I had heard it all before. If Dad only realized that this lecture had never changed a thing in the past, and never would in the future. I was on a mission and he would just have to accept that. He continued on for the next ten minutes. That was followed by a period of uncomfortable silence. I sat with my lip buttoned up. It was no use trying to defend either Sam or my chosen profession. It was hopeless.

When we finally pulled up in front of school, I was relieved. Time to escape. I reached for my backpack and was just about to make a hasty exit when I felt a hand on my arm.

"Wait a minute," my dad said. "You make me so crazy sometimes." He let out a long sigh. "Listen, as hard as it is to say this, your mom and I are amazed at some of the things you've accomplished in the past couple of months. You've done some things that even the police weren't able to do. Reading about my own son in the newspaper, or seeing him on TV, or watching him accept an award for heroism from the mayor…these are some of the things that make a father proud."

This was nothing short of a breakthrough moment for me and my dad. I wasn't quite sure where it was headed. Was he finally ready to accept the fact that I had this gift, and that it would be criminal to ignore it?

"I'm just afraid that you're going to wake up ten years from now and wonder where your childhood went. I'm glad to hear that you got involved in this school play. Those are just the types of activities I'd like to see you doing. So that's why I want you to permanently close up this agency of yours. It may be hard at first, I know, but in the long run, when you discover other new and interesting hobbies, you'll thank me."

Just when I thought we were at one of those milestones in a person's life where all the stars align and there's a meeting of the minds, I realized that nothing had really changed. I would continue to sneak around and solve cases for classmates, and my dad would continue to give me grief.

"Aren't you glad we had this little talk?" he said. "Maybe this was all supposed to happen. I have a feeling that you were supposed to sleep through your alarm so we could have this moment."

I forced a smile as I stepped out of the car. "Thanks for the ride."

"I want you to consider what I said, Charlie. Well, actually there's nothing to consider. You don't really have an option. It's going to happen. I was just hoping I could convince you to buy into this willingly. See you tonight." And with that, he was off.

I stood at the entrance to the playground and shook my head. What started out as a discussion with real possibilities had turned into another downer. It reminded me of a situation that Sam Solomon had once found himself in—Episode #47—*The His and Hearse Caper*. This was the story of a mortician who, instead of cremating bodies, was part of a black market operation that was selling corpses to unscrupulous medical schools for their cadaver collections. Instead of presenting grieving families with urns containing the ashes of their dearly departed, they would receive the ashes of animal remains. This case, a particularly gruesome one, had shaken Sam, and had caused him to question his decision to enter the detective profession.

Filled with doubts, he decided to consult his mentor, Amos Poindexter. Amos ran the agency years before and left it to Sam upon his retirement. And every so often, Sam would visit his old boss when he needed some advice. The retired P.I. could see that his protégé was confused and battle-fatigued. He advised Sam to close up the agency for a while before he was no longer able to run it. Amos suggested that he settle down, meet a nice girl, and start a family. "Do it before it's too late," the old man told him. "Don't wait like I did." As you might guess, Sam failed to listen to this advice.

It seemed obvious to me that my dad was pulling an *Amos Poindexter*. He wanted me to walk away from my passion, while still in my prime, in order to find other interests. I could no more close up shop than Sam could. He respected the advice from his old boss but managed to work through his difficulties and eventually persevered. And, fortunately, there were several more adventures to follow. What about *me*? Well, even though it might have been ill-advised, when the play was over, I fully intended to continue on despite the mandate from my dad. I had operated the agency without my parents' blessings in the past, and I would continue to do so.

"Hey, Charlie," a voice called out. It was Henry. He was waiting for me on the playground. "You weren't on the bus so I thought you were sick or something."

"No, I overslept and my dad had to drive me," I said. "Hey, did you hear about the burglary at that pet shop this morning?"

"Yeah, my mom said something about it at breakfast. Why?"

I looked around to make sure we were alone. I was about to propose a hypothesis, and if it proved to be wrong, I didn't want to be second-guessed by nosey classmates.

"Get this. I stayed up late last night to listen to The Sam Solomon Mystery Theater."

Henry looked surprised. "Sam's on the radio? Since when?"

"This just happens to be the 75th anniversary of the original old-time radio series featuring the world's greatest detective."

Henry wasn't impressed. He was tired of hearing about Sam Solomon. I was guilty of dropping Sam references into conversations on a daily basis—make that, on an hourly basis.

"What about it?" he asked.

"Would you believe that last night's show may have inspired the burglar who hit that pet store last night?"

"What makes you say that?"

"Isn't it obvious?" I said. "Whoever pulled off the heist was probably listening to the show, and by leaving the SS business card behind, he's trying to make some kind of statement about Sam. Aren't you the least bit curious about all of this?"

The bell rang. We scooted inside and headed to our lockers.

"Frankly, no." Henry worked the combination on his locker. "What difference does all of this make? It's not as if you can do anything about it. It's a job for the police."

"What if the Charlie Collier, Snoop for Hire Agency just happened to investigate the matter?"

"Here we go again—another case without a paying client. How long do you think we can operate like this? Charlie, we're not public servants. We're paid professionals. And we ought to get paid accordingly." He sneered. "And have you forgotten, the agency is temporarily closed. We've got play practice. We don't have time for any of this."

For a minute there, I actually had forgotten. I hated the thought of passing up on what promised to be a monster case. When Gram suggested that we might be able to assist the authorities, I was somewhat interested, but I wasn't quite ready to drop everything and jump in. But since Sam Solomon had entered the mix, everything had changed. A few days ago, I even had myself convinced that I'd be able to survive a few weeks away from the agency, but now I was second-guessing my decision to participate in the play. If it turned out that there was a clear connection between last night's radio drama and this morning's burglary, then I might have to politely decline the invitation from Mr. Miles to participate in his production. I hated to do that to him, but playing a private detective on stage paled in comparison to actually participating in a real caper.

"I'll see you at lunch," Henry said as he grabbed books from the top shelf of his locker.

"It's so frustrating," I said. "Something big may be happening and I can't do anything about it."

Henry dropped his books onto the floor and grabbed me by the shoulders. "You don't have to do anything about it. Let the police handle it. I'm sure they'll be able to figure everything out without our help. Just be patient."

"But they don't know what I know," I said. "They don't know the connection between Sam Solomon and this latest crime spree."

"Charlie, you know what your problem is?" Henry said. "You're going through withdrawal. Now that the agency's closed up for a few weeks, you don't have any problems to solve, so you're grabbing at some meaningless story in the news. Let it go. Concentrate on learning your lines for the play. You're soon gonna find out that's a bigger job than you think."

How could I make Henry see that this wasn't some *meaningless* story in the news? This was really important. I needed to talk to Eugene in the worst way. He'd know what to do.

"You know what you need?" Henry said. "A good brain teaser. It'll get your juices flowing and you'll forget all about this pet store burglary."

"I don't think so."

"Trust me." He smiled. "In the year 1901, a man was forty years old. In the year 1906, he was thirty-five years old. How is this possible?"

As we walked to our first class, I was trying to figure out a way to contact Eugene, not trying to solve Henry's dumb brain teaser. It looked like I was on my own now. It wasn't as if I hadn't worked solo before. I had done so plenty of times. I could do this. Heck, I would do this. Since we had different first period classes, we were just about to split up when Henry poked me in the arm.

"So, what's the answer."

I just glared. I had no time for petty word games.

"Give up?"

I sighed and shook my head. "If a man is forty years old in 1901, and thirty-five years old in 1906, the explanation is simple. The years are B.C.E., not C.E. Are you happy now?"

Chapter 10

The Wurst Case Scenario Caper

For the rest of the school day, I obsessed over the Sam Solomon connection. I don't think I took a single page of notes in any of my classes. That wasn't like me, but how could I concentrate when *I* held a key piece of information for an ongoing crime investigation and was unable to share my theory? Somehow I had to get out of play practice so that I could head over to Eugene's. He was the only person I knew who had listened to all three Sam Solomon episodes. If there was any connection between the first two programs and the crimes committed the day after each had aired, then we were on our way to solving this mystery.

During lunch and recess, Henry and I didn't speak. He was either upset that I had solved his brain teaser with so little effort, or he wasn't ready to take on another case without a client, and hence, without payment. When we walked into Mrs. Jansen's science class, the last period of the day, I knew that I was getting closer to taking some action, but which action, I couldn't say. Should I tell Mr. Miles that I wasn't feeling well? Should I make up some excuse about having to get home early? I just wasn't sure what to do. As much as I wanted to prove myself as a leading man, especially to Scarlett, I felt as though I was being pulled into a caper not of my choosing.

"Okay, gang, settle down," Mrs. Jansen said. "We're going to start out today with a chemistry brain buster."

I noticed a few of the kids glancing in my direction. So what else was new? But I wasn't sure that I was in the proper frame of mind to solve a brain teaser just then. I had other things to occupy my time. I couldn't be bothered with middle school riddles.

"Here we go. Put your thinking caps on now," she said. "Two men walk into a diner. The first one says 'I'll take a glass of H_2O, please.' The second man says 'I'll have a glass of H_2O too.' A short time later, the waitress returns with their orders. Each man downs his drink. Within minutes, one of the men is dead. What happened?"

Although I had no real interest in participating, Mrs. Jansen, as she always managed to do, was starting to reel me in. I fought the urge to solve this one. I had bigger fish to fry. But I began to imagine the scenario that she had described.

"Okay," she said. "Who can tell me what happened?"

Sherman raised his hand.

"Sherman, what do you think?"

"I'll bet that one of the men drank it too fast and choked to death," he said.

Mrs. Jansen smiled. "Good guess, but no. Who else wants to try?"

Henry, who sat directly behind me, poked me in the back. "Watch this," he said as he raised his hand.

"Henry, what exactly happened in that diner?" Mrs. Jansen said.

Henry stood. "I'm guessing that the men were spies, and the waitress was actually a double-agent. And so she put poison in one of their drinks."

"Very creative, Henry," she said. "I like the way you think. You're on the right track, sort of. But there's something else. What if I told you that the waitress gave each man exactly what he had ordered, and nothing more?"

The class quieted down. No hands were raised. I sensed that Mrs. Jansen was looking in my direction. I was determined to stay out of the competition, but I could feel the wheels starting to turn in my brain. I tried to recall the exact words she had used. "The first man said 'I'll take a glass of H_2O, please.' The second man said 'I'll have a glass of H_2O too.'" I, better than anyone, knew that most brain teasers weren't math or science problems at all, they were trick questions. You had to examine each word carefully and imagine it standing by itself. You had to consider all angles. And most of all, you had to ignore the obvious. That would always confuse you.

"Did I stump everyone?" she said.

Scarlett looked in my direction. She seemed surprised, and maybe a little disappointed that I hadn't cracked this one. The last thing I wanted to do was to disappoint her. I clenched my teeth and closed my eyes. I started to press. Now I really wanted to nail it. A few minutes earlier, I had been completely disinterested. But once I saw that look on Scarlett's face, I knew that the only way to get her to notice me was to show her that I was head and shoulders, and unfortunately one belt notch, ahead of the others.

"Charlie?" Mrs. Jansen said. "This is usually the time we call on you to enlighten us. What do you think? Don't tell me we've stumped you too."

I stood up and cleared my throat. I was trying to buy myself more time. I knew that every eye in the room was fixed on me at that very moment. By the looks on some of their faces, I could tell that a few of them were pulling for me. Then there were those who would have been perfectly happy to see me fall flat on my face. Scarlett glanced at me, and then looked away. I couldn't let her down. I just couldn't. I repeated the key words of the brain teaser under my breath. I could feel my lips moving. And then just as I was about to admit defeat and slink back into my seat, I figured it out.

"Well, here's how I see it, Mrs. Jansen. By the way, do you mind if I use the blackboard?"

"By all means," she said.

I confidently walked to the front of the room, grabbed a piece of chalk, and faced my classmates.

"The first man ordered a glass of H_2O," I said. I wrote down H_2O on the board. "We all know that H_2O is the chemical formula for water. So, the waitress obviously brought him a harmless glass of water. But the second man didn't make himself clear enough when he ordered. He accidentally asked for a lethal potion. He thought he was ordering water, but the waitress must have thought he said something else. Instead of hearing H_2O too," which I wrote on the board, "she heard H_2O_2." I wrote H_2O_2 on the blackboard and underlined the second number two. "H_2O_2 is the chemical formula for hydrogen peroxide, which can be fatal if ingested—and unfortunately in this case, it was."

Mrs. Jansen smiled and then began applauding. In all the times that I had correctly solved brain busters in her class, I didn't ever recall that type of reaction. A few of my classmates joined in. Scarlett was one of them. I thought I detected the hint of a smile on her face. That was good—very good.

"Charlie," she said, "not only did you successfully solve this chemistry brain teaser, but you explained it to the class in a clear, concise, easy-to-understand manner. Maybe we should trade places."

I could sense the stares again. Were my fellow classmates impressed or jealous? I didn't want to know. I just smiled and returned to my seat.

Henry tapped me on the shoulder. "Now you're makin' us look bad, partner," he whispered.

I maintained a low profile for the remainder of class. When your best friend accuses you of showing him up, then what must the others be thinking? I tried to concentrate on Mrs. Jansen's lecture but my thoughts kept drifting back to the Sam Solomon program the night before and the pet shop burglary. It was up to me to do something about it. If I were somehow able to help the authorities nab the perpetrator of this crime, then I had to do everything in my power to make it happen. And if that meant missing play practice, then so be it. This was far more important. There...I had finally made a decision. I would ask Mr. Miles if I could skip practice today in order to rendezvous with Eugene to discuss the latest crime spree and the possible Sam Solomon connection. He would understand. At least, I hoped he would.

*   *   *   *   *

I poked my head into the auditorium. A few of the kids were milling around the stage. Practice was set to begin in a few minutes. I walked down the hallway in the direction of Mr. Miles' office. I wasn't quite sure what to tell him when I got there. I wanted to tell him the truth but I wasn't sure if he would think it was a good-enough reason to miss practice.

I considered illness, injury, and family emergency, and I thought that with a little imagination, I could build a pretty good case for each. But I never liked to lie about things like that. I always figured that if I pretended to be under the weather or injured when I wasn't, then there were powers out there that would make those things happen. It was the same with a family emergency—lie about it, and it was sure to occur. I didn't want to tempt fate.

By the time I reached Mr. Miles's office door, I had decided to come clean. After all, he recruited me for this production because of my real-life experiences. He knew that I was a working P.I., and that conflicts of this nature were bound to happen. The more I thought about it, the more I was convinced that he would understand completely and would wish me well on my new venture. Before knocking, I rehearsed my little speech. I wanted to be able to fully explain my rationale for missing practice. I would have liked a little more time to prepare my defense but I knew that Mr. Miles' office door would be opening any time now, and I had to catch him before he left for practice. I knocked lightly.

"Yes? Come in," a voice inside called out.

I opened the door slowly and found Mr. Miles standing on his desk chair looking for something on one of the upper shelves of his bookcase.

"Oh, hi, Charlie, come on in," he said. "I'm just looking for a textbook." He fumbled for a few more seconds. "Ah, here it is."

And at the same moment, the chair he was standing on began to slide. I scooted over to steady it before the aging director came crashing to the ground.

"Oh my," he said. He held tightly onto each shelf as he negotiated his way down. "Boy, am I glad you stopped in. No telling what may have happened." He plopped into his chair and sighed. "So what brings you here today?" he asked.

"Well, it's about play practice, sir."

"What about play practice?"

I wanted to build my case and to explain my reasons in detail, but I decided to just blurt it out.

"Mr. Miles, something's come up and I'm going to have to miss practice."

The aging teacher ran his fingers through his silver hair. "It must be pretty important," he said. "Why else would your leading man abandon his fellow actors?"

I didn't like where this was going. I already was starting to feel guilty.

"You see, sir, there's this new case that I'm involved in. And the only time I can confer with my associate is after school. But it won't happen a lot, I promise."

Mr. Miles stood up, walked around and stood behind his high-backed desk chair. He leaned forward with narrowing eyes.

"Charlie, let me tell you something about the theater. In this profession, you are either all in or all out. There's nothing in between. You can't be a casual participant. It's not fair to your director, to your cast, and most of all, to your audience. They expect a total commitment at all times." He walked around and sat on the front of his desk. "Now if you were sick or there was some kind of family emergency, then we'd have to deal with it. But a conflict of this nature is unacceptable. You're going to have to decide, right now, where your loyalties lie. Is it to this production or to your little business?"

The last thing I had expected was an ultimatum. And to be perfectly honest, I didn't like the way he referred to the Charlie Collier, Snoop for Hire Agency as a *little* business. That *little* business was the reason he had recruited me. It was also responsible for the recent convictions of Rupert Olsen and Colonel Harvard Culpepper. How could he minimize the importance of my life's passion? I knew that he was devoted to the theater, and I *had* agreed to this role, but what was the big deal with missing one practice? Would he really can me for this one absence?

"So, what's it going to be, Charlie? If you choose your business, then I will be forced to recast the role of Nick Dakota. Is that what you want?"

I wasn't sure what I wanted. When I thought about giving up the chance to work alongside Scarlett for the next few weeks, it made me sick to my stomach. But when I considered walking away from the agency at such a critical time, I knew that I might be turning my back on my community, not to mention the victims of this latest crime spree. If my theory was correct, and if it might lead to solving this case, then the decision seemed easy. And then there were my parents to think about. I could just imagine how disappointed they'd be if I decided to give up my role, especially my mom.

As always, whenever I came upon a fork in the road, my thoughts turned to Sam Solomon, and in particular, Episode #52—*The Wurst Case Scenario Caper*. In this story, Sam had been hired by the U.S. government to investigate a company that imported sausage products from Germany. These were the days leading up to World War II when Adolf Hitler was commanding more and more attention on the world stage. Government officials were certain that the Nazi Party was somehow passing sensitive information to German nationals living in the U.S. through the sausage company, but were unsure how it was being carried out. Sam soon discovered that coded messages from the Führer had been imbedded onto, believe it or not, the sausage casings.

It was during this investigation that Sam met Anna Mueller, a German double-agent working for the CIA. She was instrumental in helping crack the case. As one might guess, the two spent a significant amount of time together and before long, they fell in love. Anna, who traveled around the world for the government, wanted Sam to give up his life as a Chicago private eye and join her on each assignment. Sam countered with the idea of a long-distance relationship. And like Mr. Miles just a few moments ago, Anna issued an ultimatum—he was either to leave the agency to accompany her, or end the relationship. As much as Sam wanted to make a life with her, he knew that he'd never be happy living out of a suitcase, and not being able to continue his career as a private investigator. Once again, Sam had traded in love and marriage for the agency. I knew what I had to do.

"Charlie," Mr. Miles said, "we need to get to practice. Are you coming or not?"

I swallowed hard. "As much as I'd like to show you what I can do on stage, sir, I'm afraid that I have to choose the agency over the limelight."

Mr. Miles folded his arms and frowned. "I'm disappointed, but I respect your decision. I know that you feel you must answer to some higher calling, but I hope you don't live to regret it. There's nothing on earth quite like performing in front of a live audience. It's simply magical."

"I realize what I'm giving up," I said. "It's just that I feel like I can accomplish more in my other line of work."

Mr. Miles seemed to think to himself for a minute. "I'll tell you what, Charlie. I'll make you a deal." He smiled. "If you try to attend as many practices as you possibly can, I'll allow you to be the understudy for the role of Nick Dakota. How's that sound?"

"What exactly does an understudy do?"

"Oh, it's very important," Mr. Miles said. "In the event that our new leading man is unable to perform his duties, for whatever reason, the understudy would jump back in and assume that role. So, you still need to learn everything you can about the character of Nick Dakota. Is it a deal?"

I shook hands with Mr. Miles. "Thanks for understanding," I said.

"Maybe this'll actually work out best for both of us—you'll get a chance to continue your agency work, and I'll have a quality backup for one of the main parts." Mr. Miles glanced at his watch. "Oh dear, I'm late for practice. Gotta go. Hopefully I'll see you tomorrow."

This wasn't what I had hoped for when I entered Mr. Miles' office moments ago, but it was probably all for the best. I now had the ability to pursue my dream of running the agency, and was still able to participate in the production as a member of the cast, well, sort of. I didn't like the thought of someone else with a chance to woo the fair Rebecca…er, Scarlett. But I had made a decision and I was prepared to live with it. I could see now why Sam Solomon had remained a bachelor all of his life. It wasn't just a matter of following your dream, but rather having to decide what you were willing to give up to realize it.

Chapter 11

The Hair, There, and Everywhere Caper

During the bus ride home, all I could think about was heading over to Eugene's office and sharing my theory about last night's Sam Solomon radio mystery and the pet shop break-in. If anyone would appreciate a scenario whereby a present-day perpetrator plans out his next crime based on a seventy-five-year-old radio program, it was Eugene. He loved that sort of drama. It didn't even bother me that I was sitting alone on the bus. Normally, Henry was by my side. But he was back at school at play practice. He didn't even know that I had made a decision to reopen the agency and give up my leading man role to another actor. He wouldn't be happy when he found out. I knew that his motive for accepting the role of the police investigator was to make Scarlett's life miserable. But it was doubtful that he would have ever auditioned for the part if I hadn't joined the cast first. He'd no doubt accuse me of high treason. I would just have to deal with it at another time.

When I got home, the place was empty. Both my mom and grandmother were out. Where? I hadn't a clue. It killed me that I was about to leave for Eugene's. This would have been the perfect opportunity to open up the agency for a little while. I ran upstairs to my room, threw my backpack on the bed, changed clothes, and was back downstairs in minutes. I went into the garage, hopped on my bike, and was off.

As I pedaled furiously, I thought about play practice. I wondered who would end up with my role. It bothered me to think that someone else would have a chance to give Scarlett a hug in the final scene, but what else could I do? I had thought at one time that I'd be fine with taking a brief hiatus from the agency, but I now knew that was impossible. I could never walk away from this—not even for a few weeks. And if it affected my love life, well, that was simply one of the hazards of the job.

I could see the barbershop in the distance. I knew that I was in the homestretch. I thought about saying *hi* to Mr. Dolan, the barber and Eugene's landlord, who also just happened to be Scarlett's grandfather, but I wasn't sure how long I'd be at Eugene's and I didn't want to get home late for dinner. The last thing I needed right now was to get grounded by my parents. I had a feeling that I was on the verge of something big and couldn't jeopardize it. I pulled up in front of the building, hopped off my bike, and walked to the rear entrance. I ran up the back stairs to the second floor and down the hallway to Eugene's office. I proceeded to knock twice, scrape my fingernails on the face of the door, and then knocked three more times.

"Come in," a voice called out.

I put my shoulder into the door and pushed it open. I found Eugene sitting behind his desk.

"Charlie, my man, what's brings you here today?"

I hustled up to Eugene's desk and sat down opposite him. "It's big, very big."

Eugene leaned forward in his chair and folded his hands on the desk.

"Well, let's have it then," he said. "You working on a new case or something?"

"Not exactly," I said. "It has to do with the Sam Solomon program that was on last night."

Eugene smiled. "Did you stay up and listen to it?"

I nodded.

"So, what'd you think?" Eugene asked. "Didn't Peter Wentworth do a great job as Sam? What a set of pipes. I always loved that guy. Had a short career unfortunately. I don't remember why. Those things happen in show business, I guess."

I stood up and leaned over the desk. "Eugene, have you noticed that each of the crimes that have been committed here in Oak Grove in the past three weeks all happened early on a Tuesday morning?"

"I think I heard a reporter make a reference to that. What about it?"

"Is it just a coincidence that each one occurred just hours after the Sam Solomon program aired?" I asked.

Eugene stared forward. He was deep in thought. "I guess I never realized that," he said. "So, what about it?"

"Did you also notice that in each of the crimes, the suspect left behind a business card with the letters *SS* crossed out?"

Eugene seemed more interested now. "I did read that...yes."

I strolled over to the window and looked out momentarily. And then for dramatic effect, I spun around.

"Eugene, I have a theory. I believe that the SS stands for Sam Solomon. The fact that it's crossed out may suggest that the perp has a beef with Sam. I haven't figured that part out yet. I also think that our suspect listens to each of the Sam Solomon radio shows, plots out his crime, and then acts on it."

"That's quite a theory, Charlie. Where's your proof?"

I smiled. "Still working on it."

"Let's say you're right," Eugene said. "Let's say that the SS on the card does stand for Sam Solomon. And let's say that the suspect listens to each episode and then plans out his crime. Let's say you're right about all of it...but what information do we have that'll help us identify this individual? It's an interesting theory but it doesn't get us any closer to solving these crimes."

I walked back and sat down opposite Eugene's desk. "I don't know why," I said, "but I have this feeling that he's playing a game with us. I think that each crime has something to do with the Sam Solomon programs. But it's not obvious. It's not direct. It's kind of like a brain teaser. He's making us work to figure it out."

Eugene sat back in his chair and folded his arms. "All right, counselor, make your case."

"Do you remember the plot in the first Sam Solomon show two weeks ago."

Eugene placed his finger to his lips and concentrated. "Let's see." His lips were moving but he wasn't speaking at first. "Oh, yes...yes...it was The Hair, There and Everywhere Caper. It was about a male nurse in a local hospital who used to sedate his patients, and then while they slept, he would shave their heads, and sell their hair to a local wig and toupee shop. Sam had been hired by one of the patients who woke up bald."

"Okay," I said. "And the first crime two weeks ago was the burglary of a Persian rug store. If my theory is correct, then there has to be a connection between the two. There's gotta be a common thread that links the plot to the crime."

I thought to myself for a moment. I then began reciting words that might be associated with each event.

"Let's see…nurse…hospital…shave…wig…toupee. And then there's …Persian …carpeting… store…rug…"

"Rug! That's it," Eugene said. "A slang term for a toupee is a rug. It's a stretch but it just might be the connection you're looking for."

"That's gotta be it," I said. "Okay now, what was the plot for the second program?"

Eugene smiled. "That one I remember. It was The Budding Florist Caper. It was the story of a florist whose business was failing. And he was just about to file for bankruptcy when he discovered a flower with a scent that was an aphrodisiac."

"What's that?"

"An aphrodisiac is something that can make someone fall in love with someone else. Think of it as a love potion," he said. "So this florist began delivering bouquets of this particular flower to wealthy widows. One whiff later, and they were in love with him. And more than willing to part with their fortunes. Sam was brought in by the family members of one of the widows."

I jumped up and began pacing. It was time to put our thinking caps back on.

"And the second crime was a theft at a bakery. What connects a florist to a bakery?" I walked back to the window and looked out for inspiration. It took less than a minute to figure this one out. "Eugene, I got it. What does a florist sell?"

He shrugged. "Flowers?"

"And what does a baker use to make breads and pastries and everything else?"

"Dough?"

"Before it's dough," I said.

Eugene thought for a second. He grinned. "Flour," he said triumphantly.

"Flour, exactly," I said. "Okay, now, the third show—a crooked fight promoter. And the third crime—a burglary at a pet shop."

"I have a feeling this one's gonna be tougher," Eugene said.

I closed my eyes and tried to picture a ring with fighters and trainers and managers and referees and rowdy fans. Then I envisioned a pet shop with animals and food and supplies. Nothing was coming at first. But then the light bulb moment occurred.

"Eugene, do you have a copy of today's newspaper?"

"Sure, right here," he said, as he picked it up off his desk and handed it to me.

I flipped through the pages looking for one particular article. When I found it, I skimmed it quickly. It had to be here. It just had to. If not, my entire theory was for naught. Seconds later, I let out a sigh. I had found it. I set the paper down on his desk, and pointed to a paragraph. It was part of the story from the pet shop burglary.

"Read that," I said.

Eugene opened his desk drawer, fumbled for a moment, pulled out a pair of reading glasses, and slid them on. He read verbatim from the article.

"When the owners of Pet World inventoried their animals, they discovered that four dogs were missing—a cocker spaniel, a beagle, a basset hound, and a boxer." Eugene looked up. "A *boxer*."

"Eugene, we did it. We figured this thing out. All we have to do is go to the police and lay it out for them."

Eugene scowled. "Not so fast, Charlie. It's an interesting theory but it all could be purely coincidental. We need more before we take it to the authorities."

I was all ready to bring in the heavy artillery. It seemed to me that we had all the evidence necessary to convince the police that the Sam Solomon dramas and the recent crimes were connected. And as difficult as it was to wait, I knew that Eugene was probably right. Unless we were absolutely sure, and could prove it, we couldn't expect the police to believe, what on the surface appeared to be, a pretty wild story.

"So you think we should wait at least one more week and see if our theory still holds up?" I asked.

Eugene nodded.

"Boy, if there was only a way to get the details of the next program before it aired, then we'd have the time to figure out the perp's next move, and be there to catch him red-handed."

Eugene got to his feet, began pacing for a few seconds, and stopped. "You know, Charlie, there might just be a way. Hand me that phone book over there."

I made a beeline for the far wall, grabbed a phone book from the top shelf of a tall bookcase, and ran it over to Eugene. On the same shelf, I had noticed other reference books—an almanac, a dictionary, a thesaurus, an atlas, a book of quotations, and a set of World Book Encyclopedias. Eugene was still all about hard copies. He hadn't yet made the transition to computer. And considering his advanced age, it was unlikely he ever would.

Eugene began paging through the phone book. "Here it is," he said.

"What?"

"It's the phone number for WOAK. That's the radio station running the Sam Solomon series. I have a friend over there—Ned Stewart. He owns the station actually. Maybe he can tell us what the next episode's about." He dialed from his land-line phone—no cell phone for Eugene—and waited. Then, a moment later. "Yes, I'm trying to reach Ned Stewart. Tell him Eugene Patterson's on the phone." He paused momentarily. "Sure, I'll hold."

"What's happening?" I asked.

"They're trying to track him down." Eugene waited a few more seconds. "Ned, old buddy. Eugene Patterson. How are you? Listen, I got a favor to ask. You're running an old-time radio program on Monday nights called *The Sam Solomon Mystery Theater,* and I was just wondering if you could tell me what next week's episode is about." He paused. "Oh, I see. No, don't worry about it. You take care of yourself now. And say hi to Rose for me."

He hung up the phone and frowned. "No dice. The program is fed by satellite at the time it airs. So they don't have a physical copy for anyone to look at or listen to." He sighed. "Looks like all we can do is try to figure this thing out based on the previews that ran at the end of last night's program. Do you remember what next week's show is about?"

I hadn't really concentrated much on that. At the time there wasn't a reason to. I thought hard for the next few seconds. It didn't take long.

"The announcer said something about baseball and blackmail."

"That was it?" Eugene said.

I nodded.

"Well, that's not enough to go on. Looks like we'll have to wait until it runs and then figure things out." He made a face. "But how are we gonna do that? It ends at 11:30...on a school night."

He was right. There was no way I could get over here that late at night. And even if my grandmother was willing to shuttle me back and forth, my parents would never allow me to be up that late during the week. There had to be another way. If we had cell phones, we could text—that was out. If Eugene had a computer, we could use e-mail or instant message. It looked like the only way to pull this off was the telephone. Assuming my parents were asleep, I might be able to sneak down to the basement and use the extension.

"I'll tell you what," I said. "I'll call you right after the program ends and we can discuss it then."

"That's probably our best bet," Eugene said. "That's almost a week away though. By then...who knows? Maybe we won't even be needed. Maybe the police will nab this bird in the meantime."

"And if not?" I said.

He smiled. "Since he usually strikes early morning, we'll have to work fast. I'd suggest you take notes during the show. We need to come up with a quick analysis, or we'll have wasted another week."

I walked to the door. "I'm sure we can figure this out, Eugene. All we have to do is listen really closely and try to identify a word—a key word from the drama—one that has a double-meaning—and we should be able to identify his next target."

I turned to leave. The plan was set.

Chapter 12

The Wading Game Caper

On the way to school the next morning, I was dreading the moment when the bus pulled up at Henry's stop. I knew he'd be upset about the fact that I had given up my part in the play, and had left him hanging. I should have at least tried to communicate that to him before I left school yesterday. He still wouldn't have been happy but I was fairly certain that he might handle it better. As the bus slowed down, I glanced out the window and saw him sitting on his backpack. I was preparing myself for an ugly exchange.

He climbed up the front steps of the bus, and as if he hadn't even seen me, he shot right past and plopped down in a seat in the back. I guess I had it coming. I could just let him stew for a while. That would usually work. But I was dying to tell him about my meeting yesterday with Eugene and to bring him up to speed on what was about to become our next caper. He wouldn't be happy since there were no clients to charge, but he just might buy into it because it had the potential of being a really fascinating case, and one that would require a fair amount of deductive reasoning skills.

I decided it was best to face the music. I waited for the bus to stop, and then I made my way back to where he was sitting. I noticed an open seat next to him and was just about to grab it when he picked up his backpack from the floor and set it down on the seat. Apparently he was going to make me earn this. I decided at that moment to take things into my own hands, literally, and attempted to remove his backpack. I suppose I should have expected his reaction. He would have none of it. For the next thirty seconds, without a word being spoken, we engaged in a heated tug of war. It got the attention of some of the other kids who turned in their seats to witness the altercation. And it unfortunately also got the attention of our substitute bus driver, Mrs. Marjorie Montrose, who we were certain had been a prison warden in an earlier life. Why did Milton, our regular driver, have to be out sick that day?

"What's going on back there?" she yelled out.

"Charlie and Henry are fighting," one of the girls said.

"This bus isn't moving until you two stop," Mrs. Montrose announced. "And if you make me come back there—"

That was all we had to hear. The war was over as quickly as it had started. Mrs. Montrose, better known as Shamu, had once before taken it upon herself to break up fisticuffs on the bus. It wasn't pretty. She got a little carried away and managed to get herself suspended, as had the combatants. We weren't interested in a repeat performance. Once the commotion had died down, I took advantage of the temporary truce to slip into the seat next to Henry, much to his chagrin. As the bus resumed its journey, and the other passengers were convinced the show was over, Henry broke his silence.

"You're a rat. You quit the play and you didn't even tell me? What's up with that?"

Well, at least we were speaking. It was better than nothing.

"I just couldn't turn my back on the agency. I had to."

"So you left me there with the nerd herd?" Henry said. "Nice guy."

I was feeling worse about my actions, if that were even possible.

"I'm sorry," I said. "I know I should have told you. You can hate me if you want to. I have it coming."

"I'm just wondering if I should stick it out now," he said. "It's not going to be the same without you."

I was so glad to hear him say that. It was the first step in resolving this conflict.

"Well, I'm still gonna be there," I said, "some of the time at least. Mr. Miles said that I can be an understudy for Nick Dakota."

"What's that?" Henry asked.

"I'm like a backup. I have to learn all the lines as if I had the lead role. And if something happens to the guy playing Nick Dakota, then I get to jump back in," I said. "By the way, who got my old part anyway?"

Henry smiled. He was going to enjoy this apparently. "You're not gonna like it. Would you believe that you've been replaced by…the slacker?"

I couldn't believe it. Patrick Walsh was like the laziest kid in the sixth grade—when he bothered to show up, that is. He was absent every other day, it seemed.

"The old man got desperate," Henry said. "There weren't many choices"

There was nothing I could do about it now. I had my chance and I gave it up. I had chosen career over true love. No one to blame but myself. It was time to change the subject. Too painful to talk about missed opportunities.

"Hey, you won't believe what's going on with this current crime spree," I said. "I went over to Eugene's yesterday. I wanted to bounce a theory off of him."

"Is this still about how the Sam Solomon radio show is somehow connected to the recent string of burglaries?"

"Exactly."

Henry rolled his eyes. I kind of expected that response. For the remainder of the trip, I explained to him, in a methodical fashion, everything that Eugene and I had discussed. I outlined the details of each Sam Solomon episode, and the particulars of each crime that followed. I explained my theory that the same suspect had committed each of the crimes, based on the SS cards left at the scenes, and that he was playing some sort of word association game with us. As the bus pulled up in front of the school playground, I was certain that Henry was on board with this newest caper. He definitely wanted in.

"That's it," he said. "I'm quitting the play. It's obvious you're gonna need my help. I'm not quite sure how to break the news to Mr. Miles, but the agency comes first. He'll just have to understand."

We hopped down from the bus and into the playground.

"You know, Henry, maybe you shouldn't quit the play."

"What do you mean?"

"This production is a really big deal to Mr. Miles," I said. "If we keep dropping out, it'll mess everything up for him."

Henry looked at me skeptically. "You don't want my help, do you? You want to go back to work for Eugene. Is that it?"

"No, no. It's nothing like that. I don't want to see the play get screwed up. That's all."

"If you were so concerned about it, then why did you quit in the first place?"

"I just explained that. The agency comes first."

We stopped at the front door.

"So it's okay for you to walk out," Henry said, "but not me. Is that it? Sounds kind of hypocritical, if you ask me."

He was absolutely correct. Where did I get off telling someone else not to do what I had done? He had every right to call me a hypocrite. It wasn't pleasant to hear someone say that, especially your best friend, but it was accurate.

"You're right," I said. "I have no business telling you not to quit. You do what you want to do."

And then right at that moment, out of the corner of my eye, I noticed Scarlett walking toward us. She stopped and folded her arms. She didn't seem happy to see me.

"You're a quitter, Charlie Collier," she said. "How could you do that to Mr. Miles after all the work he's done with this play? He handpicked you out of everyone else at school for the lead role, and you turned your back on him."

There were times in the past when I would have been just fine with being chastised by Scarlett. Just to have her notice me—to have her speak to me—was everything. It didn't matter that she was scolding me. But in the past couple of months, since helping her find her grandfather's parrot, and since she joined the agency and all, we had actually talked a lot. A few conversations were like this one. But most were actually quite pleasant—and I wanted more of the latter. So I knew that I needed to fix this thing right now. If our friendship was ever going to blossom into something more, then I needed to learn how to negotiate these speed bumps.

"It's not like that," I said as I tried to defend myself. "Mr. Miles is okay with this."

"And what exactly is *this*?" she said.

"He's letting me miss a few practices so that I can continue to run the agency. But I'm still a member of the cast, kind of. I'm the understudy for the Nick Dakota character."

She glared at me. "Did you ever think how I might feel about this before you decided to quit? Because of your actions, I'm stuck reading lines with Patrick Walsh. Thanks a lot."

"I had no idea Patrick would get the part," I said.

"I don't know why Mr. Miles ever gave it to him," she said. "Or why Patrick even wanted it."

Henry leaned in. "I'll tell you why he wanted it. He probably thought he could get out of class for play practice. That's the only thing that would have motivated him. If he ever—"

The school bell drowned out the rest of Henry's comment.

Scarlett turned to leave, then stopped and spun around. "I just want you to know that I'm disappointed in you, Charlie. You have real acting potential." She glanced at Henry. "Not like some people." And she was off. Hit and run.

I grabbed Henry by the arm before he said or did something that he would later regret.

"That changes everything," he snapped. "Forget what I said before. There's no way I'm quitting this play. And let me tell you something else. I plan on delivering such an amazing performance in this production that I just might be able to convince Mr. Miles to change the plot and leave the fair Rebecca in a cold, dingy cell— permanently. So there." And then just like Scarlett, Henry blended into the crowd and disappeared.

For the remainder of the day, Henry glared at Scarlett, and Scarlett glared at me. I made a vain attempt to get the three of us together at recess. Yeah, right. That wasn't going to happen. With the Charlie Collier, Snoop for Hire Agency back in business, I figured that we might want to get together over the weekend to discuss the new case, and maybe even entertain a few walk-ins. That idea would have to wait until tensions died down.

We did all meet up at play practice though. I sat in the front row and watched the others on stage. Seated on either side of me were the other understudies—the ones for Rebecca and the police lieutenant. They weren't kids who I spent a lot of time with. I was kind of embarrassed to admit that they seemed a lot more committed to their roles than I was. With scripts in hand, they meticulously followed each scene as it was rehearsed on stage. I was just kind of going through the motions. I wanted Mr. Miles to see that I was there but my mind kept drifting to other things.

Today was the day that the actors were expected to have memorized their lines from the first act. Some, like Scarlett and Stephanie, had done so. But the hisser and the slacker stumbled through their lines and kept looking to Mr. Miles for assistance. I couldn't help but notice Mr. Miles glance down in my direction a few times during rehearsal. He seemed to do so every time the slacker screwed up a line. It was almost as if he was upset with me for having bailed on him. Whenever I felt his gaze, I conveniently looked the other way.

As I sat and watched everyone on stage, as well as the other understudies, I started to feel a little guilty. They were all taking it a lot more seriously than I was. I began to read through my copy of the script. Although my heart wasn't in it, I decided that I owed it to Mr. Miles to memorize all of the Nick Dakota lines. I knew that it was a longshot that I would actually have a chance to play the character on stage but I wanted to be ready in an emergency. Mr. Miles had done me a real favor by allowing me to remain involved in the production, and to have the flexibility of occasionally missing practice to run the business. Learning my lines was the least I could do.

Every time I heard the slacker speak, I cringed. I guess there's a certain amount of truth to the old adage: you don't miss something until you lose it. It was painful not only to hear him butcher his lines but to watch Scarlett and Patrick share a scene—a scene that was intended for me. I was feeling sorry for myself and I didn't like the feeling. I was convinced that I had made a well-thought-out decision to give up the role of leading man in order to continue my P.I. business, but that didn't make it any easier. I knew the consequences going in. I knew there was a chance that I might regret my decision, but I had done so with my eyes wide open.

Henry, as promised, was on his game. Not only had he managed to remember all of his lines but he delivered them flawlessly and with passion. I noticed a smile on Mr. Miles' face each time Henry's character lit into Rebecca. The tension even heightened Scarlett's performance. At one point, she got so upset with something that Henry had said that she reached out and shoved him. All the other actors stopped to watch.

"Hey, she can't do that," Henry yelled out loud enough for Mr. Miles to hear.

The aging director shuffled over. He appeared as though he was about to reprimand Scarlett but instead he stopped and smiled.

"Scarlett, I like the way you reacted there. I should have anticipated the anger building in Rebecca's character. It makes perfect sense for her to lash out at the police detective. Good job." He pulled a pencil from his pocket and began jotting something on the script. "Let's make that a permanent part of the scene."

Henry looked at me and rolled his eyes. He couldn't believe what had just happened. Scarlett, on the other hand, grinned, flicked her hair, and walked away. She was enjoying a rather decisive victory.

The next several minutes of action paled in comparison to the Henry/Scarlett confrontation. Mr. Miles decided that the members of the cast needed to work on their enunciation, and so he had them begin a series of breathing and speaking exercises. I kept glancing at the clock on the far wall. I never realized just how boring play practice could be when you were a spectator instead of a participant. I wasn't sure how much longer I could just sit there. My mind began wandering. I thought about—who else—Sam Solomon, and a time when he was forced to spend hours just waiting for something to happen.

It was Episode #48—*The Wading Game Caper*. Sam had been hired by the Treasury Department to assist federal agents off the coast of a remote beach in Miami in December, 1938. Even though it was five years after the repeal of prohibition, smuggling was still alive and well. Prohibition, as I learned from the book, was the legal ban on the manufacture and sale of alcohol. It ran from 1920 until 1933. So, to avoid paying liquor taxes to the IRS, rum-runners, as they were called, would illegally transport alcohol from the Caribbean into the US. At one juncture in the investigation, Sam found himself in waist-deep water for hours one night, hidden behind a buoy, just waiting for smugglers to show themselves. The veteran P.I. managed to avoid a shark attack and near-hypothermia. But the worst part of the ordeal, according to Sam, was "the endless waiting." And so if Sam could sit, or rather, wade, patiently for hours on end in dangerous waters, then I certainly had nothing to complain about.

Chapter 13

The Pier Pressure Caper

At school on Thursday, I tried to play the role of peacemaker between Henry and Scarlett. It was no use. The two of them refused to meet up on the playground to hash this thing out before school. I did manage to corner them in the cafeteria during lunch though. But that turned out to be fairly unproductive and downright painful. They spent the entire time lashing out at me. It was like two prizefighters pounding on the referee. Between periods that afternoon, I tried to change the subject and attempted to discuss the current crime wave with Henry. But he would have none of it. All he wanted to talk about was Scarlett and how we should unceremoniously boot her out of the agency. That would never happen as long as my name was on the door. I made that crystal clear to him. And, as you might guess, we didn't speak for the remainder of the day. I didn't have a chance to talk to either of them after school. I decided to take advantage of my deal with Mr. Miles and opt out of play practice to man the agency for a couple of hours.

By the time Friday morning rolled around, we had made little progress. Before the bell rang, I was determined to get Henry and Scarlett to agree to a truce of some kind. We had work to do, and these petty arguments were getting in the way. On the bus ride to school, I made sure that the conversation centered around anything but the ongoing feud. I didn't want Henry to get himself worked up again. It was best to keep his mind on non-controversial issues.

When the bus pulled up in front of school, I hopped off as if everything was normal. I scanned the playground for any sign of Scarlett. I was determined to resolve this conflict if it killed me. A minute or so later, I spotted her mom's car. I waited for her to make her way to a group of friends before taking action. I started up a conversation with Henry and then slowly began leading him in Scarlett's direction. The combatants were now only a few feet away when I made my move.

"Scarlett," I called out. "Do you have a minute?"

"This is my cue to leave," Henry said.

But before he could exit, I grabbed him by the arm. "You're not going anywhere," I said. "Not until we make peace."

Scarlett had reluctantly drifted over. "What do *you* want?"

I wasn't quite sure who she was talking to. I was hoping it was Henry. But then again, it could have been me. She was still upset with the fact that I had bowed out of the leading man role in the play, and stuck her with the slacker.

"We're not going into that building," I said, pointing to school, "until we resolve our differences. This is getting ridiculous. We're a team but we're sure not acting like one."

"She hit me the other day at practice," Henry said. "I'm supposed to ignore that?"

"I barely touched you," she said.

I held up my arms. I wanted to make sure there wasn't a repeat of the alleged assault.

"Henry, no offense," I said, "but you had it coming. You're taking the role of this police detective way too seriously. You're making it personal."

Henry folded his arms. "I'm just doing my job."

"And I was just doing mine," Scarlett replied. "You heard what Mr. Miles said. He liked it. And now I get to shove you at every practice. So get used to it."

"Listen to her, Charlie," Henry said. "I can't work under these conditions."

My goal was to settle this dispute before the bell rang. I knew that I had less than a minute. And by the way things were going, I wasn't anticipating a successful conclusion. With tensions at an all-time high, we could easily spend the next couple of hours trading jabs, and accomplishing nothing. I needed to exercise my authority. It was my agency. I was prepared to issue an edict. They could follow it or they could walk. It was risky, and I knew it. But I had no intentions of wasting valuable time having to break up these petty skirmishes.

"Listen, guys, you are both bona fide members of the Charlie Collier, Snoop for Hire Agency. You both make valuable contributions to the business. I can't imagine walking into that garage and not having each of you by my side. But this bickering has to stop...now." I waited for one of them to present a defense but there was none, so I continued. "My parents are going out to dinner tomorrow night. They should be gone at least a couple of hours. The agency doors will be open from six to eight pm. I want both of you in attendance. Make whatever excuses you need to in order to be there. If a few walk-ins show up, then fine. If not, we'll lay out our strategy on how to solve this Sam Solomon radio drama caper."

"What Sam Solomon caper?" Scarlett asked.

"And that's precisely why you need to be there," I said. "I'll explain everything tomorrow night." I stared at both of them. "Remember...this feud stops here. Period."

It was almost as if I had scripted it. A half second after the final word left my mouth, the bell rang. It provided the perfect exclamation point. I walked past my associates and into school with my head held high. I had no idea how they would react. I didn't know if either would bother to show up tomorrow. I might discover that I was now a member of a one-man agency. If that was the way it had to be, then so be it. I had said my piece. I could only hope that I had knocked some sense into both Henry and Scarlett. It was now up to them.

The remainder of the day was quiet. Although we bumped into each other a few times, no words were exchanged. Either I had gotten my point across and they were willing to comply with my wishes, or they were giving me the silent treatment right before jumping ship. Since I planned to skip play practice for a second straight day, I had a feeling that I wouldn't know where things stood for the better part of twenty four hours. And that was fine. Whatever happened...happened. Now on to more pleasant things. It was at least nice to end the day with Mrs. Jansen's science class.

"Okay, quiet down, everyone," she said. "You don't want to be late for our trip, do you?"

"What trip?" Sherman said.

"Our trip to outer space," she said.

Heads turned, and smiles soon appeared on many faces in the room. Activities like this were what made this such a great class.

"Let's turn the clock ahead seventy five years," she said, "to a time when space exploration is as common as driving to the grocery store."

She immediately got our attention with that statement.

"You've all booked passage for a trip to Neptune."

There were a few ooh's and ah's in class.

"Here's the premise. All of you are really excited about the journey," she continued, "because you'll be the first group to visit a new colony that's been established on the planet. You're not quite sure what you'll find when you get there. So…you load up, blast off, and after several days of travel, you land safely. When you look out the window, you're amazed. You notice that the planet resembles Earth, but with a few differences." Mrs. Jansen paused for effect. "Before you disembark, there's something you should know—colors on Neptune are somewhat different than what you find on earth. For example—snow is red…grass is black…the sky is brown…soot is green…and blood is white."

We were all confused, but hooked.

"Now based on that color scheme," Mrs. Jansen said, "who can tell me what the color of dirt is on Neptune?"

Patrick Walsh, the slacker, who just happened to be in class that day raised his hand.

"Yes, Patrick."

"How can you possibly tell what color it is without seeing it?" he said. "It could be any color."

Mrs. Jansen smiled. "You have all the information you need to figure it out. Think about what I just said: snow is red…grass is black…the sky is brown…soot is green…and blood is white."

Henry raised his hand.

"Yes, Henry?"

"Would you mind writing those down on the board?" he said. "It's hard to remember them."

"Certainly." Mrs. Jansen grabbed a piece of chalk and began writing.

Snow = red
Grass = black
Sky = brown
Soot = green
Blood = white
Dirt = ?

Scarlett's hand went up.

Mrs. Jansen nodded in her direction.

"Can you at least tell us if this is a science question or just some trick question?"

"Then I'd be giving it away," Mrs. Jansen said. She pointed to the board. "Look carefully at what I've written down. See if you can make any sense out of it. It may seem that colors appear in a random fashion, but there's a pattern up there."

That was it. That was the giveaway. Within seconds I had the answer. I almost wished she hadn't given us a hint. I always liked to tackle a brain buster in its purest form, without any help. For the next few minutes, a handful of kids made some wild guesses. None were correct.

"Is there anyone else who wants to take a shot at this?" she said.

There was no response.

"Charlie," Mrs. Jansen said, "any help here, or have we stumped you too?"

I rose from my chair ever so slowly. I didn't want to seem overanxious. I wanted it to look more like I had been drafted. I just stood there. I decided to wait for another nudge.

"So, Charlie, what do you think?"

"Well," I said, "you kind of gave it away when you told us there was a pattern. I immediately began looking at the odd color scheme and then I started assigning the correct colors. I made it a point to notice what items were what colors, and then I saw the pattern. I started with *snow is red*. So I looked for the correct answer—white. And you had *blood is white*. I realized then that those two were a pair, and that you had just switched their colors. I did the same thing with *grass is black* and *soot is green*. I simply swapped them to make the corrections. And so that meant that *sky* and *dirt* had to be the last pair. So if the *sky is brown*...then dirt has to be...*blue*."

Mrs. Jansen smiled. "Well done, as always," she said.

"I was going to say that," Stephanie said.

"Well, Stephanie, I'm afraid you'll just have to be a little quicker in order to beat our resident brain teaser master," Mrs. Jansen said.

I appreciated the kudos but I never liked it when a teacher singled me out. As much as I loved hearing the comments, I kind of wished they would just say those things when we were alone. I was fairly certain that other classmates accepted the fact that I was pretty smart. It was just that I wanted them to think of me as popular as well. I wasn't sure if that would ever happen.

*   *   *   *   *

I did my best to kill time on Saturday just waiting for my parents to leave. I waved goodbye to them as they pulled out of the garage and left for their dinner engagement. Since it was the weekend, I knew that they wouldn't be in a rush to get home. As the overhead door closed, I began setting up the card table and chairs for a night of mystery. I was looking forward to a couple of hours of prime agency time. Although Gram was still home, she rarely bothered us in the middle of a client session. She'd probably just watch TV or read or something. I finished setting things up and then slipped on my trench coat and fedora. I wanted to look the part if a client appeared.

I glanced at my watch. It was 6:05. I wondered if Henry or Scarlett would bother showing up. I didn't like the fact that I had lashed out at my associates. It wasn't good for morale. It reminded me of a time when Sam Solomon had done the exact same thing. It was Episode #55—*The Pier Pressure Caper*.

Sam had been hired by a wealthy businessman who operated a fleet of deep-sea fishing boats at the Clearwater Beach Marina on Florida's gulf coast. Someone apparently had been sneaking onto the pier each evening and vandalizing the boats—so severely that they were no longer seaworthy. The company was forced to cancel a number of charters and was soon bleeding financially. The owner suspected a captain who had recently been fired for insubordination, but he had no proof. Sam knew that in order to keep an eye on more than twenty vessels, he needed to hire several freelance private investigators.

A week later, with surveillance crews in place, four more boats had been damaged, and they were no closer to identifying a suspect. So Sam decided to check up on his new recruits one night. To his surprise and disappointment, he found most of them asleep. Sam, as you might guess, confronted his troops and read them the riot act. He never liked playing the bad cop but this group was cheating the client. A day following his tirade, the recently-fired captain was caught in the act and handed over to authorities. Laying down the law had worked for Sam. I could only hope it would work for me.

By 6:15 I was fairly certain that I'd be running the agency solo for the rest of the night. That was fine. It was usually up to me to solve the clients' problems anyway, so it really didn't matter. If someone did walk through that door, however, there was something I wasn't looking forward to—collecting a fee for services rendered. That was Henry's territory, and he seemed to enjoy it. I would just have to cross that bridge when I came to it.

Five or so minutes later, there was a soft knock at the door. When I opened it, I had to smile. It seemed that I hadn't frightened them away after all. Henry and Scarlett stood in the doorway. I was kind of surprised to see them together.

"Well, I'm glad you guys decided to show up," I said. "Come on in."

Henry stepped back and let Scarlett enter first.

"Thanks," she replied.

Wait a minute. Wait just a minute. What the heck was going on here? Was I dreaming? The same two people who couldn't stand to be in the same room together for more than a minute were actually being civil to one another.

"What's up?" I said.

"What are you talking about?" Henry said.

"You and Scarlett. You're…you're…you're getting along. What happened?"

Scarlett folded her arms. "Don't get carried away. I wouldn't call it *getting along*."

"Yeah, it's more like…" Henry paused. "It's more like we're doing our best to tolerate one another."

I had to know what brought about this truce. "So, how'd this all happen?"

Scarlett sat down on one of the lawn chairs. "We bumped into each other on the way over here, and we got to talking," Scarlett said. "We were both thinking about what you said yesterday on the playground. You weren't very nice to us, you know."

"I did it for a reason," I said.

"And you were right," Henry said. "We've finally come to our senses. For the longest time, we've been acting like a couple of kids. We decided it was time to bury the hatchet."

"Really?" I said.

Henry laughed. "Yeah, right. Get serious. That's never gonna happen. This is a business decision, pure and simple."

"We just figured out that if we all worked together, we'd make a pretty awesome team," Scarlett said. "But if we kept fighting, it would be counter-productive…and it wouldn't be fair to a potential client."

"A potential *paying* client," Henry added. "The better we got along…the more effective we'd be…the more clients we could take on…and the more money we'd make. Get it?"

Scarlett frowned. "It has nothing to do with money. It has to do with being more efficient and helping out more people."

I couldn't believe what I was hearing. I had actually gotten through to them. I had done it. Just like Sam had done in *The Pier Pressure Caper*. The feud was over—well, sort of. And to be perfectly honest, it really didn't matter to me if it was for the good of mankind, or pure greed. We were a team again, and that's all that mattered.

"So, now what?" I said.

"Well, didn't you want to bring Scarlett up to speed on this Sam Solomon caper?" Henry said.

"Oh yeah, right." I spent the next ten minutes or so explaining everything about the case. I was just about done when we heard a sound outside. Someone—perhaps our next client—was about to walk through the door. I'd have to finish updating Scarlett another time. This was far more important. We were about to help our fellow man. A moment later, however, our worst fears were realized.

Chapter 14

The Pitcher Frame Caper

What followed was the familiar and painful sound of grinding gears. The overhead garage door was opening.

"It's my parents," I yelled. "What are they doing here?"

Scarlett froze. Henry immediately began folding up lawn chairs.

"We'll never make it," I said. I had to think quickly. I somehow had to convince my parents that we were in the garage for anything but a client meeting. But what? What would the three of us possibly be doing here? And then just as I caught a glimpse of the headlights, I had it. I discretely tore off some pages from my note pad and handed one to each of the others.

"What's this for?" Henry said.

"We're rehearsing."

"For what?" he said.

"The play, dummy," Scarlett snapped.

As soon as my dad spotted us, he hit the brakes. Through the windshield, I could see the looks on their faces. It was somewhere between surprise and disgust. I needed to douse this fire as quickly as possible. I jogged over to the passenger side of the van just as my mom's window was sliding down.

She shook her head. "Charlie, please tell me this isn't what I think it is."

"What do you mean?"

My dad leaned over. "Your little *agency*? I thought I made myself very clear that—"

"No, no, no," I said. "That's not what we're doing." I turned to the others. "Scarlett, please inform my parents what's going on here."

She strolled over to the open window. "I hope it's okay, Mrs. Collier. We were just practicing for the school play. Charlie said it wouldn't be a problem."

My mom sighed. "It's no problem at all, sweetie." She glanced at my dad and smiled, then turned to us. "How come you kids are out here? Wouldn't you be more comfortable in the house?"

"Well," I said, "you see, Gram's watching TV...and she tends to crank the volume if you haven't noticed."

"Tell me about it," my dad said.

My mom grabbed his arm. "Why don't we park on the street so the kids can continue practicing."

Henry scooted over. "Oh, that's okay. We were just finishing up. Weren't we, guys?"

We then proceeded to break down the lawn chairs and card table, and waved as we exited via the side door.

"That was close," Henry said.

"Yeah, I know," I said. "We'd better break this thing up. I'll talk to you at school on Monday."

By the time Henry and Scarlett had left the back yard, my parents had emerged from the garage.

"How come you guys are back so early?" I said.

"I learned tonight that sushi and I do not agree," my mom said. "I wasn't feeling well, and so I asked your dad to bring me home."

"How do you feel now?" I asked.

"Better, thanks." My mom put her arm around me. "I didn't realize that Henry and Scarlett were in the play too."

I nodded.

"That's nice." She grinned. "And to think that I share a last name with a handsome leading man." She hugged me.

It was right at that moment, when I saw how proud she was of me, that I thought I had better come clean.

"Mom, I've been meaning to talk to you about that."

"About what?"

We headed into the house.

"You see, I may have jumped the gun the other day."

Her eyes narrowed.

"I *thought* I had won the role of leading man...but it seems... I was wrong."

She appeared confused. "So, what role are you playing then?"

I started shuffling my feet. "I'm the understudy for the role of Nick Dakota. That's the leading man character."

"Oh, I see," she said. "So you won't be on stage at all?" She was clearly disappointed.

"Not unless something happens to Patrick Walsh. He has the role now."

My mom smiled. But I had seen that smile before. It was her way of trying to make me feel better…even though I had lost the race. I could tell that she was doing her best to console me, but it was obvious that she was the one who needed consolation. I wanted to say something that might make it easier for her to deal with it. Something warm. Something tender. Something that only a son would share with his mother.

"We can always hope that Patrick breaks a leg or some other body part," I said with a grin. It was the best I could come up with on short notice.

"Let's not wish that on anyone." She patted the top of my head. "I'm going to lie down for a little bit."

I wasn't sure if she needed rest because of the sushi or the egg I had just laid.

*   *   *   *   *

At school on Monday, things were relatively uneventful, if you don't count a fire drill that turned out to be the real thing. Well, it wasn't a fire actually. The alarm was triggered when a carbon monoxide detector went off. Most of the kids were unaware of what that was, and really didn't care. They were more interested in the fact that our last period was shortened by about twenty minutes. We happened to be in Mrs. Jansen's class when the alarm sounded. When we returned, she took the opportunity to teach us about this silent killer.

Carbon monoxide, we soon learned, is a colorless, odorless, but highly poisonous gas. It's most commonly found in the fumes produced by the exhaust system of a vehicle. But it can also be produced by a furnace that's not running properly. It was a little scary to think that something we all have in our homes, something that provides warmth during the winter months, could malfunction and cause disastrous results. But in our case today, we soon learned that it had all been a false alarm caused by a momentary power outage. It was good information to store away, nonetheless, although most of the kids paid little attention to the lecture.

I made it a point to attend play practice that afternoon. Even though tonight was a big night—another Sam Solomon drama—I didn't want to abuse the privilege that Mr. Miles had given me. I wanted him to know that I appreciated the fact that he was allowing me to miss rehearsals. So, every once in a while, I needed to show my face. I joined the other understudies in the front row and tried to stay awake. But that wasn't a problem today. Practice actually proved to be pretty interesting. When Henry and Scarlett were engaged in a rather volatile scene where the police detective shows little mercy for the accused, Mr. Miles interrupted the rehearsal.

"Henry, Henry, what's happened to you? Where's your fire? Where's your passion?"

Mr. Miles was unaware of the events that took place two days earlier when Henry and Scarlett finally settled their differences—at least temporarily.

"Well, I thought that maybe I was too hard on her before," he replied. "I thought I'd tone it down a little."

"Henry, you're not listening to your inner voice. You're a hard-nosed, streetwise, veteran cop. You scratch out a meager existence. And here's this wealthy socialite who hasn't worked a day in her life. She has no concept of earning a living. She's everything that you hate." He paused and smiled. "Does that help?"

"Sure," he said. But you could tell there was still something missing from Henry's performance.

When the scene continued, Mr. Miles stood off to the side of the stage and frowned. He knew that something had changed. Even Scarlett lacked the motivation that she had displayed so many other times. It was funny. It was almost as if Henry and Scarlett were better actors when they couldn't stand one another. It caused Mr. Miles to end practice early, which was perfectly fine with me.

At home that night, I had a hard time concentrating. I was antsy. I couldn't wait for eleven o'clock to roll around when the next episode of The Sam Solomon Mystery Theater would air. And like a week ago, I'd have to be discreet. No one could know I was up that late on a weeknight. Well, except for Gram. I wrote myself a note to set my alarm clock for morning. I couldn't oversleep again.

When it was time for bed, I set my alarm for eleven p.m., and hit the sack. But unlike last time, I never fell asleep. My eyes refused to close. I guess I was just too keyed up. I knew that as soon as the program ended, I would have to sneak down to the basement and call Eugene. I just prayed that my parents would be fast asleep. When eleven o'clock finally did arrive, I was ready. I had paper and pencil in hand. I planned to take notes during the broadcast. There was no room for error. I had to keep my ears open for words with double meanings. Then Eugene and I would have to quickly analyze our findings and try to determine the suspect's next target.

I slipped on my headphones, pulled the covers over my head, and immersed myself in the world of Sam Solomon for the next thirty minutes. This particular episode was entitled *The Pitcher Frame Caper*. It all began, as many of Sam's adventures do, when a mysterious woman walked into his office with a problem. She identified herself as Zelda Romanov, the girlfriend of a well-known major league baseball pitcher in Chicago by the name of Tommy Griffin. Tommy had recently helped his team secure a playoff berth with an amazing 17-7 record. Zelda went on to explain that after yesterday's game the ace pitcher had been approached by a notorious gambler who had offered him $25,000 if he would help fix the outcome of the opening playoff game. Tommy had been instructed to throw a series of *meatballs* to the opposing batters. (*Meatballs*, I learned, is a slang term for pitches thrown right down the heart of the plate and easy to hit.) When Tommy refused, the gambler threatened to ruin the pitcher's illustrious career by sharing sensitive information with the press.

The gambler produced a series of bank receipts which indicated that on the day following each of Tommy's regular-season losses, a sum of $5,000 had been deposited into the pitcher's personal bank account. Those receipts certainly made it look as if Tommy was in cahoots with gamblers to influence the outcome of games. Sam was certain that the records were fraudulent but even a faithful teammate or a loyal fan would have a hard time believing that Tommy hadn't accepted bribes to throw each of those games.

Zelda pleaded with Sam to help foil the gambler's evil plot and save Tommy's career. It was obvious to Sam that the pitcher was being framed—hence the title of the episode. Well, it didn't take the world's greatest detective long to solve this caper. Within days, he had identified the frightened bank teller would had been forced to falsify documents that supported the gambler's claim. And from there it was relatively easy to expose the leaders of the gambling ring, and preserve Tommy's good name.

I jumped out of bed, slid over to my desk, flipped on a lamp, and stared at the pad of paper I had with me while under the covers. It was blank. I had gotten so caught up in the mystery that I had forgotten to jot down words that might have given us a clue to our suspect's next move. There wasn't much for me to do now but continue on with the plan. I tiptoed down the stairs, through the living room, past my parents' bedroom, and down to the basement. I flipped on a light, picked up the receiver and dialed Eugene's office.

"Eugene Patterson," a voice on the other end answered.

"Hi, Eugene, it's Charlie," I whispered.

"You're going to have to speak up a little, Charlie," Eugene said. "My hearing's not what it used to be."

I scooted over to the stairwell and looked up. I had to make sure no one could hear me.

"Is that better, Eugene?" I said. I had raised my voice just slightly.

"That's fine. So, what'd you think of the show? Pretty good, huh?"

"Classic Sam Solomon as always," I said.

I opened up a folding chair and sat down. I placed the pad of paper—the *blank* pad of paper—in my lap. I wasn't sure what I'd say when Eugene asked what notes I had taken.

"Let's look at what we have here," he said. "Major league baseball…a star athlete…a pennant race…a gambling ring…a frightened bank teller…fraudulent receipts…a distraught girlfriend…and Sam. That's about all I've got. Do you have anything else?"

I was glad Eugene went first. I was basically off the hook. "That's the same list I have."

"Let's see if we can find a word with a double meaning or one that leads us to another word," Eugene said. "Where do you want to start?"

Before our analysis could begin, I suddenly felt this pain in my gut—the kind of pain you get when you're scared senseless. I had heard a sound, and not just any sound. It was the sound of someone picking up the extension upstairs. Oh, no, I was busted. I'd be grounded for a month or maybe worse. I held my breath and only hoped that Eugene would sense what was happening and would follow my cue. But it wasn't to be.

"Charlie, are you still there?"

That was it. My life was over. It was nice knowing you.

Chapter 15

The High Steaks Caper

I wasn't sure if I should play dumb and say nothing, just
hang up the phone, or run up to my room and hide under the covers.
What would be the best move for a condemned man? And then I
heard the mystery voice.

"Charlie, it's me, Gram. I know you're on the phone in the
basement."

Gram? Well, it sure could have been a lot worse. She might
not be happy about it, but I knew she would never rat me out.

"I'm sorry, Gram. I should have told you what Eugene and I
were up to."

"I know exactly what the two of you are up to," she said.
"Eugene told me all about it. I was listening to the Sam Solomon
program in my room. I'm here to help you guys figure this thing
out."

What a relief! I couldn't believe it. From execution to
pardon in a matter of seconds. I had to give Eugene credit. Teaming
up with my grandmother was a brilliant idea. Who better to help us
solve a word puzzle than an official World War II cryptologist.

"Eugene," she said, "Let's get to work. Young Mr. Collier
here has school in the morning."

And so for the next several minutes we put our heads
together trying to figure out where our mystery man would strike.
We began with the list that Eugene had suggested (major league
baseball…star athlete…pennant race…gambling ring…frightened
bank teller…fraudulent receipts…distraught girlfriend). Then we
tried to determine if any of the words or phrases had double
meanings or might be a play on words. Nothing initially was
jumping out at us. It was now close to midnight. I wasn't that tired
but I knew that I'd be exhausted in the morning.

"We have to figure this out, and fast," Eugene said. "We're
losing time. He could be out there right now."

There was a short pause and then I heard what sounded like a
chuckle from my grandmother.

"Let's try this on for size, gentlemen," she said. "The principal character in this story is a pitcher...a baseball pitcher. But there's also another type of pitcher...a water pitcher. Let's work with that."

We tried to imagine where someone might go to steal a water pitcher. If we were on the right track, we were in trouble. Every department store, supermarket, convenience store, outlet store, etc., would probably carry water pitchers. We'd need an army to stake out all of those locations.

"Let's narrow this down," Gram said. "The main character in this story isn't just a pitcher, he's a famous pitcher. So where would you go to find a famous pitcher? But not of the baseball variety."

A longer pause followed. And then all at once, I could feel the wheels and gears and cogs spinning in my brain. This is what would always happen when I was on the verge of successfully solving a problem.

"Gram, I think I've got it."

"What?" she said.

"Last month we went on a field trip to the Oak Grove Natural History Museum. And there was this travelling exhibit. I remember it because it was so boring. You know—compared to the dinosaurs and mummies and all that."

"What was it?" Eugene said.

"It was a display of pitchers...water pitchers...antique Victorian water pitchers." I scooted over to the stairs just to make sure my parents weren't standing there. "So, what do you think, guys?"

"Well, those are certainly what you'd call famous pitchers," Eugene said.

"It works for me," Gram said. "The entire plot of this story centered around the plight of the pitcher. It makes perfect sense that our suspect would choose a central theme as a trigger for his next crime."

"That's it then," Eugene said. "Constance, can you meet me over at the museum in thirty minutes?"

"Sure," Gram said. "This is gonna be fun. An all-night stakeout. Just like the old days. I'll bring the coffee. Hey, you plan to call in any reinforcements?"

"Chicken Bone is waiting for my call," Eugene said. "He's champing at the bit for a little action."

I knew that name sounded familiar but I wasn't sure where I had heard it before.

"Chicken Bone?" I said.

"You don't remember Chicken Bone?" Eugene said.

"I'm not sure."

"Well, you oughta. He's the one who helped us capture Rupert Olsen."

"Oh…yeah…I remember him now." I wasn't sure how I could have forgotten good old Chicken Bone—especially with a name like that. Of course, that wasn't his real name. It was his CB handle—his citizen's band radio nickname. Chicken Bone had helped us overpower Rupert Olsen on his farm a couple of months back when we went over there to rescue the stolen birds.

"We're all set then, Eugene," Gram said. "Chicken Bone and I will meet you at the museum in thirty minutes. And, Charlie, you'd better get to bed."

"I suppose I could do that," I said. "But I sure wish I could help you guys out tonight. What do you say, Gram, can I join you on the stakeout? Mom and Dad'll never find out." I was fairly certain that I already knew the answer to the question but I had to ask.

My grandmother sighed. "It would be good training for you," she said, "but the answer is an emphatic *no*. Now hang up and get to bed. I'll fill you in tomorrow morning."

But tomorrow was already here. The clock read 12:05. I hung up the phone, tiptoed up two flights of stairs, and deposited myself in bed. The thought of joining the others on a surveillance mission sounded pretty exciting, but the thought of a good night's sleep sounded even better. I fell back onto the pillow and closed my eyes. I couldn't wait to talk to Gram in the morning to see if we had guessed right about the water pitcher. I was just about to enter dreamland when I suddenly sat up in bed. I reached over and reset my alarm. Couldn't make the same mistake twice. And that was the last thing I remembered doing until morning.

*   *   *   *   *

I awoke to the irritating buzz of my clock radio. All I wanted to do at that very moment was to pull the covers over my head and go back to sleep. This P.I. business was starting to do a number on my body clock. I found myself thinking about how good it was going to feel to hit the sack tonight. I couldn't wait. But I also couldn't wait to talk to Gram at breakfast and see if our theory had been correct all along. I hopped out of bed, scooted into the bathroom for a quick sprucing up, and ran downstairs. My dad was reading the paper while my mom sipped coffee at the breakfast table.

"Do you think it's cleaned up by now?" my mom said.

"I sure hope so," my dad replied. "What a mess."

"What happened?" I asked.

"The office next to your dad's flooded yesterday," my mom said.

Flooded? What was she talking about? I had apparently missed part of the conversation.

"I don't understand," I said.

My dad set his paper down. "Some idiot in my office went to the cleaners at lunchtime yesterday. When he came back, he was looking for somewhere to hang the suit he had just picked up. When he couldn't find a hook, he decided to hang it on one of the sprinkler system heads. Big mistake. You can't tamper with those things. It completely flooded his office…and part of mine."

"Bummer," I said. "I didn't think that much water came out of one of those things."

"Try a hundred gallons a minute," he said. "And whenever those things go off, it triggers an alarm. So the police and the fire department showed up. It was a madhouse." My dad sighed and continued reading the paper.

"Hey, where's Gram?" I asked.

"Sound asleep," my dad said.

"She never sleeps this late," my mom said. "I wonder if she's feeling all right."

They didn't know what I knew. And it was best kept between me and Gram. I guess I'd have to wait until after school to find out what happened last night. Then again, if Eugene and company had spotted the suspect, I'm sure they would have contacted the police. And if that were the case, it would have made the morning news.

"Is it okay if I turn on the TV? Just want to catch the news."

My dad shrugged.

I took that as a *yes*. I reached over and flipped it on. The weatherman was in the middle of a forecast.

"Winds are out of the southeast at ten miles per hour, and the humidity is thirty percent. Today we're looking at partly cloudy skies with a high of 62. And much of the same for tomorrow."

"Thanks, Frank," the news anchor said. "When we come back, we'll hear from Mitzi Malone in our newsroom with word of a breaking story."

While the commercial aired, I poured myself a glass of orange juice and began devouring a bowl of cereal.

When the newscast resumed, a female reporter was sitting next to the anchor. "I've asked Mitzi Malone from our newsroom to join us this morning," the newsman began. "Mitzi, it apparently has happened again."

"Yes, Todd. For the fourth consecutive Tuesday morning, authorities are reporting an overnight burglary. This time it was at The Fontana Art Gallery on east Washington."

Fontana Art Gallery? I was expecting to hear them say that the museum had been robbed.

"Here we go again," my mom said.

"So, what was missing this time?" the newsman asked.

"About seven hundred dollars from the cash register," the reporter said. "And the thief also made off with a painting."

"A painting?" the anchor said. "What type?"

"It's a contemporary piece entitled *Summer Repose*. It's a painting of a small table on an outdoor patio. And on the table is a large water pitcher and two small glasses."

I dropped my spoon. It hit the cereal bowl and splashed milk onto my dad's newspaper.

"Charlie! Watch what you're doing!" he said.

"And," the reporter continued, "that familiar business card with the SS lined out was found by police on the floor of the gallery."

I needed to talk to my grandmother in the worst way. I gulped down my orange juice, asked to be excused, and headed into the living room where I had left my backpack. As I passed Gram's room, I thought I heard someone moving around in there. I didn't want to bother her but I just had to. I tapped lightly on her door.

A few seconds later, the door opened. Gram was in her nightgown and robe. She placed a finger to her lips. She apparently didn't want my parents to hear what she was about to say. She motioned for me to come into her room, and closed the door behind me.

"Did you hear the news this morning?" she said.

I nodded.

"Well, we were right about the pitcher…sort of."

"We were so close," I said. "We managed to figure out the double meaning, but staked out the wrong place. Gram, this guy is really clever. Do you remember the name of the Sam Solomon episode last night? It was *The Pitcher Frame Caper*. And that's exactly what he took—a painting of a *pitcher* that just happened to be in a *frame*.

She sat down on her bed and motioned for me to join her. "Charlie, we sat and sat outside the museum for hours and then about 4:30 this morning, over the police radio, we hear a report of a break-in at the art gallery."

"So, now what?"

"Now we wait a week and try to do a better job of figuring out his next target."

"It seems a shame to have to wait a whole week," I said, "and even then we're not guaranteed we'll be able to predict where he'll strike next."

"Realistically, it could take months for us to find this bird," she said. "You just gotta be patient."

I got up and reached for the door knob. "If there was only a way to set a trap, then we wouldn't be wasting all this time."

"How do you propose we do that?" she said. "Are you going to write a new Sam Solomon script yourself, with a story that'll lead him right to you?" She chuckled.

"No, that'd be crazy." I turned to leave. At least, I thought it was crazy.

* * * * *

As I sat on the bus on my way to school, I kept racking my brain to come up with a way to solve this caper. It was so frustrating to think that we'd have to wait another week to get another shot at this guy. And there wasn't really anything we could do in the interim. There were no strategies to plan out, no stakeouts to arrange, no witnesses to interview. We were his slaves. He controlled our every move. He acted, and we reacted. No one should be able to wield that kind of power over others. If there was only a way to know the details of the next episode, or better yet, to have some control over the content of the story, then we might have a shot at this guy. Maybe Gram had the right idea. Maybe we should think about creating our own radio drama. But that was impossible.

A minute or so later, Henry climbed up onto the bus. When he spotted me, he made a beeline for the empty seat next to mine.

"I heard about the burglary at that art gallery last night," Henry said. "Since the suspect's at large, I'm guessing that Eugene wasn't there waiting for him when he showed up."

"We were so close, Henry." I spent the remainder of the ride bringing him up to speed. He had apparently started listening to the Sam Solomon drama last night but fell asleep about halfway through. I told him about the conversation with Eugene after the program, and how my grandmother nearly scared me to death when I heard her on the extension. I talked about the process of identifying key words from the show and then looking for one with a double-meaning or a play on words. I then told him how Eugene, Gram, and Chicken Bone worked an all-night stakeout at the museum, but unfortunately were outwitted by the suspect.

When we got to school, we met up with Scarlett on the playground. As I had done with Henry, I shared all the details from the previous night. We were frustrated that we only had one chance each week to solve this caper, but no one had any ideas on what we could be doing until the next Monday night.

"Let's just concentrate on the play," Scarlett said. "That'll keep us busy, and at the same time, it'll take our minds off the crime spree."

It was good advice. We could think ourselves silly about this case for the next few days and still be no closer to solving it than when we started. I did my best to put the crime spree on the back burner and tried to concentrate on school matters. But it was more difficult than I was expecting. It wasn't that my classes were any more boring than usual, it was just that I was having a really tough time keeping my eyes open. The sleep I'd lost the night before was catching up to me.

When we finally made it the last period, Mrs. Jansen's class, I was relieved. I kept thinking about how good it would feel to go to bed tonight. I guess I might have been imagining my head hitting the pillow a bit too much. I remembered walking into class, opening up my science book to a page 52, and that was it. Everything seemed to stop at that point. I soon came to the conclusion that a growing boy needs his sleep.

"Charlie…Charlie…wake up." Mrs. Jansen was hovering over me.

I couldn't believe I had fallen asleep at my desk. I'd never done that before. Besides the tone of an irritated teacher, I could also hear my classmates giggling. It would take a while to live this one down.

"I realize that my lectures can be a little dry at times," Mrs. Jansen said, "but I didn't think they actually put people to sleep."

"I'm sorry. I'm really sorry," I said. "It won't happen again. I promise."

Mrs. Jansen gazed into my eyes. "You look tired. Up late?" I nodded.

"Well, just make sure you get to bed early tonight. Okay?"

I smiled sheepishly. The giggling and pointing had yet to die down. As Mrs. Jansen made her way to the front of the room, I found myself thinking about a time when Sam Solomon had suffered public humiliation. It was Episode #49—*The High Steaks Caper*. This was the story of a meat-packing facility that was suspected of dealing with poachers. Rumor had it that they would buy meat from unscrupulous suppliers who were involved in the slaughter of animals on the endangered species list. Sam had gone undercover as a meat packer in order to expose these unethical and illegal practices. When he was certain that he had determined the identity of the ringleader, he made it known that he was a private detective and informed his suspect that he'd be escorting him to jail. What Sam didn't know, unfortunately, was that the so-called ringleader was actually a police officer who was also undercover. Sam had inadvertently blown the officer's cover and had ruined six weeks of the investigation. Sam was so embarrassed that he thought he would never live it down. But in time, the veteran P.I. shared key evidence with the officer that eventually blew the lid off the illegal meat-packing racket.

So, if Sam could endure public embarrassment and survive, then so could I. It might not be easy. And it might take time to rebuild my reputation but I was determined to do so. And the best way to make that happen was to solve another high profile crime. Identifying the crook behind this recent string of burglaries was no longer an opportunity to showcase my talents. It was now an absolute necessity.

Chapter 16

The Knot Guilty Caper

When the bell finally rang, I let my eyes close for just a few seconds. If Henry hadn't nudged me, I might have been in that desk for quite some time. This had not been one of my better performances.

"Are you ready?" Henry said.

"For what?"

"Play practice. What else?"

I was not looking forward to sitting in the front row watching everyone else rehearse. Not only was it deathly boring, but I knew I'd never be able to stay awake. I thought about informing Mr. Miles that this was one of the days I needed to research the case. But I knew that I might legitimately need an off-day sometime in the future.

When we walked into the auditorium, most of the kids were in place on stage. I assumed my usual spot in the front row with my fellow understudies. Each day I was feeling less and less part of this ensemble. I knew that if the slacker missed school one day, I would be pressed into service. But for some odd reason, he hadn't missed a day since he had been elevated to leading man. Apparently he now had a reason to show up.

Always seeming to run fashionably late, Mr. Miles strolled in.

"Excuse my tardiness, thespians," he said as he made his entrance from stage left with his script tucked under his arm. "All right, let's begin with Act III, Scene 2. This is a critical scene. This is where Nick Dakota tracks down the bookie, Noah Brand, at a rundown motel on the east side of town. The bookie's been on the lam ever since Rebecca's parents were discovered missing."

The next ten minutes were absolutely brutal. I was forced to endure a half-hearted effort by the slacker and the hisser. I couldn't make up my mind who was more pathetic. And it seemed that Mr. Miles was thinking the exact same thing.

"No, no, no, gentlemen," he said. "This isn't a wake. It's one of the most important scenes in the entire production. The audience now knows that the bookie does indeed exist, and that Rebecca has been telling the truth the entire time. This is her ticket to freedom." He turned to the slacker. "Patrick, you've just found the Holy Grail. Act like it. And, Brian, the last thing you want right now is for someone to find you. If he turns you over to the police, they'll toss your sorry butt in the slammer. And if your bosses get a hold of you, they'll make an example of someone who runs out on them." He sighed. "Okay, gentlemen, I want to see some real intensity. From the top, please."

When the scene resumed, the pair of underachievers managed to kick it up a notch, but just slightly. The expression on Mr. Miles' face suggested that it was more of the same. I did my best to stay awake. It wasn't easy. I shook my arms and legs to keep the blood flowing. I hoped that would work. Then I tried actually following the storyline of the play. I had to give Mr. Miles credit. He had created a fairly interesting story, but it was painful to watch it performed in this manner. The central theme of the play was the missing bookie. The audience was reminded of that fact throughout. It got me to thinking. If this had been one of the Monday night Sam Solomon dramas, our suspect would have undoubtedly chosen *bookie* for his little word game.

Mr. Miles marched to the center of the stage and threw his arms up. He apparently had had enough.

"Gentlemen, I'll be very honest with you," he said. "Unless your performances improve, I may be forced to make some casting changes. It's not something I enjoy doing." He paused for a moment. "Why don't I demonstrate exactly what we'd like to see." He paged through his script until he found the exact passage he was looking for. "Patrick, Brian, listen carefully." Mr. Miles held the script with one hand and was suddenly transformed into character.

NICK DAKOTA
Well, look who we have here. It
just proves—if you check under
enough rocks, you're bound to find
a slug.

NOAH BRAND
Who are you? How'd you get in
here?

Mr. Miles was simply amazing. He wasn't just mouthing
someone's lines. He had taken on new personas. He altered his
voice for each role. If you closed your eyes, you would have sworn
that there were two completely different people on stage. And then I
remembered something that Mrs. Jansen had said. When Mr. Miles
first came to our class to recruit actors for the play, she had
introduced him as *the man of a thousand voices*. It was true, and it
was remarkable.

NICK DAKOTA
Put both hands where I can see
'em. And don't even think about
going for that gun under the
pillow.

NOAH BRAND
Well, I assume you're not a
member *the family*. I'd be dead
already. So that leaves a cop or a
private cop.

NICK DAKOTA
The name's Dakota. Nick Dakota.
And there's a lady by the name of
Rebecca Ramsey who'd like to
have a little chat with you.

NOAH BRAND
Listen, I had nuthin' to do with
what happened to her folks. You
want somebody else. I'm small
potatoes. Maybe we can work out
some kind of deal. I know things
that might be helpful. What do
you say?

I had never heard the school auditorium as quiet as it was at that very moment. Each and every cast member was spellbound by Mr. Miles' performance. It was easy to see why he had been so successful as an actor on Broadway and in dozens of old-time radio serials.

"Does that help?" he said to the two struggling actors on stage.

They both nodded. And for the remainder of play practice, the performance of virtually every actor on stage had noticeably improved. Mr. Miles' acting demonstration turned out to be a real inspiration. Not only had he executed a perfect teaching moment, but he made me think about something that my grandmother had said earlier. After the blown stakeout at the museum, she had jokingly suggested that we create our own Sam Solomon drama so that we might be able to lead our suspect right into a trap. The thought of doing so earlier had seemed silly, but was it really such a wild idea?

I could suddenly feel the wheels in my brain beginning to spin at breakneck speed. Wait a minute now. This just might work. It was crazy but it could be the perfect solution. I began strategizing immediately. First, I had to approach Mr. Miles to see if he would be interested in helping us out. Since he was friends with both Gram and Eugene, he might just buy in. I would have to convince him to let us produce a thirty-minute radio program based on the play that we were now rehearsing. That way he wouldn't have to write any new material. The work would be all done. We could just add appropriate sound effects and music and turn it into a bona fide old-time radio drama.

The wheels continued to turn. We could change the name of the hero from Nick Dakota to Sam Solomon. It would be easy. The toughest part would be to match up the voices from the original series. If Mr. Miles was truly *the man of a thousand voices*, then he might just be able to match his voice to that of the Sam Solomon series star, Peter Wentworth. Then, of course, we'd need other actors—adult actors—but there had to be some in the area. I knew of a community theater group here in Oak Grove that put on holiday shows. Maybe a few of them would be interested.

Then there was the little matter of approaching the radio station owner in town and asking him if we could use one of his studios to record the production, and then get his permission to substitute it for the next Sam Solomon program. This is where Eugene would come in handy. Since this was such a noble cause, I was sure that Eugene could convince his old pal, Ned Stewart, to help us out. And then all that would be left was our analysis of the program's main events. I was betting on the fact that the word *bookie*, because of how frequently it was mentioned throughout the script, would be integral to solving this crime.

I waited patiently for practice to end. I needed to talk to Mr. Miles. I wasn't sure how he'd react to my proposal. It might mean putting off play practice for a couple of weeks and pushing back opening night. He might not be too willing to do so. But I had to try. It was for the good of the community. He'd have to see that. As practice was ending, Mr. Miles pulled the entire group together on stage. He even asked the understudies to join the others. Once he had our attention, he smiled and began applauding.

"Wunderbar! Just Wunderbar! We turned a corner today, my friends. Things are progressing nicely." He waved his hand in the direction of the seating area. "Imagine this venue filled to capacity. Imagine the electricity. Oh, it's what the theater is all about. You'll do wonderfully. I just know it."

The slacker raised his hand. "Exactly how many people will be here for the show, do you think?"

"Four or five hundred, I would hope," he said. "You're not getting cold feet I hope, Mr. Walsh."

"That's an awful lot of people, you know."

"Don't even think about it. When the stage lights are on, you won't be able to see anyone," Mr. Miles said. "But you'll hear them, and you'll feed off their energy. It'll be a night you'll never forget."

"That's what I'm afraid of," Patrick mumbled.

"And so if there's nothing else, consider yourselves dismissed until tomorrow afternoon."

I waited until everyone but Henry had left the auditorium.

"You ready?" he said.

"I have to talk to Mr. Miles for a minute. I'll meet you at the bus."

"You don't want me around. Is that it?" Henry got his nose out of joint if he wasn't included in every little thing.

"It's nothing. I'll tell you about it. Don't worry."

He made a face and headed for his locker. Mr. Miles was moving props off the stage when I approached him.

"Excuse me, Mr. Miles, do you have a minute?"

"What can I do for you, Charlie?" He held up a finger. "But first, I just wanted to tell you how pleased I am so that you've managed to attend some of the practices. I know it's hard to watch the others on stage, but who knows, you might get your chance, and I know you'll be ready. So, how can I help you?"

"Do you happen to remember an old-time radio actor by the name of Peter Wentworth?"

He smiled. "Peter Wentworth was a legend. He played Sam Solomon for four or five years on radio. He was a fine actor. I don't remember him doing much else however...which is odd. With his talents, he should have been all over radio…and on the big screen." He stopped to reflect for a minute. "I do seem to recall that he got himself into some sort of a contract dispute—a particularly messy one with a producer, and then he just sort of disappeared."

"Maybe he retired."

"No, he wasn't that old. I don't recall the specific details but I think there was some wording in his contract that prevented him from working for anyone else for a period of time. There was probably more to it. I just can't remember."

I smiled. "Well, don't feel bad. That was decades ago."

Mr. Miles nodded. "You're right. And I was a young actor back then with a lot of things on my mind." He smiled. "So, tell me, why are you so interested in Peter Wentworth?"

"I'll tell you in a minute," I said. "Do you remember what his voice sounded like by any chance? I mean—could you do his voice if you wanted?"

"Well, it would help to hear it again, I suppose. But I think I might be able to." He thought to himself for a moment. It was as if he was about to morph into Peter Wentworth. And then a moment later, he had done it. "She sashayed into the office and lowered herself into a chair opposite mine. A black mesh veil covered her face but you could tell she was a real beauty. Totally out of my league. This dame would have put Helen of Troy to shame." He stopped and smiled. "So, how was that?"

That was unbelievable. His voice was so close to the actor in the Sam Solomon series that it was uncanny.

"You *are* the man of a thousand voices," I said.

Mr. Miles laughed. "Well, you're very kind to say so, Charlie."

His near-perfect Peter Wentworth impersonation was all I needed to hear. It was time to unload. I proceeded to outline the entire scenario. I told him about the connection between the recent crime wave and the Sam Solomon series currently airing on the local radio station. I explained to him that Eugene was a full-fledged member of the investigation. I knew that would add credibility. I mentioned the conversation I had with my grandmother, and her offhand comment that the only way we may be able to catch this culprit would be to produce our own episode of the Sam Solomon program. Then I dropped the bomb. I suggested that we transform the current school play into a thirty-minute radio production. I told him that all we had to do was condense the story since it was in a full-length play mode, and change the name of the private detective from Nick Dakota to Sam Solomon. And I added that it was really important for him to emphasize the word *bookie* as much as possible in the new version. It had to become the focal point of the script so that our suspect was likely to choose it for his little word game.

I talked as quickly as I could. I wanted to lay everything out before being interrupted. I asked him to think about other actors in the area who he might be able to convince to join him in the production. I told him that since Eugene was a personal friend of the station owner, we just might be able to use one of their studios to record the program. And that he would hopefully agree to substitute the new production for next week's episode. I avoided eye contact the entire time. I was afraid that if I sensed skepticism on his part, I would start to stumble and lose momentum. When I had finished my pitch, I glanced up at him.

"So, what do you think?" I said. I held my breath. I was so afraid he'd nix the whole idea, and then we'd be stuck listening to the weekly radio programs as they aired, and trying to figure things out on the fly.

"Charlie, I don't know what to say. It's either the craziest idea I've ever heard…or the most fantastic. But you say that Eugene Patterson is involved, huh?"

I nodded.

He put his hands together as if he were praying and brought them to his lips. "I have to think about it. You're asking an awful lot. Trimming this play to thirty minutes and adapting it into a radio program is no small task. Then assembling a stable of actors...not to mention the selection of music and sound effects...and then editing it all together...is a huge undertaking. And you're wanting it to air next Monday night?"

That's exactly what I was thinking but right at that moment, I was afraid to admit to it.

"Do you have any idea what you're asking?"

"I do," I said. "And I wouldn't bother you with this but you're our only hope. If we wait past Monday, another crime will definitely occur. You alone can keep that from happening." I hated to resort to a guilt trip but what else could I do?

Mr. Miles sighed. "Listen, you have Eugene call his friend at the radio station just to see if any of this is even possible. I don't want to start editing this production until I know it's a go."

"So if the station agrees to help out, does that mean you're in?"

He stared forward. "It was 1955. The 46th Street Theater in New York. *Guys and Dolls*. I was the understudy for the character of Nathan Detroit. Moments before the curtain was to rise, the actor playing that role suddenly fell ill. I wasn't even in costume when the director grabbed me and pressed me into service." He smiled. "It was a night I will never forget."

He seemed to be in some sort of a trance. I didn't want to disturb him. And then suddenly he returned to the present.

"In the acting profession, when duty calls, you had better be ready to answer the bell. Because the show must go on." He paused in thought. "All right, Charlie, if you and Eugene can work out the details, I'll do it. I have a few actor friends in the area who'd love a chance to return to the golden age of radio. Now I won't begin until I hear back from you. Let me know ASAP. You got it?"

"I got it, sir. Thank you so much. I'll get back to you first thing in the morning." I ran out of the auditorium to catch the activities bus. Henry wouldn't believe what I was about to tell him. I had done it. I had actually convinced Mr. Miles to help us create the perfect trap for our suspect. As I ran through the playground on my way to the bus stop, I started to worry. What if Eugene thought this was a really bad idea? What if his friend at the radio station said *no* to using his studio and to substituting the show? I had gotten so carried away in pitching my idea to Mr. Miles that I may have jumped the gun.

I remembered a time when the same thing happened to Sam Solomon—with near-fatal results. It was episode #51—*The Knot Guilty Caper*. In this particular case, Sam had been hired by a commodore in the Merchant Marine who suspected one of his captains of smuggling contraband into the country. In order to get close enough to observe his subject, Sam went undercover as a ship's clerk on board the vessel. But when the captain got suspicious of the new mate who was asking too many questions of the crew, he threw him in the brig and interrogated him. Now it's important to note here that before Sam had taken on his new identity, he spent a week learning everything there was to know about the Merchant Marine, or so he thought. The impatient P.I. failed to read all of the materials supplied to him by the commodore. One of those documents contained instructions on how to tie the various knots that every sailor should know. During his interrogation, the captain instructed Sam to tie the most common knot, a Spanish Bowline. When he was unable to do so, he was sentenced to walk the plank. I won't give away the ending, but let's just say that Sam came very close to actually drowning his sorrows.

Chapter 17

The Brass Tax Caper

On the bus ride home with Henry, I replayed my conversation with Mr. Miles. I didn't leave out a single detail. We were nearly at our stops when I finished.

"This is getting better by the minute," he said.

"I know. But I'm a little worried that I spoke too soon. If Eugene can't get the radio station owner to play ball, then we're back to square one."

"Eugene can be pretty persuasive when he needs to be," Henry said. "And once his old buddy at the radio station realizes that he holds the key to stopping the current crime wave, then he's bound to buy in. Heck, it's his civic duty."

"I hope you're right."

Henry hopped off the bus as it pulled up to his stop. Mine was a couple of minutes away. I found myself thinking about our next moves. Although it was nearly dinner time, I desperately needed to talk to Eugene. I knew I didn't have time to ride my bike over to his office, and I wasn't sure if I could find enough privacy to have a telephone conversation with him. I planned to ask my grandmother for help.

When I walked in the door, my mom was busily preparing dinner.

"Is Gram around?" I asked.

"I think she's out in the backyard," my mom said. "I don't know what she's up to though. And, frankly, I don't think I want to know." She smiled.

"Thanks," I said.

"Don't go far. Your dad's due home any minute. And dinner's in a half hour."

"Okay." I walked into the living room, dumped my backpack on the stairs leading up to my room, and headed outside. What I found didn't surprise me. Gram was at it again. This time she was decked out, head to toe, in S.W.A.T. gear, complete with helmet and bulletproof vest. She was holding a walking cane. It was the one she had used a couple of years ago when she fell and hurt her hip. She had it tucked in under her arm like a rifle, and was aiming it in the direction of the garage.

"Hi, Gram, you got a minute?"

She turned away from me and addressed an imaginary colleague. "Felix, maintain our position. I need to relocate another bystander." She dropped her cane and walked over. "I only have a minute, Charlie. What's up?"

"Gram, I gotta talk to Eugene in the worst way. Something big has come up and I need to discuss it with him."

"So, how can I help?"

"I don't have time to ride my bike over there, and I'm worried about calling him. I can't risk being overheard." I stared at my shoes. "I was wondering if you'd be able to drive me over there after dinner. It'd just be for a few minutes."

She lifted my chin with her hand. "Never be afraid to ask me for a favor. Never," she said. "Of course, I'll drive you over there. I assume that this has something to do with your case?"

I nodded. "But what should we tell Mom and Dad?"

"Oh, we'll figure something out. Leave it up to me."

I could hear the overhead garage door opening right at that moment.

"I hate to cut this short," she said, "but I gotta get back to work. We got a hostage crisis on our hands. And it's time to flush out our prey."

When Gram had used the term *flush out*, I didn't think she meant it literally. But as she walked away, she picked up the garden hose.

"Okay, men," she yelled out. "Now!" And with that, she stormed into the garage.

I had a bad feeling about what would happen next…not for me, but for my dad. I decided it would be best to vacate the premises. I wouldn't want to be a witness against my grandmother in court. I ran in the house and up to my room. I slid open the curtains, opened the window that faced the backyard, and watched what promised to be pure entertainment. About thirty seconds later, my dad emerged from the garage in full gallop. He was shielding himself with his briefcase. But it didn't matter. He was soaking wet. A moment later, Gram appeared with hose in hand. She was relentless. My dad was pounded by torrents of water as he sprinted to the back door.

"We got a runner!" she screamed to her fake fellow officers.

My dad stopped and the top of the stairs and lowered his briefcase. "Mom, this time you've gone too far."

I'm not really sure what my dad was thinking by letting down his guard like that. Did he really think that Gram would drop her weapon? That wasn't in the cards. With her victim's upper body now unprotected, Gram continued her assault. With her final blast from the hose, she proceeded to knock my dad's glasses right off his head. It was priceless. I knew I shouldn't be enjoying this so much but I found myself laughing so hard that my dad managed to hear me through the open bedroom window. Needless to say, dinner was filled with sneers and snarls.

*   *   *   *   *

Since no one was much in the mood for conversation, very little was said when Gram announced that she'd be driving me to the library after dinner to do research for an upcoming assignment. It wasn't a total fib. After all, we were on assignment…and we were doing research. I gobbled down the remaining portions of mashed potatoes and meatloaf from my plate and met Gram on the front porch. Moments later, we were mobile. Riding shotgun in Gram's car was an adventure in itself. I had to grab hold of the seat or anything that might keep me from sliding around. Even at her age, she never tired of putting pedal to the metal. And because of the age of her car, a 1978 Chrysler Newport, there was usually some sort of engine or exhaust issues going on. Needless to say, it was the loudest vehicle on the road.

On the way to Eugene's, I laid out my plan of having Mr. Miles rewrite his play into a condensed radio version, and having local actors assist in the production. I asked her how well Eugene knew the radio station owner and if she thought he might be able to convince him to help us out. She wasn't sure how tight the two were, but was confident that considering the gravity of the situation, Mr. Stewart might be inclined to cooperate.

When we got to Eugene's office, Gram allowed me to do the honors of announcing our arrival with the usual knock/scrape/knock password on the door.

"Come in," he called out.

When we entered, Eugene was standing behind his desk. There were opened boxes of Chinese food on the desktop.

"Oh, I hope we're not disturbing you," Gram said.

"Not at all," Eugene said. "I just finished." He began collecting the boxes and dropped them in a wastebasket. "Please sit down. So, what brings you all the way across town tonight?"

Gram nodded at me. It was time to do my thing.

"Well, Eugene," I said. "I have this idea on how we might be able to set a trap for our suspect."

He took a seat and leaned back in his chair. "I'm all ears."

"I was talking to Gram about how this guy had outsmarted us by showing up at the gallery instead of the museum. And I was complaining about the fact that we'd have to wait until Monday for him to make another move. And that even then, there was still no guarantee we'd be able to figure out where he might strike next."

"It's all very frustrating," Eugene said.

"So then Gram said something that got me to thinking. Although I don't think she was serious at the time."

She smiled. "I wasn't."

"She suggested that we somehow create our own Sam Solomon drama that might lead us directly to the suspect's next target."

Eugene put his feet up on his desk. "It's a great idea but I'm afraid you'd need a time machine to pull it off."

"Not necessarily," I said. "You know this play that Mr. Miles wrote and we've been rehearsing at school?"

He nodded.

"Well, I have this idea that if he were able to shorten it to thirty minutes—the length of the Sam Solomon dramas—and change the name of the private eye from Nick Dakota to Sam Solomon, then we might be able to drop key words into the production—and I actually have one in mind—that our suspect would hopefully use to identify the location of his next crime."

Eugene dropped his feet to the floor and sat up in his chair. "Charlie, how do you propose creating a program that's identical to the one already running? Peter Wentworth, the actor who played Sam, died a few years ago. If you used a different voice, the suspect would spot a phony in a minute. He'd know for sure it was a trap."

"You're forgetting one thing, Eugene," Gram said. "Peter Wentworth may have passed away, but his voice lives on."

Eugene scratched his head. "Constance, I'm not following you."

"Our friend, Thad Miles? He's the man of a thousand voices."

"He can do that voice?" he said.

I slid my chair closer to Eugene's. "Perfectly."

"And he'd be willing to do it?" Eugene asked.

"I think I talked him into it," I said.

Eugene stood up and began pacing. "But how are you going to pull this off? You have to find a place to record the new program, and then figure out a way to substitute it for the original."

"That's where you come in, partner," Gram said. "Since you and Ned Stewart are old pals, Charlie and I were hoping you'd be able to convince him to help us. If Thad and his actor friends could use one of the studios at Ned's station, the recording part would be easy."

"And then if you could ask him to run the new Sam Solomon program in place of the one that's supposed to run," I said, "then we'd be in business."

Eugene grinned. "You two have it all figured out, don't you?"

Gram and I smiled at one another.

"Well?" she said as she glanced at Eugene. "Are you in?"

Eugene shrugged. "Why not? It sounds like fun. I'm proud of you, Charlie." He turned to my grandmother. "And Constance, this whole thing was your idea? It's ingenious."

"I'm happy to defer to Charlie on this one," she said. "This is his baby."

Eugene reached into his back pocket and pulled out his wallet. He opened it and began looking for something. Seconds later he fished out a piece of paper. It was frayed and yellowed.

Eugene raised his eyebrows. "Home phone numbers." He smiled as he glanced at the clock on the wall. It read 7:30. "It's still early." He picked up the receiver and dialed. He held his hand up with his fingers crossed.

"Rose? How are you? It's Eugene Patterson. I was wondering if I could speak to Ned."

My grandmother leaned over and winked.

"Hi, Ned," Eugene said. "I apologize for calling you at home but something's up and we need your help."

Gram and I listened as Eugene spent the next few minutes explaining our theories about the Sam Solomon radio series and the recent crime spree. Then once he had baited his line, Eugene set the hook. He told the station owner that without his assistance, another crime would undoubtedly be committed next Tuesday morning. The senior P.I. proposed having the new drama recorded at Ned's studio, and then being inserted in the eleven o'clock slot on Monday night. Although we were only listening to a one-sided conversation, we could sense that Mr. Stewart was slightly resistant.

"I understand," Eugene said. "Can you call me as soon as you hear back?" He paused. "In the meantime, we'll get to work on our end. And again, I don't know how to thank you. So long." He dropped the receiver onto the cradle and grinned. "Looks like we're in business."

"Was there a problem at one point?" Gram said.

"Getting permission to use one of his studios to record the program was the easy part," Eugene said. "The problem has to do with substituting programs. It seems that Ned is contractually obligated to run the next episode. But what he's thinking about doing is still airing ours this Monday at eleven o'clock. And while it's running, his staff will be recording the old Sam Solomon program being fed by satellite. He'll then wait a couple of days, long enough for us to execute our plan and capture our suspect, and then run the drama that was supposed to air in the Monday night time slot. He needs to check with the supplier to get permission to delay it. But he doesn't seem to think it'll be a problem."

"That's great," I said. "So now what?"

Eugene sat back in his chair. "Now we move onto Phase II. We contact Thad and tell him to get to work."

"So, what are you waiting for?" Gram said.

Eugene studied the paper he had pulled from his wallet. He dialed Thaddeus Miles' number and waited.

"Thad? How are you? It's Eugene Patterson."

After a cordial conversation with his old friend, Eugene explained why he had actually called. He told Mr. Miles that the "table was set," and that the safety of the citizenry of Oak Grove was in his hands. He related his conversation with Ned Stewart and asked if there was anything that either he or Gram could do to help out. It was a relatively short discussion. Apparently Mr. Miles had shifted into what Eugene later described as "panic mode." It seemed that the drama teacher loved…what else, drama.

As I rode home with Gram, I couldn't ever remember feeling more satisfied. It was as if everything was falling into place. Everyone who I had hoped would step up and help out, had done so. You couldn't ask for much more than that. I recalled another time when all the puzzle pieces fit neatly together. It happened for Sam Solomon in Episode #53—*The Brass Tax Caper*. In this particular story, Sam had been hired by a trumpet player with the Chicago Symphony Orchestra who claimed that his paycheck was short each week. It seems that the symphony director, who was responsible for the financial health of the orchestra, had fallen on hard times due to a gambling addiction. He had begun siphoning off symphony funds to finance his afternoons at the racetrack.

Sam immediately sought out the services of a financial advising group to determine how much money had been taken. The accountants at the firm were so meticulous in their investigation that Sam not only discovered where the trumpet player's missing wages had gone, but he was also able to recover thousands of dollars for other musicians in the orchestra who had no idea they had been cheated. Each step of the investigation had been carried out in a flawless fashion. Every aspect of the case had fallen into place beautifully. It was one of Sam's finest performances, and one that led to many more assignments.

Chapter 18

The Rising Son Caper

I met up with Henry and Scarlett on the playground before school the next morning. I updated them on everything that had taken place the night before at Eugene's office. Henry couldn't get enough. He could feel the tension building and wanted to be included in every step of the action as things progressed. I wasn't quite prepared for Scarlett's reaction though.

"So, what does that mean for *our* play?" she asked. "Is Mr. Miles just going to cancel it so he can work on some radio script?"

"I don't know," I said. "I never thought about that."

"Even if he does, big deal," Henry added. "This is a heck of a lot more important than a bunch of six-graders getting up on a stage and pretending they can act."

Scarlett sneered at Henry. It was either because he had casually dismissed the production, or because he might have implied that the entire cast, including Scarlett, was without talent. Apparently the truce was over.

"I don't know why I ever thought being nice to you was a good idea," she said.

Here we go again, I thought. Well, it was fun while it lasted.

Scarlett glared at Henry, spun around, and headed into school. Henry just shrugged. He wasn't what you would call overly sensitive.

"So, what's my role on Monday night?" he asked. "A little surveillance work maybe?"

"I don't really know yet," I said. "Eugene and I haven't discussed where we should set up a stakeout after the program airs. But don't get your hopes up. Last Monday they wouldn't take me with them because it was a school night. Eugene, my grandmother, and their friend, Chicken Bone, handled it themselves."

"That's not fair," he said. "This is our case. They can't just squeeze us out like that. If they won't take us along, we'll just have to get there ourselves."

I wanted to agree with him but there was one important factor that he wasn't considering.

"Henry, the show ends at 11:30 at night. As much as I'd like to work the stakeout, how can we go out on our own? It's past curfew."

"Oh, bummer," he said. "You're right."

But the more I thought about it, the more I realized that in the past I had simply ignored curfew. Like when we went to Rupert Olsen's farm to save those birds. Or the time I snuck onto the Camp Phoenix compound. But somehow this seemed different. Before we were on our own. We were calling the shots. This time, however, we were working in tandem with Eugene and Gram. I knew it was best to fall in line and be a good soldier but I really didn't like the idea of missing out on another stakeout. Hopefully we'd be able to convince them to include us this time.

I fully expected the rest of the school day to drag on as usual, but for whatever reason, this one flew by. Before we knew it, we were all assembled in the auditorium after school waiting for Mr. Miles. I wondered if he'd tell the other kids about his new assignment. I wasn't sure if he'd be able to handle both—directing the school play, and adapting his production into a radio drama. It didn't take long to find out. When Mr. Miles appeared for rehearsal, he would always have his copy of the play tucked under one arm. But when he arrived today, he wasn't carrying a thing.

"Please gather round, cast. I have an announcement to make," he said.

I could tell by the looks on the faces of the other kids that no one knew what was coming.

"As will sometimes happen in the theater," he said, "I have been called away to help doctor up another script. But don't worry, it won't change things much for us. It will just delay things for a few days."

"How long?" Stephanie said.

"What is today? Wednesday?" he seemed uncertain. "We will resume our regular rehearsal next Tuesday at this same time. And, so, for the next few days, you'll be on your own. If any of you care to meet here during this time to rehearse, you are more than welcome to do so. I can ask a teacher's aide to supervise if necessary. Now I realize that this little interruption will give us one less week to prepare before opening night but these things happen. Duty calls. And like good little thespians, we will make it work."

"So what exactly will you be doing?" the hisser asked.

"Brian, I'm afraid I'm not at liberty to say at this time. I wish I could." Mr. Miles thought to himself for a moment. "Suffice it to say that by this time next week, you should all know why I had to take leave. My sincere apologies." And with that, he exited the stage.

Scarlett wandered over. She folded her arms and began tapping her foot. This could only mean one thing—an unpleasant exchange was to follow.

"Charlie Collier, I hold you personally responsible for all of this. If we stumble and fall on our faces on opening night, it will be all your fault."

Now that wasn't very fair of her. If she wanted to blame me for losing a week's worth of play practice, then she had better be prepared to thank me if we manage to catch the person responsible for burglarizing businesses in town.

"How is it my fault?" I said. "I'm just trying to help folks."

"Why don't you quit worrying about some two-bit school play and start thinking about how you're going to help us solve this caper?" Henry said.

"I'm not sure I want to work on this one," she replied.

Henry slapped me on the arm. "Looks like it's just you and me again, partner."

I knew that Scarlett would eventually rethink her last statement and rejoin us on this quest. That was her pattern. Henry would say something to upset her, and she'd want out. But as soon as he seemed happy about her departure, she'd suddenly want back in.

"C'mon," Henry said. "Let's get outa here."

I reluctantly followed him out of the building and over to the bus stop, but I kept thinking about how things had ended with Scarlett. I was worried that if she sat this one out, she might consider dropping out of the agency altogether. And I was dreading that. I wanted as much time with her as possible.

On the bus ride home, Henry and I decided to head over to Eugene's to discuss the case. Since Eugene wasn't familiar with the plot of the play, we would need to fill him in. We also needed to identify key words from the production, and analyze them in order to determine where the next crime might take place. Although that may have already been done for us. You just couldn't ignore the obvious references to *bookie* throughout Mr. Miles' production. For my money, it was the magic word. And I was hoping that our suspect would see things the same way.

Henry and I met up about a half hour later in a park about midway between our two houses. We pointed our trusty steeds—our bikes, that is—in the direction of Eugene's office and headed out. We made it there in about forty minutes. We parked our bikes in the back of the building and climbed the stairs to Eugene's office. About halfway up, Henry tapped me on the shoulder.

"With all the time we've been putting into play practice and now this case, I completely forgot about something."

"What?"

He smiled and raised his eyebrows.

I knew what was coming—a brain teaser.

"A murderer is condemned to death," Henry said. "He has to choose between three rooms. In the first one, there's a raging fire. In the second, a dozen assassins with loaded guns. And in the third, there's a group of lions who haven't eaten in two years. Which room would you choose?"

"We don't have a lot of time today," I said. "Is this really necessary?"

"Did you ever notice that whenever you get stumped, you always come up with some lame reason why shouldn't have to answer the question?"

I grinned. "I'm just buying myself a little time. That's all."

He laughed. "I knew it. Now gimme an answer."

I repeated the choices. "The first room has a raging fire. The second room is filled with assassins. And the third room has lions in it who haven't eaten in two years." I thought about it for less than ten seconds. This was an easy one. "I'll take the third room."

"Remember, those lions are pretty hungry," he said. "They haven't eaten for a while. You wouldn't last more than a minute."

"I'll take my chances," I said. "If they haven't eaten in two years? They'd all be dead."

Henry let out a long, painful groan. "C'mon," he said as he nudged me. "We don't have much time." He never was a good loser.

We continued up the stairway leading to Eugene's office. And just as we were about to use the secret password to gain entry, the door opened. It was Eugene.

"Hi, guys," he said.

"Hi, Eugene," I said.

"Hi, Mr. Patterson," Henry replied.

"It's nice to see you again, Henry."

"It looks like you're on your way out," I said. "We should have called first."

Eugene opened the door and motioned us in. "Don't worry. It can wait. So, are you here to discuss the case?"

"Yeah," I said. "Mr. Miles cancelled play practice for the next few days to work on the radio drama. We just figured we could tell you the story and then try to figure out our suspect's next target."

Eugene sat down and pointed to a pair of chairs next to his desk. "Okay, let 'er rip. I seem to recall that you had mentioned the plot briefly a few days ago. But why don't you give me all the details."

For the next couple of minutes, Henry and I relayed the entire story of Mr. Miles' play along with plot and subplots. We offered brief character descriptions as well. We tried to share every aspect of the production that we could remember.

"It sure sounds like the bookie is the key to this story," Eugene said. "You must have said that word twenty times."

"I don't think there's any question about it," I said. "Once Rebecca Ramsey is arrested, which happens in the first five minutes, the rest of the time they're trying to find this bookie."

Eugene folded his arms. "Okay, then, let's assume that our suspect will focus on that word. He may try to find a double meaning for it. That seems to be his modus operandi." Eugene thought to himself for a minute. "So the key word is *bookie*. What can we do with that? What comes to mind?"

"How about *gambler*?" Henry said.

"And bookie is short for *bookmaker*," I added.

"Good," Eugene said. "And how about *numbers runner*…or *tipster*…or even *tout*. I'm afraid I'm dating myself with that last one."

We all stopped to consider the list of words that had been tossed out. Within moments, it became clear that we had struck out. Nothing was coming.

"I think we're trying too hard," Henry said. "We're ignoring the obvious. When you look at the word *bookie*, the first thing you see is the word *book*. Why don't we concentrate on that?"

"Yeah," I said. "That makes perfect sense."

"And if that's the case," Henry said. "We'd have to assume this guy'll probably rob a bookstore, right?"

Eugene sat up in his chair. "I like that idea," he said. "Okay, then, bookstore, it is."

"Then again," I said. "It could just as easily be the library. Maybe more so. That place is loaded with books too." I found myself trying to think like our burglar. If I had decided to steal books as my next crime, where would I go, a bookstore or a library? And then it hit me. Of course. There was only one answer that made sense.

"I got it," I said. "There's a much better chance that he'll hit the library than a bookstore."

"What makes you say that?" Eugene asked.

I smiled confidently. "If our crook chooses *bookie* for his little wordplay game, and if he turns *bookie* into *book* as we're hoping, what types of books do you think he'd try to steal?"

"What difference does it make?" Eugene said. "A book is a book."

"I don't think so," I said. "This guy isn't just a thief. He's on a mission. He's trying to make some sort of statement. He's not going to grab just any old book." I waited to see if either Henry or Eugene would figure out where I was headed.

Henry jumped out of his chair. "He'll steal Sam Solomon books!"

"Exactly," I said.

Eugene stood up and walked over to the window. "Okay, let's say you're right. But why the library? He can just as easily find those in a bookstore."

"Eugene, there's over a hundred books in that series. And if you walk into any bookstore, you'd be lucky to find, at best, no more than a half dozen on the shelves. And a lot of times, you won't find any. You have to special order them. Trust me, I've had to do it." I paused for effect. "But there *is* one place where you can find the entire series."

Henry smiled. "The library!"

I nodded. "This guy has it in for Sam Solomon. Why? We're not sure. But it only makes sense that he'd want to get his hands on as many of those books as possible. And the only way to guarantee that is to head to the library."

"I just don't buy it, Charlie," Eugene said. Look at all of the places our suspect has targeted—a Persian rug store, a bakery, a pet shop, and a high-end art gallery. And what do those locations have in common? They're all commercial establishments. Besides stealing a rug, or a dog, or a painting, or whatever else, our mystery man also jimmied the cash registers. First he stole something as part of his word game, then he also made sure to fill his pockets with some green before he left. It would make no sense to hit the library. How much cash would be on hand? A few bucks from some overdue book fines? In my opinion, we're not dealing with someone who loves word games, all we're dealing with is a common thief. He's just using the game angle to throw us off. It's got to be the bookstore. It's the only thing that makes sense."

I had to make Eugene see things differently. "I don't believe he's a common thief," I said. "I think just the opposite. I think he's some misguided soul with a Sam Solomon vendetta. That's what's driving him. The money he's stealing? That's just an afterthought. And if I'm right, then he can make a much stronger statement by hitting the library where he'll find the entire series, than by visiting a bookstore where there might be a handful of books, or maybe none at all."

Henry turned to Eugene. "It kinda does make sense."

Eugene sat back down at his desk and folded his hands. "Charlie, I hate to overrule you but I'm afraid I'm going to have to," he said. "Since we have a manpower shortage, there's no way we can run multiple surveillance operations. If you kids were available to help out, then maybe we could try watching both bookstores in town as well as the library, but since it'll be after midnight on a school night, that's just not possible. I'm sorry."

"Is there any way I can make you see things my way?" I said.

"I'm afraid not," he said. "I'm going to have to ask you to defer to me on this one. Decades of experience tells me this is the way to proceed. Can I count on you to support me on this?"

I nodded…reluctantly. I knew that Eugene was the master private detective. He had solved hundreds of cases—maybe thousands—in his career. Not to mention a successful stint with Naval Intelligence. This man was a legend. And as much as I really didn't want to, I thought it best to be a good soldier and fall in line. Maybe he will turn out to be right. We'd know soon enough.

Since it was getting late, Henry and I decided to head home. We knew that we would probably need to meet up with Eugene at least one more time to work out the specifics of the stakeout, even though we wouldn't be part of it. Oak Grove had two bookstores—an independent one that had been operating for years, and a larger bookseller that was part of a retail chain. It had only been in town for a few months. I was assuming that Eugene, Gram, and Chicken Bone would find a way to keep an eye on both.

As we pedaled home, I kept thinking about the fact that no one would be watching the library after the Sam Solomon program aired on Monday night. I understood Eugene's rationale—the library wasn't like all of the other crime scenes. I got all of that. But what if Eugene was wrong, then what? Then we will have wasted hours and hours of Mr. Miles' time, not to mention everyone else who has been, or soon would be, offering assistance. I knew that I should follow Eugene's advice and forget about this library business. After all, he was the expert…the wise old sage. Everything I had learned up until now about this business was telling me to trust the pros—the people who had paid their dues in this industry—and to just follow orders. But I was having a hard time buying in.

I wasn't sure how to proceed. So I thought of a time when Sam Solomon was torn between taking the advice of his personal mentor versus doing things his own way. It happened in Episode #65—*The Rising Son Caper*. Sam had been contacted by his old boss, Amos Poindexter. Amos asked Sam to do him a favor—a favor that Sam felt could produce disastrous consequences. Amos asked him to take on his son, Julius Poindexter, as his new apprentice. Sam had watched Julius grow up and he wasn't impressed. The young man lacked initiative and confidence, and was the last person you'd want to have your back in a dangerous situation. Sam wanted to decline, but it was Amos, who years earlier had taken on a green detective by the name of Sam Solomon, and had given him a chance that no one else would.

As you might guess, Sam took on young Julius and tried to teach him the ropes of the P.I. business. Julius turned out to be a dud at surveillance work, and nearly got his boss killed due to a sloppy performance one night. But in the office, the young man proved to be a wonder at analyzing evidence and converting it into useful data. So, on the one hand, Sam had been right. But on the other hand, so had Amos. Was it possible that Eugene and I were both right? I wasn't sure…and I still had no idea of how I could persuade him to see things my way.

Chapter 19

The Pair o' Dice Caper

On Thursday morning, Henry and I met on the bus. I had to make sure that he was still in my camp. I needed him to support my theory that the library was a bona fide location for a stakeout. He had to help me convince Eugene to add a surveillance team on Monday night. The more I thought about it, the more I was certain that I was right. I had a bad feeling however that Eugene might win this one, but I decided that I wouldn't go down without a fight.

When we got to school, we found Scarlett on the playground. I told her about our conversation with Eugene. I made it point to share both hypotheses with her—mine and Eugene's. I was interested in knowing where she stood. But instead of buying into either one, she just shrugged. It seemed as though she really didn't have her heart in this case. She still seemed miffed about play practice having been cancelled because of it.

It turned out to be a relatively uneventful day at school. The highlight of the afternoon, as was usually the case, came during the final period—Mrs. Jansen's science class. She walked into the classroom holding a glass of water about three-quarters full. She set it down on the front of her desk, and then walked over to a small table-top refrigerator against the wall. She opened it and came out holding a tray of ice cubes. She dug one of the ice cubes out with her fingertips and held it up for all of us to see.

"Watch me very carefully, class," she said as she dropped the ice cube into the glass of water. "Now, who can answer this question: when the ice cube has completely melted, will the level of the water have increased, decreased, or remain unchanged?"

Sherman raised his hand.

"Yes, Sherman."

"Can you at least tell us if this is a trick question or not?" he said.

She grinned. "No trick here. The answer is predicated on a scientific principle."

"That counts me out," he said dejectedly.

"Now, Sherman," she said. "Don't sell yourself short. We talked about this principle about two months ago. I just wanted to see who remembered it. Think real hard now. You might surprise yourself and come up with it. You can check your notes if you want."

The look on Sherman's face suggested that he had little confidence in himself, or in the quality of his note-taking. A moment later, Danny Reardon slowly raised his hand.

"Danny, what do you think?" Mrs. Jansen said.

"Well, I can't remember what principle you're talking about but I just seem to think that once the ice cube melts, the water level has to be higher. And I'm not really basing that on anything but a pure guess."

Mrs. Jansen picked up the glass and began walking up and down each aisle. "I'm not saying you're wrong, Danny, but I would like to see someone reference that principle in their answer." By the time Mrs. Jansen had completed her journey, another minute had passed. "Any final thoughts before I refresh your memory?"

I knew the answer but I didn't recall the name of the principle. I wasn't sure if I should share my answer since it was incomplete. The decision was soon taken out of my hands.

"Charlie," she said, "can you help us out with this one?"

I rose from my seat. "I know the answer but I don't remember the name of the guy you're looking for."

"Well, that's a start," she said. "I'll take whatever you can give me."

For some reason the stares seemed a little friendlier than normal. It must have had something to do with the fact that I couldn't remember the guy's name. I guess it made me seem more like everyone else.

"The water level will remain the same," I said. "And it has something to do with the fact that the ice cube will displace its own weight. I remember something about *an immersed object is buoyed up by the weight of the fluid it displaces.* And so, in our example, when the ice cube melts, the water in the glass will be the same level that it was after you dropped it in."

Mrs. Jansen grinned, but before she could praise me, she was interrupted.

"Archimedes!" Scarlett yelled out. "I remember it now. It was Archimedes' Principle."

"Well done…to both of you," Mrs. Jansen said. "Now that was a real team effort."

Did you hear that, Scarlett? I wanted to say—*We do make a pretty good team. Maybe we should work together more often.* I let out a long sigh. Who was I kidding? Like I would ever have the guts to actually say that out loud. My only hope was to get her more interested in this crime spree case so that we might be able to spend a little time together trying to tackle it.

After the bell sounded, Henry and I decided to pay a visit to Mr. Miles. We were wondering how he was progressing with the rewrite of his script. When we arrived at his office, the door was closed. We weren't certain if he was in or not.

"Maybe we shouldn't interrupt him," Henry said.

"But don't you want to know what's going on?" I said. "Suppose he can't get it done on time. That changes everything, and we'd need to know that."

"All right, I guess." Henry seemed unsure. Just to be safe, he hid behind me. And considering our body types, it was relatively easy for him to disappear that way.

I knocked lightly. At first we heard nothing. Then there were footsteps, and seconds later, the door flew open.

"Charlie, what a coincidence," Mr. Miles. "I was just thinking about you."

"Oh, really?" I said.

The smile on Mr. Miles's face suddenly faded. "I was trying to remember why I had agreed to perform this impossible task." He seemed frustrated. "Killing two-thirds of your story, and still have it make sense is torturous."

"I'm afraid to ask how it's coming. Or maybe you've already answered the question."

"Come on in," he said. And just as he was about to close the door, he noticed Henry. "You don't need to hide, Mr. Cunningham. I don't hold you responsible for this."

"Thanks," Henry said.

Mr. Miles walked around his desk and plopped down into his chair.

"Well, what are you waiting for, gentlemen? Sit down."

Right at that moment, I was second guessing my decision to pay Mr. Miles a visit. I knew what we were asking of him, but I wasn't really expecting him to be angry with us.

"If this is a bad time," I said, "we can come back."

Mr. Miles seemed to sense our discomfort. He let out a long sigh and smiled.

"I don't mean to seem short with you, boys. It's just that I'm not as young as I used to be, and working on deadline is something I haven't done for quite some time. But when I get frustrated, as I've been the past couple of days, I keep telling myself that's it's for a good cause."

"A good cause? Are you kidding?" I said. "Mr. Miles, because of your contribution, you could single-handedly be responsible for catching the Oak Grove serial burglar."

"Oh, is that what they're calling him now?" he asked.

"No...I just came up with that."

He sat back in his chair. "So, what can I do for you?"

Henry chimed in. "We were just wondering if there's anything we can do for *you*." That wasn't exactly why we were here. But considering Mr. Miles' state of mind, it was some pretty quick thinking on Henry's part.

"If I keep to my schedule," he said, "we should make it." He picked up a pad of paper from his desk. "My plan is to finish up the script by sometime tonight. Then I need to run off copies and distribute them to the cast by noon tomorrow. On Saturday at 10:00 am, we meet at the studios of WOAK for an all-day recording session. On Sunday morning, we choose music and sound effects. And between Sunday afternoon and Monday evening at 11:00 pm, a technician will edit it all together."

"About the only thing on that entire list that we're qualified to do," I said, "is run off copies of the script for you. Would that help?"

Mr. Miles reflected momentarily. "That would be great, but you'd have to get here early...before school...to make copies. Can you do that?"

"The bus won't get us here early enough," Henry said. "But I'm sure one of our parents can drop us off."

"Okay, then, it's a plan," he said. "Can you be here at about 7:30?"

We nodded.

Mr. Miles got up, walked over to the door and opened it. "Great. Now off you go. I have work to do."

Henry and I sprinted to the bus stop and managed to get there seconds before the bus pulled away. We navigated our way down the aisle and found a seat away from the crowd. I wanted to talk to Henry in private.

"So you're gonna back me on this library business, right?" I said.

"Sure, but I don't think it'll do any good. Eugene sounds like he's made up his mind."

"If he refuses to give up on the bookstore idea, then we have to at least get him to agree to *add* the library as an additional stakeout location," I said. "Not only do I think that our perp will actually show up there, I have an ulterior motive as well."

Henry's eyes narrowed. "I'm listening."

I paused as two kids sat down right behind us. I leaned in closer to Henry. Maybe I was getting paranoid but I wanted to make sure that we weren't overheard.

"If we have any chance of being asked to join the others on Monday night, then there has to be at least one more location to stake out. Eugene, Gram and Chicken Bone plan to cover the bookstores. But if we can convince them to keep an eye on the library as well, then they're gonna need another surveillance team—namely us."

Henry shook his head. "So that's what this is all about? This library theory of yours is just an excuse to join the stakeout?"

"No, no, no," I said. "I really do believe the suspect will show up there. The only place where you're absolutely guaranteed to find Sam Solomon books on the shelves is the library." I lowered my voice. "Henry, it just about killed me not to be on the stakeout last Monday night. I can't let it happen again. I won't let it happen again."

Our conversation was interrupted when we reached our stops, but continued during the bike ride to Eugene's office. Henry promised to support me, but he wasn't confident that it would do any good. When we arrived at Eugene's, we found him on the phone with Mr. Miles. He was trying to determine how his old buddy was coming along with the rewrite. By his reaction, he had apparently gotten the same response we had.

"Thad, relax. Just relax," he said. "This thing doesn't have to be perfect." Eugene made a face. "Okay, why don't you call me when it's done. Good luck." He hung up the phone and rolled his eyes. "That's way too much drama for me." He stood up, stretched, and motioned for us to have a seat. "Kind of surprised to see you guys. I thought we had our plan in place."

Not as far as I was concerned. "I was hoping you might reconsider going to the library," I said.

"What about the library?" he asked.

"You know...about setting up a stakeout there, as well as the bookstores."

"Oh, oh, oh, sorry," he said. "No, Charlie, I'm afraid I haven't changed my mind. It's all about available bodies. Your grandmother and I will be at Anderson's Bookshop, and Chicken Bone and his brother-in-law, T-Bone, will be watching the big bookstore over on Fullerton. We're already stretched pretty thin."

"Don't forget about us," Henry said. "We're not worried about curfew or anything."

Eugene smiled. "Well, I am. And even if we weren't talking about the middle of the night, I'd never allow you kids to go over there by yourselves. It's just too dangerous."

"And you don't have any other associates you could ask to help out?" I asked.

"Not at this late date," he said. "If we had more time, we probably could have recruited a small army, but there's just no way that..." Eugene stopped in mid-sentence. He put his finger to his lips. "Unless..."

"Unless what?" I said.

Eugene slid open his top desk drawer and pulled out a ring of keys. "C'mon, boys, I have an idea."

Seconds later we found ourselves in the backseat of Eugene's hearse driving through town. We had tossed our bikes in the back, in the spot where a casket would normally sit. Eugene turned on Front Street and stopped in front of the Oak Grove Police Station.

"Of course," I said. "The police can cover the library for us." Even though I was dying for a chance to be included in the Monday night stakeout, I realized that it was far more important that we catch this guy than for me to be a member of the surveillance team. I was more than happy to defer to the police. If they bought in, we would certainly welcome their manpower and expertise.

"Our job, gentlemen, is to convince the authorities that the culprit picks his targets based on the storyline of the Sam Solomon programs," Eugene said.

"Why wouldn't they believe us?" Henry asked. "It's a great theory."

"To them it might seem like a series of coincidences," Eugene said. "Let's go find out."

We exited the vehicle, climbed the stone steps, and headed into the police station. We waited while Eugene spoke to the officer at the front desk. A minute later, Eugene was motioning us to follow him. We walked down a hallway and into an office marked *Detective Don Kent*. The officer immediately greeted us with a smile.

"Eugene Patterson, you old son-of-a-gun, what brings you in here?"

"Well, my friends and I need a little assistance."

Detective Kent extended his hand to Eugene and then to Henry and me. "Don Kent…nice to meet you."

"This is Charlie Collier and Henry Cunningham," Eugene said.

"Hi, boys. Why don't you all have a seat. So, Eugene, how can I be of service?"

"It has to do with this series of unsolved burglaries."

The mid-fifties detective shook his head. "We've been working on this case day and night for a month now, with nothing to show for it. I suppose you have a tip for us, huh? You'll be number…" He picked up a pad of paper from his desk. "…157."

"Well, it's more of a theory than a tip," Eugene replied.

Detective Kent put his hands behind his head and sat back in his chair. "Let me hear it."

And so for the next ten minutes or so, the three of us laid out the rationale behind our theory. We started with the first Sam Solomon program and the theft at the Persian rug shop. Then we recounted the plots of the next three programs and the burglaries that followed. We explained how the suspect seemed to be playing a word association game that was actually predicting the location of his crimes. Then we talked about Mr. Miles' connection and how he was helping create a similar program that just might lead the culprit right into a trap. When we had finished, the detective leaned forward.

"So you've got this guy pegged as kind of a copycat, is that it?" the detective said.

"Sort of a copycat with a twist," I said. "He's making us work for it."

Detective Kent smiled. "What you've got here, fellas, would make a pretty good book. But what you're missing is the hard evidence."

"What about the SS cards?" I asked.

"I suppose they could stand for Sam Solomon," he said. "But they could just as easily be the guy's initials. Some crooks are pretty vain, you know." The detective folded his hands and rested them on top of his desk. "I'm not completely dismissing your theory, and I'll tell you why." He slid open the top desk drawer and pulled out a book. I recognized it immediately. It was Sam Solomon, Episode #5—*The Steamed Carats Caper*. "We found this at the last crime scene." He handed it to Eugene.

Eugene held the book up to the light, and stuck his finger into an indentation in the front cover.

"There's a hole through the entire book," he said.

"That's because we also found this sticking in it," Detective Kent said as he pulled a large kitchen knife from the same drawer. "If you notice, you'll see that our suspect stuck the knife right through the picture of the character on the front cover—like he was stabbing him or something. This guy's a real sicko."

Eugene flipped through the pages as he examined the hole. "And you found no prints on the book or the knife, I assume?" He set the book on the edge of the desk.

The detective shook his head. "They were clean."

"Then all of this proves our theory," I said. "This case is definitely connected to Sam Solomon. It's almost as if this guy is trying to kill Sam." I picked up the book. "Look at this, Eugene," as I pointed to the hole. "This guy's gonna want to continue his assault on the book series. And the library is his best bet of finding them."

"I just don't know," Eugene said.

"Can I see that, Charlie?" Henry said as he motioned for the book. He stuck his finger right through the hole and began twirling it around. "If you ask me, I'd say we're dealing with a real nut job."

"I'll give you that," the detective replied. "Our suspect is clearly unstable. But we're still missing physical evidence. We have no fingerprints or DNA. We need more than hunches."

"I guess that means you're not going to put a detail on the library Monday night?" Eugene said.

"Listen, Eugene, I just don't have the officers to spare—and especially overnight. I'm afraid I can't help you. I wish I could."

"I know it sounds pretty crazy," Eugene said. "Thanks anyway."

And so we were back where we started. It was apparent that the police were unconvinced that the perp was somehow influenced by the radio dramas. And that meant there wouldn't be anyone watching the library. Eugene had made it pretty clear that he'd never allow Henry and me to go over there alone. So it seemed that this quest of mine had come to an end. And although it was killing me to do so, something was telling me to just back off and allow Eugene to run this investigation the way he saw fit. Having been overruled reminded me of a time when Sam Solomon had taken a stand only to be outvoted.

It happened in Episode #54—*The Pair o' Dice Caper*. In an unusual partnership, Sam had been contacted by the Chicago Police superintendent to assist the force in a series of gambling raids on the city's south side. The problem had gotten so bad that the department's resources were stretched dangerously thin. The superintendent decided to team up with local private detectives, much to the chagrin of the rank and file. Veteran officers wanted nothing to do with *cop wannabes*, as they referred to them. Sam took it all in stride. But when the gambling task force had to decide where to position their officers for an all-night stakeout and possible raid, Sam's suggestions were dismissed. There was just no way that a private cop would be telling the boys in blue how to do their jobs.

And so, while the bulk of the force sat outside a seedy bar on Ashland Avenue, Sam hid behind a dumpster alongside an abandoned warehouse on West Ogden. As it turned out, the veteran P.I. had guessed right, but his decision to conduct his own one-man raid was shortsighted. He was captured by the gamblers, and had it not been for one lone officer who shared Sam's views on the stakeout location, it might have been his final roll of the dice.

Chapter 20

The Ill Will Caper

With Friday morning upon us, we were only three days away from the moment of truth. I had asked my dad the night before if he would mind driving Henry and me to school early today. He reluctantly agreed. It wasn't that my dad wasn't in the habit of doing favors for people, it was just that he was relatively inflexible—and he'd be the first person to tell you that. Whenever something came up that wasn't on his day planner, it would throw him for a loop. So the thought of an unscheduled stop that would force a detour was asking a lot. But thanks to a dose of guilt carefully injected by my mom, we managed to secure the necessary transportation.

When we arrived at Mr. Miles' office, the door was closed and locked. There didn't appear to be any lights on inside, but just to be sure, Henry got down on his knees and peeked under the door.

"Nothing," he said. "I guess we'll just have to wait."

We dropped our backpacks to the floor and sat down with our backs up against the office door. And within seconds, we heard sounds coming from inside.

"Did you hear that?" I said, as we quickly hopped to our feet.

"It might be a prowler," Henry said. "What should we do?"

But before we were able to take action, the door flew open and standing before us was something we were completely unprepared for. Holding the door frame with both hands was Mr. Miles. His hair was mussed and his shirt tail hanging out as he rubbed the sleep from his eyes.

"What time is it?" he said. He appeared somewhat dazed.

"Just past seven thirty," Henry said.

"Oh, dear," he said as he tucked his shirt back into his pants. "I can't believe I fell asleep." He ran his fingers through his hair. "The last thing I remember is looking at the clock. It was two-thirty. I had just finished the script. I put my head down for a second. And that was it. This is so embarrassing."

I couldn't understand why Mr. Miles was embarrassed. I fell asleep in my clothes all the time. And it was pretty normal to wear the same clothes the next day. But this apparently was unacceptable for someone of his stature. I couldn't ever remember seeing him in anything but a fresh, clean, colorful outfit each and every day.

Mr. Miles motioned for us to come into his office as he plopped down in his desk chair.

"Did I hear you say you finished the script?" Henry said.

Mr. Miles nodded.

"And you remembered to emphasize the word bookie throughout the entire story, right?" I said.

"Heavens, yes," Mr. Miles replied. "I must have mentioned it fifty times. And for good measure, I managed to work it into the title."

Now that was an excellent idea. Why hadn't I thought of it?

"So, what's the new title?" Henry asked.

Mr. Miles smiled. He seemed proud of what he was about to tell us. "Okay now, get this," he said. "You know how bookies like to lay low. The last thing they want is for the police to find them with a pocketful of illegal betting slips. A typical bookie would usually maintain an alias. He'd pretend to be in another line of work to throw off suspicion. So try this for the title: *You Can't Judge a Bookie by its Cover Caper.*" He raised his eyebrows hoping for our approval.

"It's brilliant," I said.

"Glad to hear that." Mr. Miles turned and faced his computer. "I'm going to run off twelve copies of the script. That should be plenty. Charlie, make sure there's paper in that printer."

I checked and nodded.

"Now I need you boys to refill the printer when it runs out, to collate these, and then to staple them. Got it?"

"Got it," we said together.

"Just leave the copies on my desk, and please close and lock the door when you're done."

"Don't worry," Henry said. "We'll take care of everything."

Mr. Miles got up and was just about to leave when he caught a glimpse of himself in the mirror on the back of his door.

"Oh, my," he said. "What a sight." He spun around to face us. "I have to go home and get cleaned up. Not a word of this to anyone, gentlemen. I have an image to maintain. Promise?"

"I didn't see anything unusual," I said. "Did you, Henry?"

"Nope, just a typical day at good old Roosevelt."

Mr. Miles winked, smiled and shuffled out. Finding a teacher asleep in his office would actually have been a pretty good story to spread around, but Henry and I never once betrayed his trust. And how could we? Mr. Miles was doing us such a huge favor. We owed him our complete confidence.

After organizing and stapling the scripts, we piled them on the desk and made a hasty exit, barely making it in time for our first period. The remainder of the day was uneventful, and before we knew it, we were back at Mr. Miles' office minutes after the final bell sounded. When we arrived, we found him in a royal blue blazer, white slacks, with a red ascot around his neck. I wasn't sure if he was trying to achieve the patriotic look, but he sure had done it. Unlike early this morning, every hair was in place, and you could detect just a hint of after shave. Now that was the Mr. Miles we had come to know and love.

"Wonderful job, boys," he said as soon as he noticed us in the doorway. "I'm happy to report that the all of the actors now their scripts and they are enthusiastically poring over them."

"If there anything else we can do to help?" I said.

"Can't think of anything at the moment."

"So, tomorrow you record?" Henry asked.

"Yes, at 10 am over at the radio station." He paused. "Hey, if you want to, you might ask your parents to drop you off over there. I think you'll get a real kick out of watching some professionals in action. And you might just learn something."

"Really?" I said. "Now that would be sensational."

Mr. Miles stood, removed his jacket, carefully placed it on a wooden hanger, and hung it on a hook on the wall behind him.

Henry and I turned to leave.

"Oh, boys," Mr. Miles said. "Thanks. And I don't mean for the copies. I want to thank you for the opportunity to jump back into the saddle. Some of the most exciting times in my life occurred when I was doing live radio drama back in the forties and fifties. It was a wonderful experience. Thanks for making this happen."

"It's our pleasure, sir, and thank you," I said.

As Henry and I made our way to the bus stop, we decided that we would do whatever it took to get ourselves over to the radio station to watch Mr. Miles and his friends perform tomorrow morning. On our way to the bus, we noticed Scarlett getting into her mom's car.

"Hey, maybe we should tell her about the recording session," I said.

"Nah, she won't be interested," Henry said.

But I knew better. After watching her on stage the past couple of weeks, I had a feeling that she'd jump at a chance to watch actors doing their thing.

"Hey, Scarlett," I yelled out.

"Yeah?" she said. She almost seemed to be preparing herself for bad news of some kind.

"Mr. Miles and his actor friends are recording the new Sam Solomon program tomorrow morning over at the radio station. He invited Henry and me to watch. I'm sure he wouldn't mind if you came too."

She seemed to light up. "Really? What time?"

"Ten."

She leaned in to the car. "Mom, is it all right? And can you take me over there tomorrow morning?"

"I guess so," her mom said, as she slid over to the passenger side and stuck her head out the window. "Do you boys need a ride over there too?"

I couldn't believe it. Problem solved. Now we wouldn't have to tell our parents what we were up to. Immediately following the offer of a ride, however, I couldn't help notice Scarlett frowning at her mom. Apparently, she wasn't on board with us riding alongside her, especially in public.

"That'd be great, Mrs. Alexander," I said. "Are you sure you don't mind?"

"Not at all," she said. "I'll pick both of you up about 9:40ish."

"Thanks again," I said. "See you in the morning, Scarlett."

She rolled her eyes and ducked into the car.

"You just couldn't help yourself, could you?" Henry said.

I placed my hand on Henry's shoulder as we continued on our way to the bus stop. "I know you have a hard time accepting it, but Scarlett is part of the agency now. It wouldn't be right to exclude her."

Henry stewed for a minute, and then as he would always do whenever he got his nose out of joint, he flashed a devious smile and fired off a brain teaser.

"The 22nd and 24th Presidents of the United States had the same parents, yet they weren't brothers. How is this possible?"

Now this was an interesting problem. Most brainteasers are trick questions. You didn't have to be a whiz at math or social studies or whatever in order to answer them, but this one was different. This was an American history question pure and simple. And *simple* was the operative word.

"Both presidents had the same parents because it was the same man—Grover Cleveland—who just happened to have served two terms as president, but not consecutive terms." I grinned. "Happy?"

He wasn't. The bus ride home was quiet to say the least. But that was okay. I knew that once we met up at the radio station the next day, Henry would have forgotten all about it.

*   *   *   *   *

Coming up with an excuse to sneak out on Saturday morning proved easier than I had expected. Once I mentioned that Scarlett's mom would be picking me up, my parents were perfectly fine with it. I did stretch the truth a little though. I told them that I was doing research at the library with Henry and Scarlett. Come to think of it, observing Mr. Miles and his friends was like research. It was a chance to bone up on theater history in a way. The reference to the library was the only part of the excuse that made me feel just the least bit guilty. But it was for the good of mankind, so I could live with myself.

When we arrived at the radio station, Mr. Miles and his friends were in full rehearsal mode. When we sat down outside the studio and heard them read some of their lines over the speakers, it didn't take long to appreciate just how talented some of these senior citizens actually were. They had taken Mr. Miles' characters to a level that had never before existed—at least not on the stage of Roosevelt Middle School, that is. I have to say—it was a real pleasure listening to them. They were all so smooth, and their deliveries were effortless. If you closed your eyes, you would have thought these veteran actors were the real people in the story. When I heard Mr. Miles recite the lines for Nick Dakota—now Sam Solomon—I couldn't believe it. Not only did he sound exactly like the actor, Peter Wentworth, but he really sounded like a tough, no-nonsense, streetwise, 1938 private eye.

When the recording finally began, I found myself watching Scarlett. It was as if she were in a daze. I think she enjoyed this experience more than any of us. She obviously had a love for this sort of thing, and really seemed to appreciate the ringside seat. I watched her mouth some of the lines spoken by the woman who had assumed the role of Rebecca. After seeing her, I was glad that I had asked her to join us today.

At noon, the acting company, as Mr. Miles referred to them, stopped for lunch. It was a chance for us to mingle with the actors. When Mr. Miles told his friends that the three of us were part of the sixth grade cast that would soon be performing the full-length version of his play, they seemed really interested in talking to us about our futures. They wondered if any of us might choose the acting profession, either full or part time. I tried to dance around the question. I knew exactly where I'd be ten or so years from now—the proprietor of my own private detective agency—but I didn't want to say that. I wanted them to think that I was at least considering a career in the theater.

After lunch, it was back to the salt mines. These folks were real professionals. When they seemed even the slightest bit unhappy with their performances, the technician was instructed to stop the recording so that they could take another crack at it. They were perfectionists, and I guess that was why they were so good at what they did. We continued to observe for the remainder of the afternoon. It was a real treat. I was starting to regret having given up my leading man role. But when I thought about why we were doing all of this, I realized that being an actual private detective was a lot more exciting in the long run than playing one on stage.

When the recording session concluded, Mr. Miles and the other actors engaged in a hugfest in the studio. It was fun to watch people so passionate about what they did. I overheard Mr. Miles talking to the engineer about their editing session tomorrow. I hoped that everything would fall into place. Mrs. Alexander picked us up promptly at five o'clock and drove us home. She asked a lot of questions about the program, but we were pretty tight-lipped about the reason behind it. Apparently Scarlett hadn't mentioned the connection between the Sam Solomon dramas and the recent crime spree, and until we played it out, we thought it best to keep civilians in the dark.

I didn't have a chance to meet up with Henry or Scarlett for the remainder of the weekend. I actually locked myself in my room to finish up a project. We had to write an expanded book report— term paper length. And it was going to be difficult to write the paper since I hadn't read the book yet. I found it a real challenge at times trying to balance two careers—full-time student and a working P.I. Since we were allowed to choose our own book, I had asked to do mine on a Sam Solomon novel, but our Language Arts teacher, Mrs. Faulkner, wanted me to expand my horizons and pick something more classic in nature. She recommended a book called *Lost Horizon* by James Hilton. It was a book that was usually assigned in high school literature classes, but she thought that I could handle it.

And so for the next day and a half, I immersed myself in the land of Shangri-La, a Utopian society in the Himalayas of Tibet. I imagined myself as Hugh Conway, a member of the British diplomatic service, who finds inner peace and love in a strange land, only to lose it all. But the story doesn't end there. I'd rather not issue a spoiler alert. You'll have to find out for yourself. But I'm happy to report that I found *Lost Horizon* nearly as captivating as a Sam Solomon novel, and that's saying a lot.

On Monday morning, Henry, Scarlett and I made a beeline for Mr. Miles' office the minute we got to school. When we arrived, we found him making notations on the play script.

"Mr. Miles," I said, "sorry to interrupt, but how did it go yesterday?"

He waved us into his office. "It was grand, just grand," he said as he sat up in his chair. "We finished editing the program about eight o'clock last night. And if I do say so myself, it's a winner."

"And it sounds like the real Sam Solomon show?" Henry said.

"You'd be hard-pressed to tell the difference," he replied. He glanced at his watch. "We'll find out soon enough. Fifteen hours and counting. Isn't this just so exciting?"

"If it's all done," Scarlett said, "does that mean we'll resume play practice after school today?"

Mr. Miles closed his briefcase and stood up. "I'm afraid I need to go home and take a nap. We'll restart tomorrow though."

We thanked Mr. Miles for his service and were on our way. As we headed to class, Scarlett stopped momentarily, grabbed a tissue from her pocket, covered her nose and mouth, and promptly sneezed. From across the hall, we heard a distinct, but familiar sound.

"Sssssssssss." When we looked in that direction, we noticed Brian Hart, the hisser, with a book covering his face.

"Oh, relax, Brian," Scarlett said, "I don't have a cold. It's just spring allergies. I'm not contagious."

"Sssssssssss," he continued. "I'm not doing any scenes with you in that condition. I can't afford to have you hacking all over me."

We all chuckled and resumed our trek to first period. For the rest of the day, I couldn't get the hisser out of my head. His fear of germs was way over the top. It reminded me of a situation that Sam Solomon had once found himself in. It was Episode #66—*The Ill Will Caper*. This was the story of Sebastian McCloud, a reclusive millionaire who, upon his death, left his fortune to his five sons. McCloud, a germophobe, like the hisser, indicated in his will that each of his heirs would receive his share of the family fortune if he followed the father's lifestyle and remained in perfect health for one year following his death. And if any of the sons became ill during that time, then his share was to be divided among the others.

When the oldest son suspected one of his brothers of infecting the living quarters of his siblings with an active virus, he contacted Sam. The P.I. knew that he would have to do more than determine whose property had been contaminated and whose hadn't. He fully expected the culprit to leave traces of the virus in his own living quarters to throw off suspicion. Instead of bringing in medical examiners to comb the belongings of each son, Sam instead looked for motive. It didn't take long to identify the brother who had hidden a series of failed business deals, and who, instead of chasing the *dollars*, should have using good *sense*.

Chapter 21

The Hoarse Horse Caper

At dinner that evening, I felt myself zoning out. I had a hard time keeping up with the conversation. I didn't want to tell my parents that I had more important things on my mind. I couldn't be bothered with small talk when the fate of the free world rested in my hands. I felt totally invested in this caper. Not only had I determined the link between the Sam Solomon dramas and the recent burglaries, but I followed up on an offhand comment by my grandmother and suggested that we create our own old-time radio program that was sure to trap our suspect.

When I asked to be excused before dessert, I had apparently tipped my hand. It was the first time my mother could ever recall my having passed on sweets.

"Are you feeling all right?" she asked.

"Yeah…I'm fine…I just have a lot of homework. That's all."

"Okay, but if you need a snack later, there's a yummy piece of applesauce cake with your name on it," she said.

The temptation to stay put and devour a piece of my favorite dessert was overpowering, but I managed to fight it. I thought it best not to put any toxins into my system on such a fateful night.

"Thanks," I said. As I exited the kitchen, I caught my grandmother's eye. She smiled and winked. She was all set for a late night rendezvous at one of the bookstores in town. What I wouldn't give to be alongside her tonight when she and Eugene confronted the elusive man of mystery and took him down. It would be so sweet. I thought about the rush I experienced a few weeks back when both Rupert Olsen and Colonel Harvard Culpepper were taken into custody. To have been there…to have witnessed it…to have been involved in the capture…was an indescribable feeling. I couldn't believe that I wouldn't be on hand when this latest adventure reached its climax.

I went up to my room and tried to do some homework, but it was no use. I couldn't do it. I even tried re-reading a Sam Solomon novel, but I just couldn't concentrate. I found myself staring at the clock on my dresser and watching the minute hand creep ever so slowly. It reminded me of being in school during a particularly painful class. When the realization hit that I'd be up well past my bedtime again, I tried taking a nap. Even that failed. I would just have to wait this out. At one point, I began marking off each fifteen-minute interval, hoping that it might speed things up. It didn't. At about 9:30 there was a knock on my door. It was my grandmother.

"This is it, kiddo," she said. "Are you ready?"

I nodded. "So, you're all set for tonight?" I said. "You and Eugene at one bookstore, and Chicken Bone and T-Bone at the other?"

"That's the plan." She sat down on the edge of my bed. "I sure wish you were going with us tonight," she said. "But it's gonna be too late, and it might be dangerous."

"Gram, I've stayed up all night before, and I've been in my share of scrapes. I'm more than capable of handling myself in a jam."

She hugged me. "You don't have to tell me that. I've seen you in action. Maybe some other time."

I sighed.

"Listen, I'm gonna grab a quick catnap," Gram said. "It could be another all-nighter." She kissed me on the forehead. "Just be patient. Your time will come. Don't worry."

But my time had come. I was sure of it. I wanted to tell her that. There was no reason for me to be patient…to bide my time…to pay my dues. I lied down on the bed and imagined what it might be like tonight to intercept the culprit and hold him for police. It would be so satisfying to know that our strategy had worked. Then I got angry. Most of this was happening because of me. It wasn't fair that I had been squeezed out of the action. I flipped off the light in my room and hid under the covers with mini-flashlight in hand and headphones on. On a piece of scrap paper I began writing down each interval as it passed: 9:45, 10:00, 10:15, 10:30. At 10:45, I turned on the radio. It was a local chamber of commerce interview. Pretty dry stuff.

Then finally, at eleven o'clock, it was time to boogie. The first thing I heard was Mr. Miles' voice, as Sam Solomon, welcoming listeners and introducing the upcoming mystery. Then following a commercial break, the program began. It was so neat hearing the same voices we had heard only days before at the radio station, but now there were sound effects and music mixed in. I couldn't believe how closely it resembled the actual Sam Solomon dramas. Mr. Miles and the others had really nailed it. I noticed how there now appeared to be a clear focus on the role of the *bookie*. Mr. Miles had gone out of his way to feature it as well as the character throughout the broadcast. If we were to be successful tonight, our suspect had to obsess on that particular reference. It was the key to making this strategy pay off.

As the program was nearing its end, I was getting restless. I couldn't believe I was stuck under these covers while Eugene, Gram, and Chicken Bone prepared for their big night. I was upset that I hadn't been able to convince Eugene to add a surveillance team to cover the library. Not only was I sure that our suspect would show up there, but it was our only chance to be included in the stakeout. And now we'd just have to read about it in the papers. It wasn't fair. Heck, *I* was the one who had made the connection between the Sam Solomon mysteries and the burglaries in the first place. I deserved a chance to be there. I had earned it. It just wasn't right to be stuck here. And I had to do something about it.

I jumped on the computer and sent e-mails to Henry and Scarlett. I was hoping that they had managed to stay awake this time. Seconds later I heard from Henry. I had told them that I was thinking about doing something that might seem reckless, but that I couldn't help myself. I explained that I was considering sneaking out of the house, jumping on my bike, and heading over to the library. I asked for their opinions. It didn't take Henry long to respond, and it wasn't what I wanted to hear. He was dead set against it. And then right at that moment, I received an e-mail from Scarlett. She didn't hesitate in expressing an opinion. "Charlie Collier, I forbid you from going over to the library alone. Are you crazy?!!☹" she wrote.

There was only one thing I could do. I needed to think of a time when Sam Solomon was in a similar fix, when he disobeyed orders, and ventured out even though it had proven dangerous. Sam's actions would dictate my next move. After reflecting for a couple of minutes, I had it—Episode #56—*The Hoarse Horse Caper*. This story involved organized crime in Chicago, and the fixing of thoroughbred races at Sportsman's Park. Sam had been hired by the owner of a horse that had mysteriously taken ill. The animal had developed an upper respiratory infection the day before a championship race that this particular horse was favored to win. Sam soon determined that underlings in the Chicago crime syndicate had forced the horse to ingest a potion that would simulate a bronchial condition, causing the horse to be scratched. When the crime bosses realized that Sam had discovered their scam, they decided to eliminate him—permanently.

And when the police learned of this, they took the P.I. into protective custody for his own safety. Sam was escorted to a police safe house where he was under twenty-four hour guard. But to Sam, who was forbidden from leaving, it was more like prison. He felt like a caged animal. How could he help his client from in there? He needed to make a difficult decision. If he snuck out, not only would the police be looking for him, but members of the mafia as well. It was lose-lose. But his loyalty to his client came first. In a daring escape, Sam managed to elude his protectors and returned to the streets where he was not only able to secure evidence that would ultimately indict the perpetrators, but assisted the authorities in their capture.

There it was, as big as life. I now knew what I had to do. I sent another message to both Henry and Scarlett. "I'm headed to the library. Don't try to stop me." I didn't wait for their responses. I knew the dangers of my actions. I knew that sneaking out of the house at midnight meant certain punishment from my parents, but for whatever reason, it didn't matter. I had to see this through.

I dressed quickly, snuck down the stairs, tiptoed past my parents' bedroom and into the kitchen. I checked to make sure that I had packed my pocket flashlight. I then slipped out the back door, and before I knew it, I was en route to the library. I decided against using the headlight on my handlebars. I knew that it would be difficult for cars to see me, but I couldn't risk being stopped by the police since it was now past curfew. I was counting on the reflectors on the back fender to warn drivers of my presence. The library was about two miles away, not nearly the distance I had to travel to reach Eugene's office. I made it a point to stay on side streets, but avoided unlit alleys. I was on a mission but I wasn't crazy. I was actually surprised at the number of cars out this late on a weeknight. Where were all these people going anyway? Could one of them actually be the perp? I'd know soon enough.

Within a few minutes, I had reached my destination—The Oak Grove Public Library. The building was completely dark except for a light in the lobby area. I rode my bike slowly around the perimeter, checking out all possible entrances. There was the front door, an employee entrance on each side, and a loading dock in the back. I soon realized that that there was no way I could keep my eyes on all of them at the same time. This is where a little backup would have come in mighty handy. I decided to hide my bike in a clump of bushes, and work on foot. And so, every few minutes I would change my vantage point, from one entrance to the next.

I had been worried about falling asleep but there seemed little chance of that happening. The cool, night air kept me wide awake. I had been observing things for about twenty minutes when I heard a sound. I wasn't sure exactly what it was. I hid behind a dumpster and tried to see who or what was out there. When the sound got louder, I knew that someone was only yards away. Part of me was hoping that it was our thief. But another part of me was hoping that it was anyone but him. When I heard footsteps scraping against the pavement, I crouched down and closed my eyes. I wasn't feeling particularly brave right at that moment. The mystery man was now behind me and moving in my direction. I stayed perfectly still…until I felt a hand on my shoulder.

"Ahhh!" I opened my eyes and turned. It was Henry. "You scared me to death. What are you doing here?"

"What do you think?" He crouched down next to me. "I couldn't very well let you come out here alone and get yourself killed, now could I?"

I felt my heart beating all over my body. I was having a hard time catching my breath. But I was thrilled to see Henry.

"I just got to thinking that I'd probably be the one asked to give the eulogy at your funeral," he said, "and since I hate public speaking, I thought I'd rather be with you if the unthinkable happened."

I wanted to smile. Then I got to thinking about the funeral reference and it made me kind of nervous.

"So, have you seen anything?" he asked.

"Not yet. But it's hard to watch all of the doors at the same time. I might have missed something."

"Maybe we should split up," he said. "What do you think?"

It was a good idea. It made perfect sense. So why did I *not* want to do it? The answer was simple. I was nervous, and I wasn't proud of it.

"We could, I guess," I said. "Or we could just stick together and check each entrance one by one."

Henry was tough—a lot tougher than me. It wouldn't have bothered him in the least to split up. But sometimes, and I can't explain why, there is this unspoken language between friends. It was almost as if he knew exactly what I was thinking. And it probably was the reason why the two of us had been inseparable for years.

"You know, why don't we do that," he said. "Why don't we stick together. Like they always say: there's strength in numbers."

And so we began our rounds...once...twice...three times. We would walk up to each door and tug on it just to make sure that the building was secure. We made it a point to stay as close to the outer walls as possible, and to duck behind whatever shrubs were available in order to stay hidden. After we had circled the property at least a half dozen times, we sat down to rest.

"How long are we gonna keep doing this?" Henry asked.

"I don't know. Are you getting tired?"

"I'm not tired. I'm just not sure this guy is ever gonna show up," he said.

I didn't know what to do. It was probably getting close to two o'clock. I was starting to believe that Henry might be right. This guy apparently wasn't coming. And my theory was all wrong. I guess I should have listened to Eugene. It serves me right for thinking that I knew more than the expert. It was, however, kind of nice to be a member of a surveillance team and to be part of the action though. And if we ended up packing up and going home, I was doubtful that I would ever tell anyone that we were here. I wouldn't want to admit that my strategy was flawed.

"Let's check the doors one more time," I said. "If he still hasn't shown by that time, then I suppose we can head home."

"I know you don't want to hear it," Henry said, "but this guy may have gone to one of the bookstores like Eugene figured, and may very well be in custody by now."

"I'd be fine with that," I said. "I just want the guy caught. Although I was positive he'd show up here."

Since we were facing the loading dock, we began there. It was secure. Then we worked our way to the east side of the building. Again the door was locked. We crept to the front of the building, the most unlikely place for a break-in considering the lighting. And as we had expected, there was no one in sight.

"One more door and we're done," Henry said. "Then we have to make it home without being nabbed for a curfew violation. I don't want to even think about having to explain that one to my parents."

As we approached the employee entrance on the west side of the building, I felt this tightness in my chest. I sensed that something just wasn't right. The closer we got, the more uneasy I felt.

"Hey, that door doesn't look right," Henry said. We ran up to it. The door was slightly ajar, and there were scratches on the lock. When we tugged at the handle, it opened. "Paydirt!" he said. "Looks like you may have been right, partner."

I nodded nervously. Flashlights in hand, we entered the building. It was dark. Really dark. In the past few years, ever since I had discovered the Sam Solomon mystery series, I had spent untold hours at the library. But since we were now in a restricted area, accessible only to employees, I wasn't exactly sure where we were. We followed a long hallway until it we reached another set of doors.

"This way?" Henry said.

"Why not." We flipped off our flashlights as we opened a heavy steel door. If our suspect was out there, we didn't want him to know we were here. When we didn't see or hear anything, we turned them back on and proceeded. We found ourselves in the main part of the library. I knew exactly where we were now. We hadn't gone more than a few feet when we heard footsteps. We hit the floor. Flashlights off. There was a reddish glow on Henry's face from the overhead exit sign. He looked concerned. The footsteps seemed to be coming from the hallway we had just passed through. We could hear the doorknob turning. We huddled together up against the nearest wall. The door opened slowly and we could see someone holding a light of some kind, a colored light. It didn't appear to be a flashlight. We held our breaths and prayed we weren't detected. The figure moved closer and closer and then we felt something....

"Ahhhhhh..."

Chapter 22

The Fur Real Caper

Henry and I jumped up and ran in opposite directions. With flashlights tucked in our pockets, we were running blindly. And so it wasn't a surprise when we each came to a screeching and crashing halt—me into a table, and Henry into a floor-to-ceiling bookcase. Each of us, afraid to speak, and now in a prone position, reached for our flashlights and flipped them on. As soon as I saw the glow from Henry's flashlight, I aimed mine in his direction. We gave each other a thumbs up, and began to scan the area, looking for our uninvited guest.

It didn't take long to locate the intruder. We spotted him crouching behind a waste basket. Now on all fours, I began to crawl toward our prey. I could tell from the glow of Henry's flashlight that he was also moving in for the kill. Right at that moment, I wasn't quite sure if what we were doing was the smartest thing. We had no idea who or what was waiting for us. I stopped in my tracks. I wondered if we should just get up and run for our lives, or should we see this through? Part of me wanted to hightail it out of there, but the other part of me—the part who claimed to be a disciple of Sam Solomon—had to continue on. Why come this far, I thought, only to back out now?

I could see that Henry was only about twenty feet from the figure. And then all at once, he climbed to his feet, darted forward, and ducked down behind a cart of books. He was now close enough to get a good look. He lifted his head and peeked out over the cart. Then he aimed his flashlight at the wastebasket.

"Oh, no. You've got to be kidding me," he said.

The intruder…the mystery man…the uninvited guest…the person who had scared us half to death…just happened to be one Scarlett Alexander. She stood up, sighed, and folded her arms. I couldn't tell if she was relieved or furious. I soon found out that it was a little of both.

"What are you doing here?" I asked.

She marched in my direction, shaking her finger at me the entire time. "What am I doing here? What am I doing here?" She was beside herself. "Because you don't go out alone. Because you don't go out alone...at night. And because you don't go out alone...at night...and place yourself in a dangerous situation. Did anyone ever tell you that? You have no business here. None of us do."

"So what do you expect us to do?" Henry said.

"You two are going to help me find my cell phone so we can get out of here. I dropped it when I tripped back there."

"So that was the colored light you were carrying," Henry said. "I should have known you wouldn't be smart enough to bring a real flashlight."

But before Scarlett could fire off a volley, we spotted a light...a moving light. It was all the way across the main floor on the other side of the library between two shelves of books. We all dropped to the floor.

"That must be him," Henry said.

"I guarantee that's him," I said. "He's in the exact spot where they keep all of the Sam Solomon books."

"Let's just get out of here," Scarlett whispered.

"Are you nuts?" I said. "That's the reason why we're here. We can't turn back now."

Scarlett seemed frightened. She shuffled a few feet in my direction, which was perfectly fine with me.

"Listen, I'm not crazy," I said. "I don't want to be a dead hero. Why don't we just try and get a look at this guy. Then we can go find Scarlett's phone, call the police, and get the heck out of here."

"I don't like it," she said.

"Then you can just wait here for us," Henry replied.

Scarlett grabbed my arm. "Don't you dare leave me here alone."

I motioned for the others to follow me. We slowly made our way across the main floor and over to where the mystery books were kept. We stopped just a few yards short of our subject.

"This is close enough," Scarlett said.

"We just gotta get a good look at him," I said. "Then we'll take off. No need to confront him."

I rose from a crouched position ever so slowly, shuffled over, and peeked around the end of a bookshelf. In the dark, I could barely make out a figure. It appeared to be a male, dressed head to toe, in black. He slid out a book and then set his flashlight down on one of the shelves. The light, now facing him, illuminated his face just enough for me to see his features. He had a long face…with a goatee…and sunken cheeks…maybe about fifty years old. His hair was salt and pepper. I made a mental image of the suspect. I was sure that I could either pick him out of a line-up, or help a police artist create a composite sketch. My work was done here. I lowered myself back to a crouch and snuck back to where the others were waiting.

"Did you get a look at him?" Henry whispered.

I nodded, and then pointed to the door we had come from. "Time to go." But before we were able to make our way across the main floor and out of the building, something unexpected happened. And I can only blame Mother Nature. I noticed that Scarlett's mouth had started to open…but not to speak. She was about to sneeze. Her spring allergies were about to expose us. I couldn't let that happen, but what could I do? Right at that moment, without thinking, just as she was about to sneeze, I reached over and squeezed her nose, trying to suppress the sneeze. But what I managed to do was far worse. The petite sneeze that she might have produced had been transformed into a monster that came directly out of her mouth. It was the most hideous sound you could have imagined…and one of the loudest I had ever heard.

Scarlett looked up at me in horror. But that was the least of our problems. The suspect immediately came running down the aisle, spotted us on the floor, and pointed his flashlight directly at us.

"Who are you? What are you doing here?" he said.

My partners glanced in my direction. Apparently this question was for me. "We're just messing around. That's all." I stood up and smiled sheepishly. "Well, we'd better get going, gang. Sorry to have bothered you."

"Well, you're about to be real sorry," he said. "I can't afford to have anybody recognize me."

"We won't say anything," Scarlett said. "We promise."

"Oh, I know that," he said. The perp stuck his hand into his pocket as if he were hiding a gun.

I doubted if he really had one but we couldn't take a chance.

"Okay, start walking," he said.

"Where?" Henry asked.

The burglar surveyed the area. "Over there," he said, pointing to a stairway that led to the library basement.

I led my friends in the direction of the stairs. I thought about where we might be headed. If he takes us downstairs, it could be a good thing. This was the spot where I had spent countless hours in the past couple of years curled up with any number of Sam Solomon novels. I knew every inch of the library basement. As we approached the stairwell, he motioned with his flashlight for us to head down.

Good. When we reached the lower level, he flipped on the light switch. We were staring at a room filled with stacks of books, along with a small reading alcove with a couch and a table and chairs. That was my hideaway when I wanted to be alone with the world's greatest literary detective.

"Stay right there and don't move," the man said, as he checked out each corner of the room. When he reappeared a moment later, he nodded in the direction of the far wall.

I knew exactly where we were headed. We walked, in single file, toward a door marked *Library Archives*. This was where they housed the rarest and most expensive volumes—ones that weren't available for public consumption. Our captor slipped by us and tried the door. It was locked—naturally. He reached into his pocket, pulled out a handful of small tools, and selected one. He then slipped one end of it into the lock, moved it around for a few seconds, and then, just like that, turned the knob and opened the door. Our friend was the proud owner of a set of burglary tools. I was actually familiar with these. They were similar to the ones that Rupert Olsen had given to Sherman to break into pet stores a couple of months back when all the exotic birds had been stolen.

The man waved us into the room, followed us in, turned on the lights, and pulled the door closed behind him. The first thing he did was to walk over to one of the air vents. He jiggled the metal cover and then popped it off. He did the same with another vent on the opposite wall.

"Say hello to your new home, or should I say *tomb*," he said.

I didn't like the way he had phrased that. By the looks on my partners' faces, I could tell that we shared the same sentiment. I wasn't sure what this character had planned for us, but whatever it was, I was confident that I would be able to figure out a way to get us out of it. I had done so in the past when our lives dangled in the balance, and this was no different. My goal, for the time being, was to engage our suspect in conversation. I would either try to convince him to let us go, or at least learn enough about him to share with police after we escaped.

"Why are you doing this?" I said.

"Don't worry about it, kid. Your timing was bad. Let's leave it at that."

"I think I know what's going on here," I said.

He chuckled. "Oh, really? Well, why don't you enlighten me."

"Here's how I see it," I said. "For whatever reason, good or bad, you have this thing for Sam Solomon."

The look on his face suggested that I had hit a nerve.

"You listen to the dramas on Monday nights. You identify some important word or phrase from the program, you look for a double meaning, then you find a business associated with that word, and burglarize it early the next morning. Am I close?"

The man smiled, pulled out a chair, sat down and put his feet on a table. He began applauding.

"Well done, my pudgy friend. I'm impressed," he said.

"And if you have any thoughts of trying to shut us up," Henry said, "then you should know that a professional private detective, as well as the police, know all about it."

He grinned. "Wonderful. I couldn't be happier. I want people to know where my inspiration comes from. I want them to know that Sam Solomon is behind all of it."

"Have you got some kind of beef with Sam Solomon?" I asked. "Does it have anything to do with the business cards you leave at every job—the ones with the *SS* lined out?"

The man pulled a similar card from his pocket and tossed it on the table. "You mean this? It appears my little plan is working beautifully."

Scarlett took a step in the direction of the suspect. "Who are you, and what exactly do you want anyway?"

He stood and bowed at the waist. "My name is Jonathan Wentworth. So pleased to make your acquaintance."

Wentworth. Wentworth. Where had I heard that name before? It didn't take me long to figure it out.

"Are you any relation to Peter Wentworth, the actor who played Sam Solomon in the radio show?"

"Peter Wentworth was my grandfather," he said.

Now I was even more confused. "I don't get it," I said. "What do you have against Sam Solomon? He made your grandfather a star."

The man slammed his fist down on the table. "Sam Solomon killed my grandfather. And now I'm going to kill Sam Solomon."

I had heard a lot of wild things in my twelve short years on this planet, but this guy was seriously off his rocker.

"Sam Solomon is a fictional character," Scarlett said. "How can you possibly kill him?"

"And how could Sam have killed a real person?" Henry asked. "It makes no sense."

The suspect stared forward. He wasn't even looking at us any longer. "When my grandfather was cast in the role of Sam Solomon, he was thrilled. This was the break of a lifetime. And as the show got more popular, so did he. The producers talked him into signing a long term contract...and that was the beginning of the end."

I glanced at the others. This guy was scary. It was as if he was in some sort of a trance.

"My grandfather was a simple man. He didn't believe in lawyers or agents. He conducted business with a handshake and a signature. But what he didn't know is that he had signed an exclusive contract that prevented him from accepting any other acting jobs while he played Sam Solomon. Well, that was the kiss of death. No one does that anymore. It's a career killer."

"I don't get it," Scarlett said. "If he was working steadily and getting a nice paycheck, what difference did it make?"

The man shook his head. "You don't understand the acting business, little girl. When the show fell out of favor with the audience...and it did...my grandfather was cut loose, and that was the end of his acting career."

"But he was famous," Henry said.

"Yeah," Wentworth shouted, "so famous that no one would hire him. After playing the same role for five years, he was stereotyped. Don't you see? The public wouldn't accept him in any other role." He began to breathe heavily. "But if he had been able to take on other jobs while playing Sam Solomon, he could have shown people how versatile an actor he really was. He could have been a superstar. Instead, he died penniless."

I could see that Wentworth had reached a boiling point. I was almost afraid to say anything. But I had to.

"You got it all wrong," I said. "Your gripe isn't with Sam Solomon…it's with those producers."

He spun around, cocked his arm and put his fist right through the plaster wall.

"Wake up, kid. They're all dead. And that's just how you're gonna end up."

I needed to defuse this situation, and fast. In Wentworth's current state of mind, he was capable of anything. I wasn't sure what to say to calm him down. How would Sam have handled a situation like this? In all of the cases that he had investigated, he had to have dealt with a character who was emotionally unstable. And suddenly I remembered. It was in Episode #59—*The Fur Real Caper*.

This was the story of Jacob Altman, an aging furrier from the Bronx, long past retirement age, who was swindled by a fur wholesaler. Realizing that the furrier was not as sharp as he once had been, the wholesaler managed to sell him a truck full of fake furs. When Jacob's sons realized that the new shipment was filled with phonies, they chided their father and insisted that he retire. The sons then hired Sam to track down the scoundrel who had cheated them. Halfway through the investigation, however, Sam received a call from the sons informing him that their father was missing. He immediately began to search for the old man. Sam eventually found him clinging to a railing on the George Washington Bridge and threatening to leap to his death in the cold waters of the Hudson River.

Jacob was apparently disgraced and embarrassed about what had happened. After hours of trying to coax him to safety, Sam soon realized that he needed a new tactic. Instead of minimizing the mistake the old man had made, he reminded Jacob of the successful business he had created, and how much more he would still be able to accomplish, if he would only step back off that ledge. Sam continued to pump up the furrier until the old man finally abandoned his desperate act.

So that would be my new strategy. Instead of reminding Wentworth of what would happen to him when he was eventually caught, I would compliment him on his ingenious scheme, and hope that he would start to look at us as allies. I wasn't sure if it would work. But it was the only chance we had. And if it failed, I couldn't bear to think about the consequences.

Chapter 23

The Shore Thing Caper

I continued to watch our captor. He seemed agitated, nervous, upset. He ran his fingers through his hair. He stared at us and then at the open vents. I still wasn't sure why he had removed the covers from them. Whatever it was, it couldn't be good. I decided it was time to try out my new strategy.

"Mr. Wentworth, if you don't mind, I have a question for you" I said.

"A dying man's last request. Is that it, kid?"

I ignored his comment and tried to stay positive.

"I was just wondering about the word play and double meanings you used to pick each business you burglarized. It was really clever. Why'd you do it?"

He grinned. "Have you ever read a Sam Solomon novel?"

Henry and Scarlett looked at me. They knew the answer to that one.

"Yeah," I said. "A couple of times."

"Well, did you ever notice that the title of each book is a play on words? That's why. I just wanted to keep it consistent with the Sam Solomon theme. *And* I didn't want to make it too easy for the cops to figure out my next move. I wanted them to work for it."

"If you're so smart," Scarlett said, "then how come we figured out how to find you?"

Please, Scarlett, don't make him mad, I thought to myself. It'll mess up my plan.

"You just got lucky, sweetie," he said. "I listened to the show tonight." He paused and seemed to reflect momentarily. "Grandpa's voice sounded a little different." He shrugged. "Must have had a cold or something. Anyway, since it was about a *bookie*, I decided to lay my hands a few *books*. But not just any books. I wanted the ones about my dear friend, Sam Solomon. That's where I was when you so rudely interrupted me."

"What did you intend to do with those books?" Scarlett asked.

"I was about to throw a little party—a book-burning party."
He chuckled. "I suppose I could just shred them but this'll be so
much more satisfying."

"I notice that you always manage to rifle through the cash
register. Is that part of your little word game?" Henry asked.

"A man's gotta eat, doesn't he? Although when that runs
out, I rely on my training as an HVAC guy to pay the bills," he said.

"HVAC?" Henry said.

"Heating, ventilation, and air conditioning," Wentworth
answered. "And, boy, are those skills gonna come in handy
tonight." He winked. "You'll see."

Right at that moment, I decided to make a bold move. I
walked up to the table that Wentworth was standing next to. I pulled
out a chair and sat down.

"There's just one thing that still confuses me," I said. "How
will all of this kill Sam Solomon?"

"Well, you look like pretty smart kids," he said. "You tell
me."

I tried to figure out where he was going with this. I wasn't
certain. But I was pretty sure that after this last burglary, the police
would put some stock in our Sam Solomon theory. I found myself
thinking out loud.

"When the police finally buy into the connection between the
Sam Solomon dramas and the burglaries," I said, "they'll probably
decide to…" I was still stuck.

"Wait a minute," Scarlett said. "If they're smart, they'll just
cut off the food supply."

"Yeah," Henry said. "That's it. They'll make the radio
station take the program off the air to stop the burglaries."

"Bingo!" Wentworth clapped his hands. "And goodbye,
Sam Solomon. When word gets around that there's someone out
there committing crimes based on the series, there won't be a radio
station in the country that'd risk putting it on the air. Because if they
did, then they're asking for a crime spree. And knowing that, there
wouldn't be a police department around that'd let them run it."

"I have to hand it to you, Mr. Wentworth. Your plan is
ingenious."

Henry and Scarlett both glared at me. They obviously
thought that I was cozying up with the enemy.

"And once the radio series is buried," Wentworth said, "then we go after the books. Imagine a crime spree across the country all inspired by the book series. It'll be great. And how do you stop it? You simply pull every Sam Solomon book off of every shelf in every bookstore and library. You cut off the *food source*, as the little lady suggested. And then Sam Solomon will officially be dead. No one'll ever hear about him or read about him again. It'll be as if he never existed. And my grandfather will have his revenge."

Wentworth reached into his pocket for his tools. He walked over to the door and began to disassemble the lock.

"What are you doing?" Scarlett said.

"Just making sure that no one can get *in* or *out* of here," he said. He turned to us. "Listen, kids, I'm sorry about this. No one was supposed to get hurt. But I can't have you telling the cops about me, and especially being able to identify me." He grabbed the knob, opened the door, and stared at us. "Don't look at me like that. It'll be quick and painless. I can promise you that. Now I need to go find the furnace in this place so I can do my magic. Then in a few minutes, it'll all be over. Don't worry, I'll check back in with you in a little while just to see how you're doing. But by that time I'm sure you'll be fast asleep…or worse. Sweet dreams, kids." He picked up the vent covers, tucked them under his arm, and pulled the door closed behind him.

Henry ran over and tried the door. It wouldn't budge. Even though the lock was on our side of the door, Wentworth had done something that made it impossible for us to open it. Screaming for help wasn't an option. There were no windows in this place, and no one else, other than our captor, was in the building. And the worst part of this whole thing? No one would be looking for us.

"Well, you've done it again, Charlie," Scarlett said.

"Me? You were the one who sneezed."

"No thanks to you. When you squeezed my nose, you made it ten times louder."

Henry was kneeling in front of one of the air vents. "What do you suppose he has in mind for us anyway? Is he gonna try to poison us or something?"

I knew exactly what Wentworth's intentions were. A fire drill at school a few days earlier had provided the answer.

"He plans to get the furnace to leak carbon monoxide into the vents," I said. "Don't you remember when Mrs. Jansen told us about it...about how it's a colorless, odorless gas that can kill you. And that it can come from a furnace."

"Are you sure?" Scarlett said.

"What else could it be?" I said. "It all makes sense. And if anyone would know how to rig a furnace to leak this stuff, it'd be him. Didn't you hear him say he was a heating/air conditioning guy."

Henry grabbed a chair and pushed it up against one of the vents. "We gotta block these things."

"That's too loose," I said. "Why don't we jam as many of these books as we can into both vents."

"But it's a gas," Scarlett said. "It'll get right though the books."

"I know that," I said. "But it might slow it down and buy us a little more time to find a way outa here." We immediately began stuffing as many books as we could into the vents. "Try to fit them in as tightly as possible. We don't want to leave any holes where the gas might seep through."

We spent the next ten minutes jamming books, many of them rare first editions, into the vents and trying to keep them flush against the sides of the air ducts and each other. When it was clear that no more books would fit, we stopped and stared at one another.

"Now we need a real escape plan," Scarlett said. She pointed at me. "And I'm counting on you to figure one out. You got us into this. You get us out. And to think that if I had stayed home tonight, I wouldn't be here fighting for my life."

"Charlie," Henry said, "We gotta get that noodle of yours working. And I know just how to do that." He thought to himself for a minute. "Okay, got it. A mother has seven children and six potatoes. How can she feed an equal amount of potatoes to each child?"

"A brain teaser? You've got to be kidding," Scarlett said. "A poisonous gas is about to come through those vents any minute, and you want him to answer a brain teaser. You're crazy."

I knew what Henry was trying to do. He wanted to get the juices bubbling in my noggin. And I knew that to a normal person, it seemed nuts. But it had worked in the past. And it just might work again.

"Give it to me one more time," I said.

Scarlett threw her arms up. "You're both crazy."

"A mother has seven children and six potatoes. How can she feed an equal amount of potatoes to each child? And I should mention that the answer can't include fractions."

I assumed it had to be a trick question of some kind. That was Henry's style. I didn't think this was a math problem. Therefore the answer had to lie within the wording of the question. I repeated it to myself. *A mother has seven children and six potatoes.* Nothing tricky there. *How can she feed an equal amount of potatoes to each child?* Wait a minute now. There was something funny about the way that last part was worded. It didn't say *how many potatoes.* Instead, it said *an equal amount of potatoes.* Since we can't use fractions, then we can't slice them up and give each kid an equal number of pieces. But what if we....? And then it hit me.

"Give up?" Henry said.

"I think I smell something," Scarlett said nervously.

Henry glanced at her nonchalantly. "It's odorless." He turned to me. "Well?"

"There's only one solution," I said. "You make mashed potatoes, and give each kid an equal portion."

"Oooooh," Henry groaned.

I walked to the center of the room and looked around. I had hoped that the brain teaser would have jarred something somewhere. I made a mental inventory of everything in the room...books...bookcases...shelves...step stool...wall clock...rugs...table...chairs...sprinkler head...light fixtures...wait a minute. I stared at the sprinkler head on the ceiling. I thought back to the conversation I had with my dad a couple of days earlier.

"I got it," I said. "I figured a way out."

"What? How?" Scarlett said.

"Do you see that sprinkler head on the ceiling. That's our ticket to freedom."

"I don't get it," Henry said.

I began to push the table to the center of the room and positioned it directly under the sprinkler. I climbed onto the table and motioned for Henry to hand me a chair which I placed on top. The sprinkler head was nearly within my reach.

"Hand me one of those books," I said. "A light one that I can throw."

"What are you doing?" Henry asked.

"If I can tamper with that sprinkler head just enough, it'll go off. And when it does, it'll send a signal to the alarm company, the fire department, and the police. And they'll be able to tell exactly what room it's in. And we'll be saved."

"If we don't drown first," Scarlett said.

Henry handed me a pile of books. I took the lightest one, cocked my arm and was just about to toss it at the sprinkler head when I thought about what Scarlett had just said. The water. I had forgotten about the water. I began shaking my head.

"What's wrong?" Henry said. "Throw the book."

"I can't. I just can't do it."

"Let me do it then," he said.

I climbed down from the chair and hopped off the table. "I don't mean I *can't* do it, I mean I *won't* do it."

"Why?" Scarlett said. "What are you talking about?"

"Look around you," I said. "What do you see? Hundreds and hundreds of volumes of first edition books. Some of them more than a hundred years old. They're irreplaceable. Imagine what will happen to them when the water comes pouring out?"

"We'll cover them up or something," Henry said. "We can protect them."

"Not when a hundred gallons of water come rushing out every minute. There's no way to save them. That's why we have to think of another idea."

"Let me get this straight," Scarlett said. "We're probably gonna die, but at least the books will survive. Is that it?"

Henry cocked his head to the side. "I hate to say it but she has a point, partner."

I handed a book to each of them. When it actually came down to it, I wanted to see which one of them would really pull the trigger.

"Go ahead," I said. "The blood will be on your hands."

After a minute or so, they both set the books on the table.

"All right," Scarlett said. "You'd just better figure out another way to get us out of here."

I knew that my decision to save the books was a noble one. But it also meant that I'd have to come up with another escape plan. And to be perfectly honest, I couldn't think of a single thing. We had reached the point of desperation, and that always meant it was time to call upon my mentor—Sam Solomon. I tried to think of a time when Sam had to abandon a great idea, and then come up with an alternative plan. After a minute or two, I had it. It was in Episode #58—*The Shore Thing Caper.*

Sam had been hired to investigate an international smuggling ring that was moving shipments of Mexican rifles from Tijuana into a port in San Diego. The yacht of a wealthy U.S. businessman was the suspected mode of transportation. At one point in the investigation, Sam managed to get himself captured and thrown into a storage room—a makeshift jail in the hull of the yacht. While a prisoner, he searched for a way to free himself. With boxes of ammunition that he discovered in the compartment, he ingeniously fashioned a crude homemade explosive. With it, he planned to blow a hole in the side of the yacht, and since it was only about a mile off shore, he would easily be able to swim to safety.

But when Sam thought through his plan, he realized that he might not have considered the big picture. The veteran detective was a fine swimmer who was more than capable of saving himself. But what would be the consequences of his actions? With a hole in its hull, the yacht would certainly sink. And the plight of everyone on board was in jeopardy. Some might survive, but others would surely drown. Granted, they were all criminals, but Sam was uncomfortable in playing the role of judge, jury, *and* executioner. The plan would surely have guaranteed his escape, but he opted to dismiss it. Instead, he constructed a fortress with the boxes of ammo and the rest is history. If it worked for Sam, it could work for us.

Chapter 24

The Santa Claws Caper

It was time to put the next, and hopefully final plan, into action. I began grabbing as many books as I could carry and started piling them on the table. Then I pulled the table over to the doorway.

"What's going on?" Henry said. "A new escape plan?"

I nodded.

"What can I do?" he said.

"I need books, books, and more books…the bigger the better."

Scarlett, who had been sitting on the floor in the far corner of the room, scooted over.

"What's happening?" she said.

"You told me to come up with an idea. Well, I've got one. I don't know if it'll work, but it's worth a try."

Right at that moment, Henry yawned. A second later, Scarlett did the same. And then so did I. It made me a little nervous. It could have been the fact that it was the middle of the night and we were all tired. But it bothered me that we had all yawned at the same time. I was worried that the carbon monoxide was now slowing seeping into the room. I thought it best not to say anything, at least not yet. We had to keep moving. We couldn't allow ourselves to fall asleep. Just to be safe, I asked Henry and Scarlett to build a wall of books in front of the air vents. Since we had already jammed books into the vents, this would give us a second line of defense. We wouldn't be able to stop the gases completely but we might just be able to delay them long enough to make our escape.

I knew that Wentworth would be stopping in relatively soon. Once he had tampered with the furnace, and had gathered the entire Sam Solomon series from the main floor of the library, it was safe to assume he'd be back. He couldn't risk having us survive and being able to identify him. As for me, I needed to explain my new strategy to the others, and to have us execute it as quickly as possible.

"Here's what I think we should do," I said. "It was something that Sam Solomon once had success with." I walked to the door and waved my hands as I explained. "I want to build a wall of books all the way around the door, in a semi-circle, as high as we can stack them. Then I want to take some of those loose wooden shelves off the bookcases and build a roof for our book wall. We'll place one end of each shelf over the door. They can rest on the top of the molding just above the door. Then the other end of the shelves will rest on the wall of books we've built. Finally, we pile as many books as we can on top of those shelves."

"I don't get it," Henry said. "That won't stop Wentworth. He'll walk in, see the books, and just knock them down."

I smiled. "And what do you suppose will happen when he does?" I said.

At first neither Henry nor Scarlett could picture the scenario I was describing. A moment later, Scarlett saw the light.

"When he knocks down the wall of books," she said, "all of the books on top will come crashing down...right on him."

"I doubt if it'll knock him out," I said, "but if it buys us enough time to slip past him, run upstairs and escape, then it's certainly worth a try."

Henry was all in. He immediately started stacking books around the door. "It just might work," he said. "When Wentworth sees that wall of books, he'll figure we're up to something, and he'll bust through for sure. Charlie, you did it again. At least, I hope so."

"Me too. Let's get to work." For the next several minutes we built our wall. By standing on the table, we managed to construct a wall nearly nine feet high. Then we took some of the long wooden shelves from the bookcases and carefully placed them on top. Finally, and what proved to be the most difficult chore, we piled the heaviest books we could find on our makeshift roof. We found some old Webster's dictionaries from the 1930's and 40's. Man, were they heavy. In some cases, it took all three of us to lift them up and place them on our makeshift roof. And then we sat back and waited.

In order for our plan to succeed, Wentworth would have to make a return visit. If he didn't, and if he had successfully rigged the furnace to emit the deadly vapors, all our plans will have failed. But I was certain that he wouldn't leave without making sure that there was no one left to identify him. The fear of what might be seeping through those vents made the minutes that passed seem more like hours. I tried to engage the others in conversation to take their minds off of the obvious, but also to make sure that none of us fell asleep.

Thirty minutes later, I was starting to get worried. Scarlett was complaining of a headache, and Henry was holding his stomach. These were early signs of carbon monoxide poisoning. We had to hold on. We had to beat this. If anything happened to either one of these people, I would never forgive myself. The only reason they were here is because they were worried about me. They could have just as easily have stayed home and avoided all of this. I decided at that moment to take on the role of cheerleader. I had to keep their spirits up. I had to make them believe we would prevail. But to be perfectly honest, I was starting to lose hope myself.

Then suddenly we heard something right outside the room.

"This is it," I whispered. "Not a sound."

I motioned for Henry and Scarlett to join me up against the wall next to our fortress of books. When Wentworth pushed through, we wanted to be out of the line of fire. We needed to sneak past him before he realized what had happened. When we heard metal against metal, we knew it was him. He was using one of his burglary tools on the lock. Seconds later, we heard the door open, and then his voice.

"Hey, what's going on here?"

Then, just as we had hoped, he pushed through the wall of books. And right on cue, the wooden shelves full of oversize books came crashing down. We stepped back out of the way to avoid being hit ourselves. One of the dictionaries plunked Wentworth right on top of the head, knocking him to the floor. We heard him groaning. This was working. This was actually working. We were going to pull this off, I thought. And then suddenly, my hopes began to fade. I saw the door slowing closing and I couldn't reach it in time to catch it. With the lock now broken, if the door closed, we wouldn't be able open it. I couldn't believe we had gotten this far only to fail. But at the last second, I had an idea. I began kicking books in the direction of the door. And just as it was about to close, one of the books wedged itself between the door and the frame.

I stepped over the pile of books, threw the door open and motioned for the others to follow. We ran out of the archives, through the basement, and up the stairs to the first floor. I reached into my pocket and dug out my trusty flashlight. I pointed it all around and began searching for the door we can come in through.

"There it is," Henry said.

We sprinted to it, made our way down the hallway, and then before we knew it, we were outside, and under the most beautiful starlit sky you could have imagined. We were free. The plan had actually worked.

"Okay," I said. "Let's find our bikes and get out of here."

But before we were able to escape and enjoy our freedom, we heard footsteps from behind. It was Wentworth. He was in full gallop.

"Split up," I yelled. "He can't catch all of us."

We immediately ran in different directions. I was hoping that our hunter would accept the fact that he was licked and would just hightail it out of there. But when I looked behind me, my greatest fears were realized. Wentworth had chosen to chase me. These were always the times when I would wish that I had a smaller, sleeker frame. I was a lot younger than my pursuer, but the extra weight was a real handicap. He was gaining on me. And when I felt his warm breath on the back of my neck, I knew it was over. I only hoped that either Henry or Scarlett would find help in time to save all of us.

"Gotch ya," Wentworth cried as he grabbed my shoulder. He pulled me down to the ground. "Hey, kids," he yelled out. "I got your little friend here. You better come back or you may never see him again."

"My friends are smarter than you think," I said. "They won't come back. They're headed to the police station as we speak."

"I don't think so," he said.

I figured that if I could keep him talking for the next few minutes, it would buy enough time for my partners to get help. I could only hope that they'd be able to contact the authorities in time. Then out of the corner of my eye, I saw something move next to one of the dumpsters. It had to be a person but it was too dark to tell who it was.

"Looks like your friends aren't as smart as you thought," Wentworth said.

Oh, no! Why had they come back? I appreciated their loyalty but right at that moment I would have preferred if they had exercised a little common sense. There was no way this guy was going to let any of us go. Our only chance now had been dashed. It was as good as over. I watched as the figure emerged from the shadows. And then, as it got closer, I soon realized that it wasn't Henry…or Scarlett. It was Eugene.

"If you know what's good for you, friend, you'd better let that kid go," Eugene said.

But before Wentworth could respond, another figure appeared from behind a pillar. I couldn't believe my eyes. It was Gram.

"Don't make me come over there, pal," she said. "It won't be pretty."

Wentworth began to laugh. "You don't scare me. You old codgers oughta head back to the home."

Eugene smiled and pointed up over our heads. "What about them? Do they scare you?"

Floodlights suddenly lit up the scene. And a half dozen police sharpshooters, perched on the edge of the library roof, were poised and ready.

"It's all over," Eugene said.

Wentworth threw his head back and dropped his arms to his sides. And then from behind every bush and parked car, uniformed officers appeared. They rushed their suspect and ordered him to the ground.

"He might have a gun in his pocket," I yelled out.

One of the officers immediately checked for weapons. "He's clean," the patrolman yelled out, and proceeded to handcuff his prisoner.

"And you'd better not go into the library without gas masks," I said. "It's full of carbon monoxide. He did something to the furnace to make it leak."

I watched as one of the officers pulled out his radio and called for a hazmat team to join the party. Then, out of the corner of my eye, I spotted Henry and Scarlett in the company of police. I was so glad to see they were safe.

Eugene walked up and put his hand on my shoulder. "Looks like you were right all along about the library, Charlie. I should have listened to you."

"Yeah, but none of that would have mattered if you hadn't shown up tonight," I said. "So how did you figure out we were here?"

"Well, after staking out the bookstores unsuccessfully for a couple of hours, we decided to call it a night," he said. "Then about twenty minutes later, I got a call from your grandma. She apparently went up to your room to check on you when she got home. She found the bed empty and knew something was up. We figured you had gone to the library. Then we both came over here, and when we found your bike in the bushes, we decided to call in reinforcements."

"I'm sure glad you did," I said.

Gram walked up and joined the conversation. "If you kids hadn't gotten out by yourselves, these fellas were prepared to rush the building. I don't mind telling you we were awfully glad to see the three of you come running out of there."

As the police escorted Wentworth to an awaiting squad car, he stopped and stared at me.

"Hey, kid, don't think you're a hero or anything," he said. "You did me a favor. This is gonna work out even better. Now I'll have my day in court, and everyone will know how Sam Solomon killed my grandfather. I ought to thank you."

An officer tried pulling Wentworth away but the criminal continued to babble.

"I'll tell the world about it. Radio, TV, You Tube. You'll see. The name of Sam Solomon will finally be disgraced...forever," he shouted. "And justice will be served."

We watched as police loaded their prisoner into the back seat of a squad car.

"What's that all about?" Eugene said.

"I'll tell you on the way home."

After sharing our story with the police, Henry, Scarlett, and I jumped into Eugene's hearse, along with my grandmother. And for the next few minutes, we brought both of them up to speed on what we had learned from having spoken to the suspect. We told them about the actor who played the role of Sam Solomon, Peter Wentworth; his ill-fated contract with the producers of the series; and his grandson's pledge to destroy the memory of the literary hero. We told them about our near-death experience in the library archives, and how we created a fortress of books that helped us escape.

When police later searched the residence of Jonathan Wentworth, they found the majority of the items taken in the burglaries, along with most of the cash, not to mention a box full of the SS cards. Wentworth pleaded not guilty but it didn't matter. This was a slam dunk for the prosecution. Even the defendant's court-appointed attorney encouraged him to cut a deal, but Wentworth would have none of it. He was on a mission...and the world would know about it.

However a funny thing happened at the trial a few months later. As Wentworth had hoped, the case drew the attention of the press—even the national press. But his plans to destroy the good name of Sam Solomon backfired. Instead of discrediting the hero, the trial actually stirred interest in not only the book series but the radio drama. Dozens of radio stations from across the country began running the series. And many Sam Solomon books, some out of print for decades, were brought back, and for a time, even made best seller lists.

It was a renewal…a renaissance for America's greatest detective. As for Wentworth? At least he wouldn't have to see it. He was eventually sentenced to a long stint in a federal prison. Besides the burglary convictions, a jury also found him guilty of attempted murder. His plans to do us in by tampering with the furnace were taken very seriously by law enforcement officials.

There was one more little matter that needed to be settled. It had to do with how I had snuck out of the house without my parents' permission. I had to thank Gram for stepping in and bailing me out on this one. She told my parents that she had invited me to join them on the stakeout. My folks didn't like the fact that Gram had given me permission without telling them first, but they eventually got over it. And then we had to deal with two other sets of parents— Henry's and Scarlett's. They were equally upset that their kids had up and left in the middle of the night. But when it was explained to them that they had taken action to save me from danger, their folks went easier on them. Their parents didn't approve of their tactics, but understood their need to answer the call and rescue a fellow classmate.

*   *   *   *   *

A couple of days following the arrest, things began to quiet down at school. But they soon heated up as opening night of the play approached. Mr. Miles was now in full panic-mode. He scheduled a series of two-a-day rehearsals to help us catch up. When Scarlett reassumed her position on stage, it was clear that she hadn't missed a beat. Henry, on the other hand, was a bit rusty. And I had forgotten most of my lines. Since I was just an understudy, I guess I hadn't really put my heart into the memorization, even though Mr. Miles would continually remind me of how important it was to be ready for any theatrical emergency. I then took it upon myself to get serious about the role of Nick Dakota. It was the least I could do to thank Mr. Miles for dropping everything and helping us set a trap for Wentworth. We couldn't have done it without him.

At dress rehearsal on Friday night, the nodder, the hisser, and the slacker were up to their old tricks. Stephanie was as irritating as ever. She decided that it might boost morale if she pointed out everyone's mistakes. She soon discovered that her input was not appreciated. We could thank Henry for that. Brian the hisser's insistence that he stand no closer than six feet from anyone else on stage threw Mr. Miles' blocking directions for a loop. And Patrick the slacker appeared relatively nonchalant about things even though opening night was only a day away. Mr. Miles seemed concerned about the slacker' attitude. After all, this was his leading man. He should have been taking dress rehearsal much more seriously. Besides Scarlett's portrayal of Rebecca, the role of Nick Dakota was by far the most important. By 10:00 pm, we had somehow fumbled our way through the performance, but not without a meltdown or two from Mr. Miles.

Less than twenty four hours later, we found ourselves stage left peeking out between the curtains at the capacity crowd in the auditorium. Most of the kids were rattling off lines under their breaths. I asked around if anyone needed help rehearsing. Most of the actors were in their own little worlds. The moms who had volunteered to make costumes had done a masterful job. Everyone was dressed to the nines. When Mr. Miles entered the green room, he appeared as nervous as an expectant parent. And that nervousness soon morphed into total panic when he took a head count and discovered that one of his actors was missing.

"Patrick! Patrick! Where is my Nick Dakota? Has anyone seen Nick Dakota?"

He was met with a sea of shrugs. Mr. Miles spotted one of the moms who was moving a prop onto the stage.

"Mrs. Nelson," he said. "Patrick Walsh is missing. Can you call his house and see if he's there?"

Mrs. Nelson nodded as she pulled her cell phone from her pocket and began dialing.

I suppose we should have anticipated this. The slacker's attendance record was legendary. Maybe he never planned on showing up tonight. That may have been why he was so cool at the dress rehearsal. He knew he'd never have to face this audience. But how could he just ditch? This wasn't just another day at school. It was one of the most important nights of the year. Even Patrick wouldn't just blow it off—or would he? If he had, that meant only one thing, and I couldn't even bear the thought of it. I couldn't make myself say it. I wasn't ready for this. I needed more warning. I hadn't concentrated on learning my lines the way I should have. Maybe the kid was stuck in traffic. Maybe he had gotten the date wrong. Maybe he was in the parking lot. Or maybe he was never coming at all and never planned to.

"Mr. Miles?" Mrs. Nelson said. "There's no answer. Maybe he's on his way."

Mr. Miles began wringing his hands. He appeared to be in deep thought. A moment later, a determined look appeared on his face.

"I'm afraid it's too late," he said. "We can't wait for him." Mr. Miles spun around and grabbed me by the shoulders. "Charlie, are you ready? I told you that things like this can happen. Your country needs you, son. This will be your finest hour…your moment of glory…your Super Cup."

"You mean Super Bowl?" Henry said.

"Whatever," he said. "Are you with us?"

I suddenly felt as if I were standing in Mrs. Jansen's class about to rattle off the answer to a brain teaser. Except in class, I knew what I was doing. This was different. I was completely out of my element. I felt the stares of my fellow actors burning holes right through me. I was worried about screwing up and embarrassing myself. I might never live it down. And even if I did agree to do it, then what? It sure didn't guarantee a flawless performance. How would I be remembered following a less-than-stellar debut? Would it go something like "Well, at least he tried"? That wasn't nearly good enough. But if I told Mr. Miles that I was unable to perform— that I just wasn't prepared—then they would have to cancel the show. And that would be on me.

What I needed right now was a pep talk, and it had to be
from the one person who could talk me into doing almost anything—
Sam Solomon. I tried to recall if Sam had ever found himself in
such a predicament. I thought hard…and fast. There was no time to
waste. And then all at once I had it—Episode #64—*The Santa
Claws Caper*. In this story, Sam was hired by officials at Yosemite
National Park in California following a series of bear attacks during
the Christmas holidays. The ranger service had been unsuccessful at
tracking down the beast. During his investigation, Sam made a
connection between the firing of a department store Santa and the
bear attacks. Apparently the Santa, who had been hired by park
officials to entertain children of campers, had been arriving for work
in a state of drunkenness. Sam soon determined that the Santa, in a
desperate plot to seek revenge against those who had fired him, had
dressed up as a bear, and had attacked campers while they slept.
One night, Sam managed to corner something in a remote cave—it
was either the alleged Santa or a real bear. He wasn't sure. When
he entered the cave and approached his prey, he was uncertain if he
were up to the challenge. What if this turned out to be a seven-foot,
eight hundred-pound grizzly? But Sam knew that it was now up to
him and him alone to end the attacks on unsuspecting campers.

I walked up to Mr. Miles and held my head high. If Sam
could dispel his fears and face danger head-on, then so could I.
Neither of us knew what the future would hold but that wouldn't
stop us.

"I'll do it," I said.

"Marvelous," Mr. Miles cried. "Now get to wardrobe and
make it snappy."

I promptly walked into wardrobe and found a dozen
exasperated moms and a wall of sewing machines that had been
running non-stop for days. When I announced that I would be taking
on the role of Nick Dakota, you should have seen the looks on their
faces. You see, the slacker had a slimmer physique than yours truly,
and the clothes that had been made for him would never fit me. But
that didn't stop the moms. They were driven. They had me in
costume in less than twenty minutes.

As I stood in the wings waiting for my cue, I realized that there was actually one good thing about being pressed into service. My mom would be delirious when she saw me on stage. She and my dad had come to the play with Henry's parents to support both him and Scarlett. Never in a million years would they have expected to see me in the spotlight. This would be a great opportunity to win a few points. I knew they'd come in handy the next time I got caught in the garage taking on new clients. But I was worried about what my parents—make that everyone in the audience—would think when I botched my lines. I wasn't looking forward to embarrassing myself but I had given Mr. Miles my word, and there was no going back now.

When Scarlett eventually delivered the words that were supposed to trigger my entrance, I froze. I might still be standing there had not Stephanie rammed me from behind. I remember stumbling onto the stage, and from there everything was a blur. I only recall bits and pieces of what took place for the next hour. And when the curtain finally fell on Mr. Miles' playwriting debut, despite my fears, it turned out to be a magnificent night at the theater. Scarlett was her usual perfect self. Henry managed to turn his character into a memorable villain. Stephanie, believe it or not, was nearly flawless. She did, however, work a few nods in whenever the audience would applaud. Then, of course, there was Brian the hisser. I saw Mr. Miles roll his eyes whenever Brian would pull away from anyone who got too close to him. There was one especially trying moment when Scarlett needed to hand him a wad of cash. Brian would have none of it. And for a while there, it looked like the two were playing a game of tag on stage. She eventually just threw it at him. The crowd seemed to love it though. The other assorted cast members did themselves proud. All in all, the production was nearly glitch-free.

And then there was me. I actually surprised myself by remembering most of my lines. But there were a couple of times when I had no idea what I was supposed to say. I had gone totally blank. It could have been a disaster. But once again, Sam Solomon came to the rescue. Instead of freezing in front of scores of onlookers, I found myself trying to recall specific dialogue from one of the Sam novels with a similar theme. And then I simply rattled it off and hoped for the best. It confused some of the actors momentarily, but Mr. Miles would later call it a masterful job of ad-libbing. I was still, however, somewhat nervous about the last scene—with Scarlett. Our characters were together in the courtroom when the jury returned from deliberations. And then right on cue, as if we had practiced it a million times, the jury foreman rose, delivered a not-guilty verdict, and Scarlett leaned over and hugged me. But that wasn't all. For good measure, she planted a kiss on my cheek.

I don't have to tell you what that meant. I got so flustered after the big moment that I nearly forgot the rest of my lines. But, in true Sam Solomon style, I pulled it together and finished strong. The audience couldn't have been more receptive. There were three curtain calls. And it was so nice to see Mr. Miles get the biggest hand of all, including a standing ovation. He gathered us all together backstage after the show and told us how proud he was of the group. Then he singled out two of us.

"Scarlett," he said. "You are a natural. I expect to see you on this stage many more times. And I hope you'll continue your acting in high school. Will you think about that?"

She nodded and smiled.

"And Charlie, what can I say? You became an understudy so that you could concentrate on your private detective business. I wasn't sure if it was the right decision at the time. But in the end, you managed to excel at both. I couldn't be more proud of you." He grinned. "Okay, everyone…group hug."

We all swarmed Mr. Miles and then hugged one another. All except the hisser, that is.

"Please tell your parents to join me at The Burger Factory on Chestnut in thirty minutes. It's the official cast party, and it's on me."

Collective cheers followed as we made our way to the boys' and girls' locker rooms to change into street clothes. Afterward, as we waited for our parents to find us, I enjoyed a quiet moment with Scarlett in an outer hallway.

"Well, you did it again, Charlie," she said. "You not only helped capture the Sam Solomon copycat, but you were amazing on stage tonight. And to think you pulled that off with only a handful of rehearsals."

"Listen, I'm no star," I said. "But you were unbelievable. I think you should consider what Mr. Miles said. This could be a new career for you."

"I've got plenty of time to think about that," she said. "Right now I'm wondering if there's any more excitement in store for us."

"What do you mean?" I asked.

"First, we're mixed up in a life and death caper, and then…" she pointed in the direction of the stage. "…All of this. Life's about to get pretty dull, I'm afraid."

A few more kids stepped out of the locker rooms and high-fived us.

"On the contrary," I said. "Who knows? Tomorrow someone may walk into our office and present us with a killer caper. That's how these things work. You just gotta be patient."

Mr. Miles emerged from one of the offices and smiled at us as he walked by. And seconds later, the principal, Mr. Reeves, ran up to Mr. Miles, smiled, patted him on the back, and then took off in full gallop.

"I wonder what that's about," I said as I watched Mr. Reeves sprint down the hallway.

And then before Scarlett could respond, Sherman walked up. He seemed out of breath.

"Great job, tonight, guys," he said. "But enough of that, I need your help. I'm in big trouble. I'm being framed."

"Framed? What happened?" Scarlett said.

Sherman looked around to make sure he wasn't overheard. "Word has it that someone emptied an entire container of powered laxative into the principal's water cooler. And for some reason, he thinks it was me."

I smiled. "Well, that would explain why he was in such a hurry."

Scarlett chuckled.

"Come to my office after school on Monday," I said. "We'll get right on it."

"Thanks, Collier, you're the best," Sherman said. He waved and disappeared.

I turned to Scarlett. "And you thought it was going to get boring around here, huh?"

She grinned and grabbed my sleeve. "Come on, it's time to party."

And so off we went to celebrate with Mr. Miles. When we got to the restaurant, the parents decided to let all of the kids sit together. I'm not so sure they really had our best interests in mind. They just wanted to sit with other grown-ups and talk about the boring things that grown-ups talk about. It was fine with us. And it got even better when I managed to sit next to Scarlett. We spent the evening laughing and talking about some of the funny things that had happened at rehearsals. All in all, it was the perfect night. And it capped off the perfect week. First my partners and I had put an end to a crime spree that had plagued Oak Grove for weeks. And then we managed to dazzle the crowd on stage. It didn't get much better than that.

At one point when everyone else was joking around and having a good time, I found myself thinking about the future—the future of the agency, and the future of Scarlett and me, or Scarlett and *not* me. I was never quite certain how that would work out. But there was one thing I was sure about, even if Scarlett wasn't. I was confident that there was plenty of excitement just waiting for us out there. To tell you the truth, I couldn't wait for tomorrow, or the day after that, or the day after that. And you know why? Because as long as there were people with problems, people in trouble, people with nowhere else to turn, then there'd always be a need for someone like me…and Henry…and Scarlett. So, despite my parents' best efforts, the Charlie Collier, Snoop for Hire agency is destined to keep its doors open, and ready to take on its next adventure. Won't you join us?

And there you have it, another case—opened and closed. I hope you enjoyed it, and I hope we kept you thinking along the way. Were you able to solve any of Henry's brain teasers? And how about the science problems posed by Mrs. Jansen? Did you see the connection between the Sam Solomon radio series and the crime spree? Did you have any idea what the "SS" cards were all about? And when it was determined that the culprit did indeed have a gripe with Sam, were you able to figure out why? This was a tough case. I don't mind telling you that I was pretty worried when we were locked up in the library basement. For the benefit of my partners, I tried to appear confident, but to be perfectly honest, I had my doubts if we'd ever get out of there alive. I'm just sooo glad that I'm here today to talk with you about it.

And so if you were able to correctly solve any of the problems above, you just might be ready for your next challenge. In order to be considered agency-material and worthy enough to join our little firm, you'll need to tackle one more brain teaser. Here goes: Write down the word LIVING. That's L-I-V-I-N-G. Tell me how can you eliminate four letters from that word and still have six remaining? Think about it. You have to take four letters away, and still have six left. Did you figure it out yet? Do you need more time? Did we stump you? For those who can't quite crack this one, here's the answer. Take away the first two letters, L and I, and the last two letters, N and G. And what's left. That's right...V-I. The correct answer is now staring you right in the face. VI is the Roman numeral for, you guessed it, six.

If you were able to figure that one out, you're well on your way to joining the agency. If not, don't worry, there are plenty more brain teasers and more mysteries to come. If you'd like to sharpen your deductive reasoning skills, you might want to visit my official website: **www.charliecolliersnoopforhire.com**. *You'll discover a page of brain teasers that you might find pretty challenging. And if you have a favorite brain buster that you'd like to try to stump me with, just send it in an e-mail to* **charlie@charliecolliersnoopforhire.com**, *and I'll do my best to figure it out. So, until next time, keep reading and keep solving brain teasers. That's one way to stay sharp. Because you never know who may come calling. Someday there just might be a knock on your door, and one of us will be standing there with a personal invitation to join the Charlie Collier, Snoop for Hire Agency. Will you be ready to answer the call?*

John Madormo is an author, screenwriter and college professor. He lives in Naperville, IL, with his wife, Celeste. He has three daughters. He is a professor at North Central College.